THE DEADLY FLOWERS

Strange thoughts are coming, the Guardian whispered through its roots.

Slowly Brightseed awoke. Strange thoughts could mean danger. Thousands upon thousands of flowers opened and shook off the heavy dew in preparation for what was to come.

A towering spike of yellow blossoms straightened. Energy focussed on the spike as it transformed the message and echoed it back to the colony.

The Guardian speaks. Strange thoughts approach from the seeking Heart-of-One.

Gerard Manley stumbled through the brush into Brightseed's meadow. A deafening buzz in his head drove him to his knees.

Peace, Brightseed whispered. *Peace.*

Fireballs of pain danced behind Gerard's tightly squeezed eyes. Jagged edges of fear scraped their way slowly up his spine. He clutched his helmet as he fell forward and clawed at its psi-damper switch. Bright agony screeched through his nerves . . . .

THE WINDHOVER TAPES

PLANET OF FLOWERS

Warren Norwood

BANTAM BOOKS
TORONTO · NEW YORK · LONDON · SYDNEY

THE WINDHOVER TAPES: PLANET OF FLOWERS
A Bantam Book / March 1984

ISBN 0-553-23963-5

Published simultaneously in the United States and Canada

Bantam Books are published by Bantam Books, Inc. Its trade-
mark, consisting of the words ''Bantam Books'' and the por-
trayal of a rooster, is Registered in U.S. Patent and Trademark
Office and in other countries. Marca Registrada. Bantam
Books, Inc., 666 Fifth Avenue, New York, New York 10103.

PRINTED IN THE UNITED STATES OF AMERICA

H   0 9 8 7 6 5 4 3 2 1

To Margot,
who gave me the opportunity to get it out of my system,
and to Anne McCaffrey,
who asked the intriguing questions.

*   *   *

All characters in this book are fictitious, and
any resemblance to actual persons living or dead
is entirely coincidental.

THE WINDHOVER TAPES

PLANET OF FLOWERS

1

Time and memory marked the seasons for every colony. Each sunrise was a blessing to be treasured. Each sunset was a signal for pleasureful rest. Days were filled with idle thoughts and concentrated study. Nights were given over to the wonder of dreams.

Thus it had always been until the coming of the kinous, the strange colonies from outside full of incomprehensible thoughts and a disquieting mobility. With their coming the old colonies had changed. Never again would an old colony enjoy the full sleep of dreams. Always some of the Guardians would stand attentive to the activities of night, ever vigilant against dangers which had no names.

One colony stood nearest to the largest group of kinous. The colony's name, if such a name could be translated, was Mountain-Offspring-High-Fertile-Meadow. Neighboring colonies called it Brightseed. And it was one of Brightseed's Guardians who stood so attentively in this pale dawn and listened.

The Guardian's umbel of tiny, pink, trifoliate flowers spread in an arched crown over its tall, woody stalk. Sepals peeled back. Petals opened. Golden anthers wavered in the morning breeze at the ends of hairlike filaments and picked up the thoughts. Synapses closed.

Nanoseconds later the information reached the tuber at the center of the Guardian's root system. From its heart three meters below the umbel and a full meter below the spongy surface of the ground, the message went out to the colony.

They are coming, the Guardian whispered through its roots. *The strange thoughts are coming.*

Slowly the colony awoke. Thousands of plants stirred under their silvery coatings of dew. Millions upon millions of ganglia reinforced the colony's first waking thought. *They are coming*.

Morning had brought a new challenge to the colony and, as they had many times before, the thousands of plants which comprised the totality of Brightseed responded. Beneath the message sent by the Guardian ran quieter messages of excitement and anticipation, and more than one small flash of anxiety.

Strange thoughts meant another kinous, perhaps one like kinous Amsrita which could share its wonderful knowledge with them. But strange thoughts could also mean danger. Thousands upon thousands of flowers opened and shook off the heavy dew in preparation for whatever was to come.

Near the center of the colony a towering spike of yellow blossoms straightened. Its woolly basal leaves flattened themselves against the moss-covered rocks from which it grew, as though trying to steady the four-meter spike. Energy focused on the spike as the verbascum transformed the message and echoed it back to the colony.

The Guardian speaks. The strange thoughts approach from the seeking Heart-of-One.

Slowly the undercurrent of messages subsided. Each Guardian stood alert, straining to find some coherence in the thoughts which approached it.

Curiosity, a Guardian whispered.

Peace, the verbascum answered.

PEACE, Brightseed responded.

Gerard Manley stumbled through the brush into Brightseed's meadow. A deafening buzz in his head drove him to his knees.

Peace, Brightseed whispered. *Peace*.

Fireballs of pain danced behind Gerard's tightly squeezed eyes. Jagged edges of fear scraped their way slowly up his spine. He clutched his helmet as he fell forward and clawed at its psi-damper switch. Bright agony screeched through his nerves.

Pain, the Guardian whispered. *Confusion*.

Be still and wait, the colony answered.

Gerard opened his eyes to the clear light of morning and deafening silence. "Shttz?" His voice was a muffled echo in

2

his head. ShRil and Junathun had suggested that he wait for them to accompany him, but he had been too impatient.

"Shttz?" he called again, hoping his ghost-friend was close enough to hear him.

No answer.

Slowly Gerard sat up. Then he remembered Junathun's crude psi-damper and reached for its controls. As he touched the switch over his right ear, his fingers trembled with hesitation. Suppose...There was no way to complete that thought. He would have to take a chance. Resting his elbows on his knees and his helmeted head in his hands, he turned off the damper.

A faint buzz greeted him, but nothing more.

"Shttz?" he asked hesitantly, his right forefinger poised to switch on the damper again.

"Come back from there," Shttz's voice answered faintly.

They return.

Be still.

ZZZ-zzz-buzz. ZZZ-zzz. Gerard felt the rhythm as much as he heard it. It was coming from the colony of flowers which spread in multicolored splendor in the meadow in front of him.

A subtle buzz under the rhythm rasped painfully against his thoughts. He had to retreat. But even as he forced himself to his feet, fascination kept him from turning away. Beauty and pain, he thought as he stared across the meadow.

And organization!

Suddenly he saw a very clear pattern. The flowers filled an almost circular space in the center of an elliptical meadow. At regular intervals beyond the edge of that circle, pink, umbrella-shaped plants grew like boundary markers. The closest one was thirty meters down the slope from him. The dense colony of flowers began about ten meters beyond that. The locus around which the flowers grew was a tall spike of yellow flowers which stood in the only patch of bare ground in the circle.

Gerard stared in wonder. How? Why?

Questions.

A louder buzz swept past the pain in Gerard's head. He backed up the slope, unable to take his eyes off the circled colony of flowers. When he reached the line of thick bushes which marked the meadow's edge, the buzzing subsided to a tolerable level. Then he saw something which his earlier perspective had hidden from him.

Most of the flowers in the circle were shades of blue, purple, violet, and red. But stretching radially from the tall plant in the center, faint yellow lines traced fine divisions of color out to the circumference.

Gerard shook his head to clear his vision. Was this some kind of garden? Had someone planted the flowers in this pattern? It must be. The layout was too regular to have happened by chance. But if someone had planned and planted this garden, a larger question rose in his mind. Who?

Our-Gatou, the One.

Pain! Vertigo! Gerard squeezed his eyes shut and lost his balance. Only the bush behind him kept him from falling. As he struggled to stand straight, he opened his eyes. For the briefest instant he thought he saw an image superimposed on the meadow, a geometric image of burning lights. Then it was gone. Gerard felt a strange sense of peace.

Stillness.

A light breeze plucked at the meadow. Silence filled Gerard's head. Weakness tugged at his knees. He heard a squeaky voice behind him and turned slowly. Still dazed by what had happened, he blinked, then saw Shttz.

Actually, he only saw Shttz's floppy hat. The ghost's translucent blue isosceles shape was hidden by the bushes. Gerard didn't want to leave the flowers, but he didn't want to lose Shttz again either. "Where did you go?"

"There is confusion here," Shttz answered. "Come away."

Gerard took one last look at the flowers. Then he reluctantly pushed through the bushes and followed Shttz's hat toward the narrow path which had led them there from the settlement station.

They are gone, the Guardian said quietly.

The One is whole, the colony answered. *They will return.*

"What do you mean, confusion?" Gerard asked as he sat down at the edge of the path. Shttz's incorporeal form wavered in front of him like a bright shadowy counterpoint to the buzzing echoes in his head.

"Dangerous confusion. Did you not feel it?"

"I don't know. I don't think so." Gerard rubbed the back of

4

his neck, then looked up at his strange friend. "I felt overwhelmed in some way, but not in real danger."

"You doubt me?"

"No, I don't doubt you. I just don't understand."

"Confusion, as I said. Perhaps Junathun..."

"Yes, perhaps Junathun can explain it." With a sigh Gerard got to his feet. "Let's go back to the station. On the way you can tell me what you felt."

"Confusion," Shttz repeated as though that were the answer to everything.

"Can't you be more specific than that?"

"Yes, but not in languages which you and I share. Confusion is the only word you have for that, that... thing."

Gerard asked no more, but as they walked he couldn't shake the feeling that he had missed something important, some message or symbol he should have understood. Damned mindwipers, he thought. But he knew it wasn't the mindwipers this time. They had indeed wreaked havoc with his memories and probably destroyed a small prescient talent he had once possessed, but he could not blame them for this lack of understanding. No, this was something else.

Gerard shook his head with a grim smile. He and Self had picked enough holes in the mindwiper blocks for him to know at least part of what had happened to him back in Ribble Galaxy. And in the process he had gained more confidence than he was willing to admit in the power of mind over mystery. He was sure he had missed a message in the flowers' buzzing. He was just as sure that if there were a way to do it he and Self would dig out that message. If there were a way.

ShRil did not know if she was more frustrated because Gerard and Shttz had gone to look at the flower colony without her, or because she had failed to arrange CrRina's meal so that she could accompany them.

CrRina called to her from the floor. "See hi, Mummum," she said with a smile. "See hi!"

The demand for her attention made ShRil smile. CrRina had learned to get Gerard's attention with cries of "Dedo!" and Shttz's attention, when he was around, with "Seets!" But it had taken her much longer to say "Mummum," because she already had half-a-set of ways she regularly called for her

5

mother. The word was hardly necessary. Still, CrRina's use of it pleasured ShRil.

"See what, you little spacer?" ShRil said as she sat on the floor facing her daughter.

"See HI! See HI, Mummum." CrRina held her hands high above her head and wiggled her fingers.

ShRil laughed and mimicked her. "Hi, CrRina," she said, wiggling her own fingers. "Say hi."

CrRina got clumsily to her feet. "See hi, Seets!" she called in her high-pitched voice as she ran across the room.

ShRil turned to watch her daughter just in time to see Gerard follow Shttz into the room. "That did not take long," she said sweetly.

"Danger there," Shttz squeaked as CrRina ran giggling through him to be swept up in Gerard's arms.

"What are you talking—" ShRil cut herself short when she realized that Shttz had faded away. She got to her feet and smiled at Gerard as he carried CrRina over to her. "What was Shttz talking about?"

Gerard held his smile for CrRina, but his voice reflected his concern. "We went to the near colony Junathun told us about. I tried to get close for a good look at the flowers, but something stopped me. Shttz thinks it's—"

"What stopped you?"

"See HI, Dedo."

"Yes, CrRina, Daddy says hi. I don't know what stopped me. Something buzzed in my head, made me dizzy. Had to use the psi-damper on the helmet. That cut it off. Cut everything off. But you know what was really interesting?" Gerard set CrRina on the floor and sat down at the table. "The really interesting thing is that the flowers in that meadow seem to be arranged like a spoked wheel around a central hub."

ShRil sat down across from him. CrRina looked at them both curiously. "See hi," she said quietly with her arms half raised over her head. When neither of them responded she turned and walked out of the room and into the sleeping quarters. In the four days since they had landed on Brisbidine in their spaceship, *Windhover*, CrRina had already made herself at home in the small geodesic building which had been assigned to them. "See hi," she said as she disappeared through the doorway.

Gerard watched her go and smiled. Then he turned back to ShRil. The smile disappeared. "I think Junathun has been holding some information back from us."

"Why do you say that?"

"Because he never mentioned how precisely the flowers are arranged. Because he didn't tell us there's a pattern, a rhythm in the buzzing noises, a pattern which obviously means something. And because—"

"Why does the buzzing obviously mean something?"

"It just does. I know it."

"Another of your intuitive judgments?"

Gerard paused before answering. Was it intuitive? Or had he really heard something he knew had meaning? "I don't know, ShRil. I really don't. But I couldn't avoid the feeling that I was missing something, a message of some kind wrapped up in all of that static."

"So you think Lorrane may have been right?"

"Who knows? There's a long distance between my feeling that some kind of message was being directed at me, and Lorrane's conclusion that the flowers have some level of sentience."

ShRil smiled and patted his hand. "I suspect you plan to make the journey between those two positions."

"And I suspect that's why I love you," he said softly.

"Why?"

"Because there's so much I don't have to explain to you. Yes, I'd like to find out if Lorrane's right. But we need a lot more information than her records gave us. And a lot more understanding than Alvin's cram course at Jelvo U. I think Junathun has to be the one to provide—"

A loud crash and a wail from the sleeping quarters interrupted his sentence and sent them both hurrying into the next room to see what CrRina had done this time.

7

2

"Are you sure?" Spinnertel's voice was as coarse as his fur was soft.

"Of course not. Gracietta was not sure either. However, she observed him for a considerable span of his time and felt strongly enough to report her findings." Gatou-Drin made the last statement with a slight smile of satisfaction.

"She cannot be trusted."

"In this case she can. She knows him and his species far better than we do."

Spinnertel leaned back with a sigh of resignation and curled his soft tail around his feet. The Verporchting had been his idea. For centuries it had amused him to watch the spirit of his idea as it went through its mortal incarnations. But when the last Verporchting had died, he let the idea disperse, glad to be rid of the duty it imposed on him. Other projects had become far more interesting.

Now the exile, Gracietta, dared to suggest that his duties were unfinished. "We will need proof," he said finally.

"Indeed. But when the proof comes, and I am inclined to think it will, what will you do then?"

Spinnertel ignored Gatou-Drin's malicious smile. "I shall watch him, of course. If he bores me again, I shall let him die for good."

Gatou-Drin's smile quickly turned into a frown which furrowed the grey skin between her multifaceted eyes. "You did that once already. I seriously doubt if the Constant will vote to approve such an action again."

"Are you suggesting I failed before, my dear Drin?"

"Obviously. If your Verporchting has truly been reincarnated, then you failed. And, it has won its right of existence. Those are the Constant rules, rules that you voted to approve, I believe."

Spinnertel had indeed voted in favor of those rules, and that was part of what bothered him. But more than that, for the first time since their conversation had started twenty-six day-cycles before, Spinnertel felt a prick of vulnerability. It was just a prick, for Spinnertel was actually vulnerable to very little beyond the decisions of the Constant and the ravages of time. But that little point of annoyance was more than enough to upset his balanced view of the universe.

If his Verporchting had in fact won its right of existence, Spinnertel would be asked to contribute a counterweight which would have to come from his personal store. He shook his shaggy head and wondered if the accumulated millennia of his life were finally eroding his mental powers.

"We shall see," he said to Gatou-Drin with a careless wave of his taloned hand, "if the proof meets the exile's claims. Where is my Verporchting supposed to be now?"

"Cosvetz," Gatou-Drin answered with a barely controlled smile. "He and his female have gone to Cosvetz."

A second prick of vulnerability touched Spinnertel. Cosvetz was one of Drin's ideas, one that the Constant had watched with great interest and proclaimed highly successful. Even he liked what she had done there, if for no other reason than the aesthetics on Cosvetz seemed particularly harmonious.

But if his Verporchting was there, Spinnertel would have to be doubly careful before doing anything. A mistake there and he might find himself banished like Gracietta to some powerless planet to live out the rest of his long, long life in exile.

"Is there a way to get proof on Cosvetz?" he asked, after carefully choosing his words. He did not want to offend Gatou-Drin in any way—at least not yet. He might very well need her assistance before this game was finished.

"I suspect there is, Spinnertel, but perhaps we should deliberate on the problem separately before attempting any initial test. Does that meet with your approval?"

"Certainly. However, I would like to observe this one who Gracietta claims has taken the spirit of my idea."

"That can be arranged if you will allow me a little time."

Spinnertel laughed. "Do we have anything but time?"

"We have time," Gatou-Drin said with a trace of smugness,

"but if this one is truly your Verporchting, *his* time may be limited."

Before Spinnertel could answer her, Drin retreated and left him with his thoughts. The Verporchting would have to be dealt with. However, everything concerning him would also have to follow the strictest forms. Any deviation could cause Spinnertel more trouble with the Constant than any ten ideas were worth.

It was annoying, terribly annoying, to have a matter one thought was concluded suddenly reappear laden with new questions and problems. Especially when it happened for all the others to see, Spinnertel thought, as he rolled lazily up into a ball and let sleep take his cares away for a while. Terribly annoying.

The discussion was lengthy and heated. All through the day Brightseed had shared ideas with its neighboring colonies, and they had conversed with their neighbors. Then, Brightseed sent a request which surprised each colony it reached. Brightseed wanted to continue the discussion into the night. That would mean the loss of energy, and most certainly the sacrifice of a small number of plants in every colony which agreed to participate.

With the coming of twilight, most of the colonies declined, unwilling to make sacrifices for a matter which did not directly involve them. It was not that they were selfish—it was merely a matter of little concern to them what Brightseed decided to do. For those who had closer, more regular contact with the strange thoughts, Brightseed's ideas were always listened to with great interest. But as the darkness deepened, most of those also dropped quietly out of the lines of communication.

Finally only Brightseed and two of its farthest neighbors were left exchanging their thoughts in the cold night air.

How will you make the probe? East-Slope-Spread-by-Hard-Winds asked.

By searching for the thoughts of one of the kinous.

That does not answer East-Slope's question, Low-Riverside-Bend responded. *How will you search for their thoughts?*

By using the groundsel.

That is dangerous.

And costly.

10

Our groundsel are well established. Our root ties are strong. We shall not tax them.

East-Slope sighed with its heavy imitation of the night wind. *There is the danger, Brightseed. If you burn out the root ties to your groundsel, how much will you lose when the cold comes again?*

The root ties will be protected. But that is not the problem on which we seek your counsel. Our-Gatou has promised our safety, yet the strange thoughts continue to spread. Must we wait for them to make contact? Is that what Our-Gatou meant by her guidance to us? Suppose the kinous are like the night eaters? Are we to open ourselves to them? These are the problems which plague the high meadow.

And not only the high meadow, East-Slope added.

Change is the stability of life, Riverside-Bend quoted from the Accumulated Words.

Brightseed waited for the rest of the quotation, knowing what came next as well as every colony. Finally Brightseed finished the quotation itself. *What you have I will give you: what you do not have I will take away.*

Thus is the One always whole.

East-Slope's addition of the common refrain brought a stillness to their thoughts. Our-Gatou had given them life and guidance, but she had also shown them there was a greater life of which they were an integral part, and from which they were ever separated. That was part of the contradiction they lived in constant awareness of.

We will rest now, East-Slope and Riverside-Bend. Perhaps the morning will bring fresh thoughts and other views on this.

But Brightseed did not rest, it only stopped broadcasting its thoughts. Somewhere in those alien colonies there had to be another kinous like Amsrita, one with whom they could communicate and learn more about the greater life.

The groundsel can listen—
And speak—
As we have the way—
So Our-Gatou gives it to us.
Understanding will come—
When the morning warms us—
And the Guardians' watch—
Will keep us from harm.

11

*　*　*

The violet hues of Junathun's skin darkened in the sunlight as he turned to face Gerard. "This is premature," he said in his normally harsh tones. "What can you learn from questioning the pioneers if you do not already understand the records?"

"Additional information," Gerard said, more and more annoyed by Junathun's seeming unwillingness to volunteer anything.

"And opinions," ShRil added as she joined them from the door of their dome.

Junathun frowned. "I have given you both, have I not?"

"Have you?"

"Were you not here under the grace of Alvin, I would take offense at that."

ShRil put her hand on Gerard's arm. "Forgive us then, Junathun. Perhaps you are right. Perhaps it is premature. But there is so much the records do not explain, so much we do not understand—"

"Like the patterns in the flowers, and the rhythms I heard."

Junathun snorted. "That has been explained to you. Gel told you that others have reported the same phenomena."

"Yes. But Geljoespiy would not have done so had we not asked him. Why are you all holding information back from us?"

"We will go then and see the one who can tell you the most," Junathun said, as he turned away from them and headed for the old skimmer he took such loving care of.

Gerard cocked an eyebrow at ShRil and shrugged his shoulders. She gave his arm a gentle squeeze, and together they followed Junathun across the station yard.

Gerard thought back to that day they had stood in one of the libraries of Jelvo Universal Institute and reviewed the first of many reports about the strange flora of Brisbidine. He wondered now as he had wondered then why Alvin had been so adamant in his belief that two ex-diplomats could find answers here when several trained botanists had failed.

Or not failed. If Amsrita Williviic Lorrane had kept her sanity, would her colleagues in science have put more store in her reports and theories? Was it her discovery which had pulled the already strained threads of her sanity to the breaking point? Was that why her last reports had been so garbled?

Even as he speculated, Gerard knew that there was little to be gained from it. If there were clues in Lorrane's reports, clues which might help them unravel Brisbidine's mysteries, he doubted that either he or ShRil had managed to absorb enough understanding along with the training they had been given to find those clues and put them to good use.

ShRil sensed his pensiveness as they rode along in the skimmer and contented herself with watching the scenery. But a question nagged at the back of her thoughts. It was a meaningless question. Yet it refused to be ignored. CrRina had asked it just before they left the station.

"Where is the one, Mummum?"

"The one what, dear?" ShRil had answered automatically.

"The ONE, Mummum. The ONE!"

ShRil had been too busy getting ready for their outing to pay much attention, but now as Junathun guided the skimmer through the gently rolling hills she realized that it was not the question CrRina had asked which bothered her. It was the fact that CrRina had asked such a strange question at all.

Shttz, she thought suddenly. CrRina must have picked the question up from Shttz. She smiled at the silliness of it all and snuggled closer to Gerard.

"Hunh?" he asked distractedly.

"Watch the scenery, dear."

Gerard heard her and moved his arm slightly to accommodate her closeness. But his eyes saw little that they passed. Somewhere out there were the answers he was seeking, and somewhere out there were the answers Amsrita had found. Deep in the reaches of his mind Gerard felt a strange stirring. A slight smile moved across his face. For some unaccountable reason, he knew that Amsrita was right, that the plants were sentient.

"Why are you smiling, companion of my heart?"

"Because it fits," he said absently.

ShRil could tell by the look in his eyes that his mind was far away in the midst of some puzzle that he would explain to her later.

13

3

In a postpartum fit of perversity Chizen Dereaviny had named her son Hopeman. Then as though wanting to deny the blatant meaning in his name she referred to him thereafter as Hap.

Now Hap was fourteen Standard years old and Chizen wondered if there was hope for either of them in the future. They were headed to the colony planet, Brisbidine, under a special clemency ruling handed down by the commissioner of emigration on Sun's March.

There had been many applicants ready and willing to give up their hard lives on Sun's March for a freer life on a remote planet outside of any galactic control. But for unknown reasons she and Hap had been singled out, and Chizen had been told to report to the commissioner of emigration.

She had gone to her meeting with the commissioner with some trepidation, wondering if she had revealed the secrets of her past by some inadvertent word or action and would soon be told that her name had been stricken from the list of acceptable applicants. Much to her surprise, the commissioner had been cordial and even somewhat deferential toward her. After they had worked their way awkwardly through the amenities of hostess and guest, Commissioner Dusea had told Chizen that she and Hap had been granted emigration rights. They along with a small group of others from Sun's March would travel to Brisbidine aboard the freespacer *Rowlf*.

The right, of course, had been subject to a condition, but it was a condition so simple that Chizen had accepted it immediately. She was to carry with her a sealed directive, a directive which Commissioner Dusea herself claimed not to know the contents of. Upon arrival on Brisbidine, Chizen was to break the seal, read the directive, and do her best to fulfill its terms. If she would swear on her honor to do that, she and Hap were free to board the *Rowlf* and leave Sun's March and Ribble Galaxy forever.

As the huge pioneer transport *Rowlf* made its way slowly from system to system picking up volunteers, Chizen had been tempted more than once to break the seal on the directive and find out exactly what it said. But as she had sworn on her honor to do her best to fulfill its terms, so she had sworn on her honor not to open it until they were planetside on Brisbidine. And honor was something Chizen had come to understand during her exile. She would wait to read the directive as she had agreed to do.

"Eat time, Mother," Hap said, as he poked his head into her cramped cabin.

"Go ahead. Shortly I will join you."

"Eating with the team?" he asked, referring to the recteam she had joined and which was leading the ship's competition in four of its six chosen sports.

"No. Not until tomorrow."

"Shall I wait for you?"

His handsome face reminded her constantly of his father. "No. Eat with your friends if you wish." He left without comment, and she thought how unlike his father that would have been. Odd memories scrolled through her thoughts for a moment or two before she automatically cut them off.

That part of her past was gone. She was a pioneer now, destined to build a new life for herself and Hap, a life free from any entanglement with what had gone before. Except for that directive, she thought, with a glance toward the small personal locker where she had safely stowed it away.

The old skimmer whined in protest as it came to a stop. The small group of brown geodesic domes looked like they almost belonged in this little valley. Gerard wondered how long these pioneers had been on Brisbidine.

"We're here," Junathun said, as he climbed out of the skimmer. He held one dark, hairy hand up for ShRil, and she gave him a smile as he helped her down.

Gerard got down by himself. As he looked around the area,

he noticed that, despite all the lush growth, there were no flowers to be seen anywhere. He suspected—

"Hallo." A female voice broke into his thoughts.

"Hallo yourself, Liana Tracy," Junathun answered cheerfully. "I brought some visitors to impose on your grace, and bother you with questions about the Wheezer's Bane."

"They'll not bother me, Junathun," she said with an odd look. Then she turned to Gerard and ShRil. "You're welcomed here, you are," Liana Tracy said with a broad smile that seemed to naturally divide her narrow face, "even if you do come with this hairy do-nothing."

"Peace, Liana. Peace. I do my turns."

Her smile faded slightly and amusement twinkled in eyes so clear that for a moment Gerard thought her irises had no color at all. But when she turned back and held out a callused hand to him, he saw a flash of pale green around her pupils. Still, he wasn't sure if it was color or reflection.

"So you're Gerard Manley," she said as she gave his hand a firm rhythmic shake. "And this would be ShRil. But where is the little one Junathun told us so much about? And is it true you have some kind of ghost-thing with you?"

Gerard liked her. "Yes, we have a ghost-friend."

"A real ghost? I mean, what is it like?"

"That's hard to explain," Gerard said with a smile. "Shttz is the integrated spirit, the essential essence of an alien—"

"Can he truly talk, as Junathun said?"

"Yes. He talks and thinks, appears and disappears, even walks through walls when he wants to."

Liana shook her head as though unwilling to believe what he had said. "So where are he and your daughter now?"

"Back at the settlement station," ShRil said before Gerard could answer.

"Well, next time bring them with you. They can probably do their turns as well as Junathun."

"Liana—"

"Hush. See if you can find Carson up on the south ridge and tell him our company has arrived. If you two want to know about the Wheezer's Bane, he's the man to ask."

Junathun grunted in protest, but climbed back aboard the skimmer. "Where on the south ridge?" he asked.

"He's clearing again. Look for smoke. He'll be near."

They moved aside as Junathun turned the whining skimmer and headed back the way they had come. "We hate to be so much bother," Gerard said, as the skimmer disappeared around a small hill.

"Ah, no bother. That's just Junathun's way. He thinks everything's a bother. Especially work. Us, we don't see that many people, so visitors are never a bother. Now come into the house and we'll put some food on. Carson will want to eat when he comes in."

ShRil gave Gerard a brief smile as she took his hand and they followed Liana Tracy toward one of the smaller domes. "How long have you and Carson lived here?" she asked.

"I've been here all my life. Born here, right here in this valley," Liana said as she held the door for them. "Carson ... well, this time he's been here almost five years."

"This time?" Gerard watched Liana seal the door back in place with a well-practiced movement of her hands.

"You got to understand Carson, I guess. Sometimes he has to wander. Been offplanet twice, once for almost ..."

As soon as she paused Gerard knew she would not finish her sentence. He had obviously touched a tender area of her life. ShRil gave him a look that told him she knew also.

"Is that why he knows about the flowers? Because he wanders, I mean?" ShRil asked quietly. She understood about men who wandered. Gerard had certainly done his share of it.

Liana waved them to some chairs around a well-used, handmade wooden table. "I'm glad you've come," she said as she sat down opposite them, "but you can't tell about Carson. After Junathun's call he just grunted and went on eating. He might be glad you're here, and he might not.

"He and Junathun, they know more about Wheezer's Bane than anyone, except maybe Lorrane. And she's dead. And don't mention her name to Carson. He loved that woman dearly, but he's odd about that. Sometimes he'll talk his head off about her, and other times you just have to wait for him to bring her name up. But ... well, you'll see what I mean soon enough."

CrRina cocked her head and listened. The noise was funny. She laughed.

Shttz bobbed up and down in front of her, then stopped when he realized she was not laughing at him. A strange

17

warmth filled him as he let himself dissipate to escape the buzzing which flooded his mind.

Essenne, the old woman who was taking care of CrRina while her parents were gone, dozed noisily in the corner. Several of the station hands were building a new gate to the yard and their banging could be heard in the distance.

CrRina heard only the noise in her head. Then it spoke to her. The words were funny. She giggled. They spoke again. Mummum and Dedo didn't talk that way. Seets didn't talk that way. "Where is the ONE?" she asked suddenly.

Essenne jerked and opened an eye. The child was playing on the floor talking to herself. Essenne slipped back into sleep.

"Where is the one?" CrRina whispered.

Coming soon, the voice answered.

"Coming here? With Dedo and Mummum?"

Yes, coming here.

CrRina laughed. She liked the voice. "Look, Seets," she said. Seets was gone. "Seets?" she called. "Seets?"

Seets did not come back. The smelly she-mum snored. CrRina listened to the voices. Happiness jingled out of her in little giggles.

Touched by morning dew we drink with great happiness in the streams of early light.

One of the station hands yelled across the yard. The voices fell to a whisper. CrRina listened, head cocked to one side, eyelids drooping until she fell gently to sleep.

Gerard's first impression of Carson was that he needed to be fed. Never had he seen a human alive who looked so emaciated. But when Carson shook his hand, Gerard dismissed any idea he might have had about Carson's being weak. His grip felt like cables wrapped around Gerard's hand.

"So, you've come to ask about Wheezer's Bane, have you? Well, I'm the man to ask. It was me and Amsrita who first discovered that they was thinking plants."

ShRil liked Carson immediately. Something about him spoke of an honesty and sincerity as full as he was lean. But at the same moment as she felt attracted to this rail of a man, she felt a distance also, as though he were physically far away. She shook off the odd combination and asked, "Can you tell us about it?"

18

"Easy enough after I eat. And you, too. Won't do to have us talk and not eat." He turned toward Liana with a grin. "Well, boss, you gonna feed the help, or you gonna let us all starve to death?"

"Them I'll feed. You can starve," she said, letting him pull her into his arms.

With no sign of strain Carson lifted her off the floor and gave her a noisy kiss on the nose. "Then you'll be starving with me, boss. The help gets grumpy when it's not fed."

Liana blushed. "Put me down, Carson! Imagine!" she said, when he set her gently back on the floor. "In front of strangers yet. You have no manners." The look on her face only half belied her words.

"None at all," Carson said as he pulled a chair up to the table. "And less when I'm hungry."

"I'll agree to that," Junathun said from the doorway.

"Then I guess I'll have to feed you all. Get the trays, Junathun, and you the mugs, Carson."

Gerard watched the three of them move around the room and realized that they had been through this routine many times before. Each seemed to anticipate which way the others would move, and no one got in anyone's way. Within minutes there were five places set with steaming trays of meat and vegetables, and mugs filled to the brim with a liquid topped by golden froth. He and ShRil followed their example and ate without talking.

It was only after Carson had finished a second helping that he leaned back and said, "They do think, you know. Oh, sure, there's no proof for it. You can't go out there and talk to them. But they do think. Amsrita proved that." A scowl paused momentarily on his brow, then faded away.

Gerard swallowed quickly. "How did she prove it?" he asked. That odd feeling stirred again in his mind and he did not want to lose this opening.

"Talked to them, she did. I heard her."

ShRil looked startled. "You talked to them, too?"

"No, not me. I just listened. I used to hear them pretty good, but . . . well, damn, I wish Amsrita were here."

A heavy silence surrounded the table. None of them looked directly at Carson, and his eyes were bright and unfocused. Then as he sighed, the silence broke apart. "See, Amsrita was special, real special. She could hear them and

19

talk to them. Not for long, you understand. Even she couldn't do that. But longer than I could—lots longer."

"Her reports on that were—"

"Damn the reports, man. I wrote those reports, wrote them after she...after she couldn't any more."

This second silence refused to break. ShRil looked at Gerard and shook her head ever so slightly. Carson might have a wealth of information they could use, but this was not the time to try to pry it from him. She doubted it could be pried from him anyway. He would give it at his own pace, she suspected, or he would not give it at all. "May I have some more of this?" she asked, holding up her mug.

"It's called blend around here, ShRil, though others call it other things."

Liana answered her, but Junathun filled her mug from a heavy tap beside the triple sink. When he gave it to her his smile seemed approving.

"It wasn't easy for her, you know," Carson continued as though he had never stopped talking. "She had to work at it all the time. And still did her turns when they came around, she did. Maybe that was it. She had to work at it too hard, had to dig inside herself and root out too much to make room for it all. Fara knows she never complained though."

Gerard was slightly surprised at the mention of Fara. He had no idea that belief in his god had spread this far. But then he had always regarded his relationship with her in a very personal way. She was *his* god, after all, and that was how he thought about her. As far as he was concerned she didn't figure in other people's lives.

But his reaction to Carson's use of Fara's name almost masked a second reaction, a feeling, a hard, cold feeling that Carson was hiding something, something dangerous.

"And Fara knows I couldn't help her too much." Carson looked around the table as though they all understood exactly what he meant. "So what do you want to know about that damned old Wheezer's Bane?"

4

Gracietta smiled with her lower mouth and frowned with her upper mouth and eyes. That expression disconcerted Spinnertel, and for a moment he lost his concentration. "Well, then, our exiled colleague," he said as he took time to regain his composure, "it would seem to me that your assumption is only that—an assumption, one which—"

"Speculation is always legitimate."

Halido's interruption only added to the growing annoyance Spinnertel felt with this preliminary debate in the Constant. He knew better than to try to rush the discussions, but he wanted to get on with it. Now, perhaps for the first time he realized how very much he wanted to put his Verporchting behind him. He smiled inwardly as that realization gave him back the self-control he needed to continue.

"As I was saying, this assumption of Gracietta's seems too unsubstantiated to me. However," he added quickly with a wave of his hand to delay any further comments, "I am more than willing to agree that it should be investigated. If it should *eventually* prove valid, then I will act in accordance with the dictates of the Constant."

"Of course you will," Gracietta said sweetly with double knowing smiles. "We all must act in accordance with the dictates of the Constant."

"I have some further questions."

Everyone's attention turned immediately to Askavenhar. As the twenty-third of the twenty-three immortals, she was not only the oldest, but also the most respected. Even though the Constant was a democratic body with no delineated leadership, Askavenhar, by virtue of her vast experience and

21

the respect she had earned over the millennia, was in fact the voice of leadership. Her questions and her opinions were always listened to. Her advice determined the Constant's decisions more often than not. It was she who had suggested Gracietta's exile, and she who had suggested this gathering of the Constant based on the exile's information.

"Those of you who would rush hither and yon spreading your ideas like seeds throughout the universe might ask yourselves these same questions, but for the moment my inquiry is directed solely toward Spinnertel. Tell us, young one, what will you do if this is indeed your Verporchting?"

Spinnertel resented being called "young one," but he knew that Askavenhar referred to almost every member of the Constant by that appellation. He quieted his resentment quickly and stroked his feelers for a moment knowing that he had to choose his words very carefully. "I shall present a course of action to the Constant designed to allow the Verporchting to live this life, but no further reincarnations."

Silence greeted him from all sides, but Spinnertel refused to give in to that censorship. "Since I feel that my idea has run its natural course, I also feel—"

"You *feel*?" Gracietta interrupted. "We care not what you feel. Give us rational reasons for destroying an idea that has gained a life of its own."

"Seemingly gained a life of its own," Spinnertel corrected.

"As you will, Spinnertel. What Gracietta asks is valid. Surely you have a rationale for your proposal."

He had no quick response for Askavenhar. "Yes," he said finally, "I do have a rational reason. However, I wish to explain the historical pattern I followed with the Verporchting, and the processes by which I made my decision. Then I—"

"Spare us, Spinnertel. Spare us. If you have one logical reason or a galaxy full of them, we will listen. But spare us your historical dissertations."

"No!" Spinnertel immediately regretted speaking so sharply to Gatou-Drin, but he was tired of being interrupted. "No," he said more quietly. "If you want my reasons, you will have to listen to how I came to them. Otherwise..." He paused for effect.

"Otherwise we can only assume that your reasons are based on whimsy and emotion," Askavenhar said with a stern look on her oval face and a dark gleam in her wide-spaced

22

eyes. "Thus we will have to find your reasoning invalid if it will not stand alone. The consequences of that conclusion might more than fill all the otherwises you wish to stall us with."

She waited, but Spinnertel did not respond. "Gracietta made a similar plea before the Constant. I am sure that if you asked her she would be more than willing to give you the historical basis of the decision which forced us to exile her."

Spinnertel seethed with anger. He could never defend his reasoning if they would not let him explain. But he was not so rash as to risk exile. "Very well," he said slowly, "I will give you the logic and let you decide."

The Guardian relayed the message to Brightseed. Another of their number had been caught by fire. Plain-Hollow-Below-the-Trees, born of their own seeds ten seasons before, had died. A link in the family had been destroyed.

It had happened before, but none of the surviving colonies could ever explain why or how. Some had suggested a connection to the kinous. Others had suggested that the One was displeased. Most of the colonies accepted the deaths as natural occurrences, some inevitable phenomena they accepted as simply as they accepted the rising sun, the changing seasons, and the existence of the One.

Brightseed knew something the others did not, something which it had decided not to share. More than one of the deaths by fire had been caused by the strange thoughts. Kinous Amsrita had confirmed that. But Amsrita was gone now, gone to bring new colonies, it said, gone for some inexplicable purpose which called it to seed elsewhere.

Now their listening through the groundsel had found a new colony, but its thoughts were so different from colony Amsrita that at first they were not recognized. This colony was very different. Where Amsrita had been closed to certain ideas, this colony was open to all. Where Amsrita had fixed opinions, this colony had none. But where Amsrita had possessed great understanding, this new colony, kinous Sirreena, was innocent of understanding.

Still, the presence of kinous Sirreena offered hope, hope that contact would be reestablished, hope that a firmer, more lasting connection would be made.

The One is whole, Brightseed said. *The One is all that is, and all that will be. If we have life, the One will provide life. If we have no life, the One will take it away. The One is the seed before it is formed. The One is the form beyond all form. The One is here and gone, but the One always returns. Thus Our-Gatou has promised.*

Voices whispered in her dreams. CrRina's lips quivered in a quiet smile. Drool dampened her cheek. Her eyes darted about under her closed lids. "One, one, all is the One," the voices sang. "The One is here and everywhere. One, one, all is the One, the One is here and everywhere!"

In the music of her slumber CrRina saw flowers, pretty flowers in a big field. "Come," sang the flowers, "come with the One, come when the music is everywhere."

"Gerard!" the voice screamed.

A bloody hand reached out for him. A sea of agonized faces moaned in the background.

"Gerard," the voice screamed again. Its face spread in fury. Its eyes bulged wildly in their sockets. "Gerard!"

He awoke with a start. It was Fairy Peg.

The dream was unexpected, but not new, and it was no longer a nightmare. His nights of horrid dreams and fragmented memories of Fairy Peg seemed mostly behind him now. The treatments he had received from Chief Headfoot at Jelvo U. had eased the pattern of his dreams and helped him live with them.

Fairy Peg and Ribble Galaxy were part of a past he was gradually learning to forget. He would never know whether or not he had actually betrayed them and caused the deaths of hundreds, maybe thousands of people. But he was learning to live beyond even those thoughts, learning that whatever he might have done could not, and must not, destroy his new life.

ShRil pulled him close. "The dreams again?" she asked in a sleepy voice.

"Yes."

"Are you all right?"

"Yes."

"Can you go back to sleep?"

"Yes."

"Good."

24

She wiggled a little and relaxed against him, the sounds of her breathing quiet and reassuring. Gerard shut his eyes and tried to relax, waiting for the heaviness that would pull him down to sleep.

He drifted. His eyes rolled back in his head. A face appeared. With a start he opened his eyes. ShRil mumbled and twitched beside him.

It had been Fairy Peg's face, but not Fairy Peg's face. Whose? He shut his eyes and tried to recapture that face from the depths of his memory.

It was Fairy Peg's face, but hard years and toil had written their history in lines across her furrowed brow and wrinkles in the corners of her eyes. It was a worn face, a tired face, a face pulled down at the corners by having frowned more than smiled. It was a face he fervently hoped he would never see again.

Once more he drifted. Thoughts tumbled lazily through his mind. Words echoed back at him, from another place.

"Wheezer's Bane is a killer, if you ask me."

"See the one who can tell you the most."

"Talked to them, she did."

"Talked to them . . ."

"Talked to them . . ."

"Are you ready, Hap?" Chizen asked.

"Ready, Mother-of-mine," he said as he threw his duffel into her cabin.

"Be careful with that."

"I'm always careful."

"You are not. Now, are you sure you are ready?"

"Quit worrying. We're not scheduled to board the landing shuttle for another ten hours." Sometimes he didn't understand her at all. She should be excited now. Instead she acted as though she were expecting something terrible to happen.

"I wish you would not look at me like that."

"Like what?"

"You know very well what. It is your oh-Mother-quit-acting-silly look. I dislike it terribly."

Hap tried to change his expression, but it made his face feel funny. He had no idea how he looked when she accused him of that, so he had no idea how to change it. As far as he was concerned, he looked natural.

"That is much better. Did you get my locker properly stowed?" Almost everything that had personal meaning to her was in that locker, and she hated letting it out of her sight. She knew Hap had taken it to the loading area, but she had to ask him anyway.

"Yes, Mother-of-mine," he said with a tired smile. "I told the handler it contained the family jewels and he should be sure that it was safely stowed."

Chizen shivered with fear. "You did not tell him that . . . did you?"

"Of course I did. Will you please calm down? You don't have anything to worry about. The handler knew I was joking. When he asked what the family jewels were, I told him they were the trophies you had won and we both laughed."

She thought of the trophies with a slight smile, but it quickly turned into a frown when she remembered the directive tucked safely beneath them. "I'm sorry, dear, but . . . well, I just will not feel right until . . ."

"I know, until we are down on Brisbidine. But we have a long wait yet before that happens, so there's no sense in letting yourself get all worked up like this. We're due for a meal soon and it will be our last until we land, so why don't we go enjoy it and save our worry until the time comes."

"You sound like me."

"I had a good teacher."

"All right, we will go eat . . . together."

"Of course together," Hap said with a smile as he offered her his arm. "We're a team, Mother. A team."

5

Liana Tracy laid out enough food to feed ten people, and Carson and Junathun started eating as though they were trying to consume double their share. "It is delicious, Liana," ShRil said, after tasting several of the unrecognizable portions on her tray.

"Staples," Liana said quietly. "Nothing fancy like I'm sure you're used to."

"I wish we were used to this." Gerard had to force himself to eat, but not because he didn't like the food. The dark disturbances from his dreams had carried over into the morning. He deliberately took a larger bite than he wanted and smiled around it.

"I should have guests like you more often," Liana said as she returned his smile. "Some people don't appreciate good food."

"Don't be talking about us, Liana," Carson said, after wiping his mouth with one of the rough, grey napkins. "You never hear complaints from us, and I don't hear no compliments from you about my clearing and fences."

The look that passed between them told ShRil more than anything they said. Gerard nodded ever so slightly when she caught his eye. There was a tension here that lay all too close to the apparent tranquillity of Liana and Carson's relationship, and she suspected it had something to do with Amsrita Lorrane. Junathun seemed to be ignoring everything and concentrating on the food. ShRil decided to do the same.

Despite the fact that Carson and Junathun ate twice as much as anyone else, they finished breakfast first. Carson wiped his mouth and then leaned forward and stared at Gerard. "You sure you want to take a look at another patch? Them flowers really start to get nasty about this time of year and I can't say as I much like the idea of wandering up to them for no good reason."

Gerard pushed his plate away, and with it the last of the lingering distractions from the night before. "You said we only have a couple of weeks before they start to release their pollen. If we don't make the best of the time between now and then, we'll have to wait another season."

"So? You got someplace you gotta be?"

"No."

"Then what's your hurry?"

"Please, Carson," ShRil said quickly, "we do not mean to be rude, but neither do we wish to waste time that might

27

be valuably spent. If there is a reason why we should not—"

"There's always a reason not to tangle with the flowers."

Carson's interruption of ShRil angered Gerard. "And always a reason to put us off," he snapped.

"Yes. Good reasons, too."

"Nice guests I brought you, Liana," Junathun said with just a hint of a smile.

Suddenly the tension broke. Carson looked at Junathun and let out a brief, exasperated sigh. "My fault," he said. "Shouldn't be so touchy, I guess. But you've got to understand, both of you, that as soon as the patch starts to talk you'd damn well better turn on your psi-dampers. I won't be responsible if you don't. Can't be."

"We agreed to that last night."

"Good. Let's get started. Junathun needs to be back at the station after midday."

"You did not tell us that," ShRil said with the smile she had learned disarmed Junathun's natural aggression.

"I didn't know. Geljoespiy wants my help with the greenies landing this evening, and I said I'd do it."

"Greenies?"

"He means new pioneers. Colony ship got here a little early, it did," Liana explained. "The new folks are called greenies, though Fara only knows why."

"It's how I do my turn," Junathun said.

"And earn a few extra credits," Carson added.

Gerard was disappointed. He had hoped they might take most of the day exploring the "patches" Carson had talked about. Now that they had a time limitation nothing was going to work out the way he had hoped. Surprisingly, his disappointment quelled his anger. Best not to spoil what time they did have.

"Consequently," Spinnertel said with a feeling of satisfaction, "I contend that our ideas, however good they may be, should not be allowed unlimited existence, and therefore, I would limit this one Gracietta believes to be my Verporchting to a natural completion of this life." Rather nicely done, he thought, as he leaned back and casually combed his silky beard with his talons.

Everyone waited for Askavenhar to speak. "I see a problem with your line of reasoning, young one, but not necessarily a flaw in your plan so much as a problem for the Constant. If we take what Spinnertel says and strip away his rather pretentious logical construct, his case can be simply stated. The ideas we foster and propagate are unnatural, and therefore should not be allowed existence beyond the limits we set for them."

Spinnertel was startled. "That was not what I meant at—"

"You had your say, young one. Now keep your peace."

Askavenhar's cold stare stopped his interruption. However, it was plainly evident to every member of the Constant that Spinnertel was furious.

"Does anyone else wish to offer an opinion?"

"Yes," Gracietta said without hesitation. "Since I am at least partially responsible for this discussion—"

Spinnertel snorted and cleared the phlegm from his nostrils.

"I would like to say that I totally disagree with our young colleague. Ideas are neither natural nor unnatural. It does not matter where nor how they arise. What matters is if they take hold, if they put down roots and establish themselves as valid."

"Even bad ideas?" Askavenhar asked.

"Even bad ideas. Any idea which can exist on its own will go through many changes, good and bad. Cosvetz is a perfect example of that. The migrations of the flowers were not part of the original idea, and it has caused the other sentients not only problems, but also loss of life. Would Spinnertel suggest that we raze the flowers from Cosvetz because the brilliant idea that Gatou-Drin put forth there has been modified?"

Spinnertel sensed a trap much deeper than the obvious one, and waited a moment before answering. When it became obvious that Askavenhar expected him to reply, he did not know what to say. "Of course not," he said finally, unwilling to risk any more than that.

"I should hope not," Gatou-Drin said. "But if you can say that about Cosvetz, why does the same principle not apply to your Verporchting?"

"Because the Verporchting is not confined to one planet."

"And is Askavenhar's idea of liberty confined to one planet?"

"No, but that is not a living thing."

29

"Ah, so now you are saying that an idea embodied in a living being is unnatural and—"

"Of course not!"

"Then what are you saying, young one?"

Spinnertel sucked in his breath and let it out with an ugly rasp. There were times when he hated being one of the immortals, and this was one of them. "I'm saying that ideas have to be controlled, that they can't be allowed to spread and wander willy-nilly through the universe."

"So much for liberty," Gracietta said quietly.

"Stop it, exile! What is the matter with all of you? This Constant is supposed to be a forum of equals. Yet when I propose a simple solution to a simple problem, you act as though I were some unworthy outsider attacking you."

"Ah, but you, young one, you act as though we are joined against you when all we are doing is asking questions and expressing opinions. Are you so uncertain in your arguments that you cannot accept this forum's analysis?"

There was the trap. Askavenhar had revealed it. But for Spinnertel it might already be too late. He had assumed that the Constant would accept his arguments. The first steps in his plan had already been initiated. Now if he admitted he was wrong, he would have to modify that plan, and quickly. Either way he was trapped. By acting without the Constant's approval, he risked exile. By admitting he was wrong, he risked losing stature in the Constant, and worse, life and responsibility for the damned Verporchting. "I can accept the Constant's analysis."

"Then accept this, young one. I shall be greatly disturbed if anything happens to your Verporchting before this matter is resolved. Will anyone else be disturbed?"

Signals of assent came from every member of the Constant except Spinnertel.

"I believe that is a consensus."

Spinnertel nodded agreement and wondered at the same time if he could merely slow the motion of his plan without being detected.

CrRina smiled as the she-mum stacked the pretty wooden blocks in front of her. Then with a giggle she knocked them down. The she-mum laughed and stacked them up again. CrRina giggled and knocked them down.

"Your parents will be back soon," the she-mum said.

"Play!" CrRina demanded.

"Later," the she-mum said as she rose slowly to her feet. "Now it is time I fixed us something to eat."

The she-mum left the room and CrRina quickly forgot her. The voices were back, laughing inside her head. This time they brought pictures. CrRina listened, and looked at the pictures. They were pretty pictures. Then the voices and the pictures went away. CrRina was alone again.

She wanted the happy voices back. She wanted the pictures back. "Mummum?" she called. "Dedo? Seets?" No one answered her. She looked at the blocks and thought of the pictures. With a giggle she mixed the blocks up with her hands. Then one by one she started moving them around. A red one here. A blue one here. A yellow one here.

Hap had bribed the handler for a seat assignment beside one of the shuttle's few windows. Now as they pulled slowly away from the *Rowlf* he wasn't so sure he had spent his credits wisely. Everything was upside down. Brisbidine hung at a forty-five-degree angle above them with the *Rowlf* partially obscuring the view. The shuttle had no artificial gravity, and Hap's stomach twisted and turned in unhappiness. But he was determined to enjoy himself.

He glanced quickly at his mother and saw that she had taken the drugs offered her and seemed to be sleeping peacefully. Hap would never have made the descent asleep. He had no idea when he might get to space again, and he didn't want to miss a thing. As he stared out the port he forgot about his stomach and lost himself in the wonder of what he was seeing.

Chizen was not asleep. She had taken the drug, but only enough to help her overcome the nauseous feelings that always came to her with weightlessness. For the moment she was pleased that Hap was enjoying their descent and she was unwilling to spoil his pleasure with her concerns. He would have to face the problems of their new life soon enough.

Watching him made her feel better. He was like his father in many ways, especially in his looks and his naïve acceptance

31

of the twists and turns life had presented to him. She started
to shut off her thoughts about Hap's father, then consciously
decided to let them flow.

He was dead now. Chizen knew that, but knowledge that
he had died did nothing to lessen the vividness with which
she could call his image into her mind... strong, brown-
haired, with a broad face that blushed easily... oh, how she
had tried to impress him, tried to make him see her for
herself.

She remembered the night of Hap's conception, the night
she had come to him with the full knowledge that she was at
her most fertile, the night she had offered him a moment's
reprieve from his misery and he had taken her into his
arms. . . .

Anger burned through the memories which followed that
night.

It was too much. Chizen shut the memory down again.
Then she vowed once more to keep that memory buried.
This was the beginning of a new life for her and Hap, and
they would be better served if she left the past well behind
them and concentrated on what they could make for themselves on this new world.

"It is agreed, then? The Constant will meet aboard this
ship four cycles from now and make the journey to Cosvetz.
Are there any who do not wish to participate?"

"Perhaps I should not go."

"Why, Gatou-Drin? We understand that Cosvetz is your
idea and that you are biased accordingly."

"Thank you, Askavenhar, but—"

"You have an obligation to be there, Gatou-Drin."

She paused for a moment, the pleasure apparent in her
multifaceted eyes. "Very well. I will come."

"Any others?"

There were none. Spinnertel left as quickly as he could
without appearing to rush. As soon as he was back aboard his
ship he downed two quick liters of his favorite tranquilizer, a
mixture of alcohol and the oily essences of several rare herbs.
He needed to relax, and he needed to think. But for the
moment relaxation was more important.

He had been humiliated in the Constant, and there was
nothing, absolutely nothing he could do about it. He poured

32

himself a third liter of the spicy alcohol and reclined on his favorite contoured mat.

Damn the Verporchting, he thought, then smiled ruefully to himself. He had created the Verporchting as a counterego, an innocent opposite, expendable and amusing, useful for stirring up a minor tempest here and there. But the last reincarnation had shown too many mutations and too much independence. It had annoyed Spinnertel and he had arranged a convenient and—he thought—final death for it.

Now it appeared he would have to get rid of another one. But he would have to do so without jeopardizing his status in the Constant, however little that status might currently be worth. He would have to find the most ingenious way. Then maybe those old stuffed-heads, Askavenhar and Gracietta, would grudgingly acknowledge that he was a force to be reckoned with.

Somewhere through the fourth liter Spinnertel fell asleep.

6

"There it is," Carson said simply.

The patch, as Carson referred to it, filled the open space below them. Gerard estimated it to be roughly one hundred and fifty meters in diameter and from their perspective on the edge of the low cliff, the flower colony's geometrical layout was clearly visible. "Do they all look like this?" he asked.

"All I've seen. Same shape, same colors, same umbrella plants on the edges. Amsrita measured eight or ten of them."

"Why wasn't that in her reports—or your reports?"

Carson looked away from them and ShRil thought he was

not going to answer. When he turned back there was an odd look in his eyes and a softness in his voice that surprised her.

"She said not to. Said we had to be careful what we told and that telling too much was just as bad as telling too little. Made me promise—later, when I had to write them for her—that I'd only say what had to be said to get others to come here. I promised . . . but, well, you might as well know it now if you haven't figured it out for yourselves. I didn't want no one else to come here."

He had turned away and the last sentence was almost whispered. ShRil put her hand on Gerard's arm and shook her head. When he arched his eyebrows in question she touched the corner of one eye with a forefinger and tilted her head toward Carson.

Gerard understood. Carson was crying. The fact that ShRil was physically incapable of shedding tears made her understanding of Carson's emotion no less real. But why was Carson crying? Was it because they had stirred up his emotions about Amsrita? Somehow Gerard didn't believe that. He was beginning to think Carson was a little unstable. Yet he had no logical explanation to offer for Carson's tears other than sentiment. They would have to wait until Carson was ready to tell them.

"Sorry," he said finally with his back still to them. "Didn't mean to let go like that." He wiped his face on the dark cloth of his jacket, then turned to face them. "You got to understand, if you can, that what I told you is true. Those flowers are killers. There's no way to get rid of them all, but that doesn't mean that we've got to put up with them any more than we have to. I hate them. It'll come the day when you'll hate them, too."

"I still don't understand," Gerard said quietly. "If they're so bad, why wouldn't you want someone to come in and study them, and find a way to help you get rid of them permanently?"

Carson's eyes showed red around the edges, but his gaze was steady and his voice firm when he answered Gerard. "Can't do that either. Amsrita understood it and tried to explain it to me. Has something to do with the whole planet. They're all over it, you know. Eleven major continents and every one has its colonies of flowers. They're necessary here, part of the ecology, and more than that, too . . . maybe."

"Something else that was not in the report?" ShRil asked.

34

"Weren't no place in them for that 'cause, well..." His voice cracked slightly, but he shook his head with an odd jerk and cleared his throat. "Let's sit." Without waiting for them he brushed the loose debris off a long, knee-high, black rock and sat down. Gerard and ShRil sat next to him.

"See, at the end Amsrita wasn't making much sense most of the time. Told me to put down lots of things that didn't fit together. I wrote them down, but I didn't put them in the reports. Then after she died...well, I did something pretty stupid, I guess. I burned those notes. Didn't want to have them around. Didn't want to be reminded of what she'd been through."

"And did not want anyone else to know?" ShRil added softly.

"Truth," he said, giving her a little smile. "But I shouldn't have burned them."

"Because there was something in them you now think might be valuable?" Gerard offered.

"Yes. And because you two could've read them, and maybe understood better how dangerous the flowers are if you could see what they did to her mind."

Gerard didn't want to push Carson, but he knew there was something he had started to say which he was now avoiding. "You said the flowers might be more than ecologically necessary?"

"Sounds crazy, but a lot of the stuff she kept repeating before she died was about something she called the One. The One knows this. The One knows that."

ShRil quivered as a strange chill passed through her. The one? That was what CrRina had said.

"Like I said, it didn't make much sense, and lots of it I didn't put down. Now I wish..." Carson laughed grimly. "Wouldn't have made no difference, would it? That part would have been burned up, too."

"Can you tell us anything specific?" ShRil asked suddenly.

The urgency was so apparent in her voice that Carson and Gerard both looked startled.

"Please, Carson, it may be important. Right before we came out here our daughter, CrRina, asked me a question about 'the one.' I thought maybe she picked it up from Shttz, but—"

"Sheets?"

"Yes, our ghost-friend. But after what you just said, I am afraid for her."

A vision of CrRina sitting in the midst of one of the colonies flashed through Gerard's mind. Then it was gone. Almost immediately one word ricocheted through his mind—prescience. He heard Carson ask ShRil a question, but it seemed distant and foreign, and he had to drag his attention back to hear ShRil's answer. Even then he could feel Self digging furiously for understanding.

"She asked me where the one was. When I said, 'the one what?' she insisted, 'The ONE! The ONE!' It frightens me."

"A child?" Carson said. There was a dark, haunted look in his eyes. "I don't know. It could be. But perhaps I should go back with you. There are some questions we could ask her which might prove you wrong. At least I hope so."

The subtle change in Carson's speech pattern startled Gerard to full attention. "What did you say?"

"I said there are some questions which might prove ShRil's concern unwarranted. And I think we should ask them as soon as possible."

Gerard stared at him. "Who are you, Carson? Two minutes ago you were talking like a pioneer. Now..."

Carson looked away for a long moment before he turned back and answered. "Guess my education's slipped through. I'll explain as we go back to Liana's. But first there's something I have to ask you. Has CrRina ever guessed what was about to happen next?"

"You mean prescience?" Gerard asked quickly. "No," he said without waiting for an answer, "but I have."

"So did Amsrita."

The pair stood out from the other greenies in subtle ways which Geljoespiy detected easily. She carried herself with a certain graceful set of her shoulders and a tilt of her chin that spoke for a level of living denied by her clothes and belongings. He not only looked the right age, but also had the same broad face and wide-set eyes as his father. They were almost definitely the two Gel had been told to watch for.

Gel could not guess the reasons behind his mentor's interest in these two, nor did he wonder about fathers and unclaimed sons. He would keep the boy and his mother temporarily at his place as requested, and attempt to win

36

their confidence and trust. In the long accounting of what he owed Letrenn that small act would not begin to make repayment.

"You two," he said to the chosen pair, "move your gear over to that blue skimmer over there."

Chizen looked carefully at the small, dark man who had spoken to them. "Are you the administrator?" she asked.

Gel laughed. "Don't have any administrators around here, lady, at least not like you mean. I'm just doing my turn." Without Junathun's help, he thought. "You'll be staying at my place until you decide what it is you want to do. Then we'll set you up with a place of your own or find you more permanent quarters. Now get your stuff over there. I've got to get all these people sorted out and assigned before it's too late to move them." Gel turned away without waiting for a reply and began to visually assess the rest of the group the shuttle had dumped in his sector.

Chizen watched him for a moment then said, "Come on, Hap. Let us do as he says for now."

"I don't like him, Mother."

"You do not have to like him or anyone. But for the time being we have little choice but to follow his directions. Do you want to sleep outside tonight?"

"Might be fun."

"Will be cold. Move."

Hap moved. It took them three easy trips to carry their meager belongings from the assembly area to the blue skimmer the dark man had indicated. Without waiting for instructions, Hap opened the small cargo hatch and loaded their four duffels and two personal lockers neatly into the available space.

"He keeps a clean skimmer, anyway," Hap said as he closed the hatch. "Looks pretty old, but . . ." He let the sentence go when he realized that his mother was paying no attention to him. She was staring back toward the assembly area lost in some thought of her own.

The late afternoon sun cast long shadows from the volunteers and pioneers sorting them out in the assembly area. A skimmer full of people had pulled up to the edge of the area and caught Chizen's attention. One of those people looked familiar. She could not be sure but . . . She shaded her eyes and squinted, hoping in some way to cut the hundred meters between them and make a positive identification.

Her hand shook. Her breath stopped. For a moment her world stopped with it. Then the skimmer turned and moved away, taking its mysterious passenger with it.

Chizen let her hand drop to her side with a shaky sigh. It was impossible. He was dead. There was no way he could be here on Brisbidine. No way. An arm encircled her shoulders.

"Are you all right, Mother?"

"Oh. Yes, Hap. I, uh—"

"Maybe you'd better sit down."

"Yes, maybe I should. The trip down seems to have gotten to me. I feel a little dizzy."

They sat beside the skimmer and Chizen took deep breaths of the strange air laden with its warm scents of growing things. But she could not tear her thoughts away from that vision of a man in the distant skimmer, a man who looked anything but dead.

"She was no trouble at   l," Essenne said with a smile. "She's a fine child and you've a right to be proud of her."

"Thank you, Essenne. We owe you a turn."

"Oh, no, ShRil. You don't understand that as yet. A turn would be far too much for the little I have done. Some small favor in the future, perhaps, but nothing more. Now I'd best return to Gel. He'll be bringing some greenies home tonight and if they hold the pattern, they'll be hungry and tired."

Essenne left without further ceremony and Gerard and ShRil looked into the sleeping room where CrRina was curled peacefully on their bed, a beatific smile floating on her lips. As they turned away, Gerard spotted the blocks on the floor.

"Look," he said with a quiet tremor in his voice. Then he turned in the doorway and motioned to Carson. "Look at that."

The colored wooden blocks were arranged in a rough circle at the foot of the bed. The hub and spoke pattern was clearly evident, and around the edges of the circle at regular intervals stood solitary red blocks.

"Maybe Essenne," ShRil offered, doubting her words even as she spoke them.

"I don't think so."

"Neither do I," Carson said. They both looked at him, and

the way he pursed his lips made his face look even narrower than normal. "Can we wake her?"

"Please, let her sleep. It cannot be that important, Carson. Can it?" The urgency in her voice revealed how very much ShRil wanted to protect CrRina.

"Don't know. Can't say. Still, I guess it won't hurt to let her sleep."

Gerard quietly closed the door to the sleeping room and they sat around the table in the kitchen area. He realized how much had changed from yesterday afternoon when they had sat with Carson for the first time around Liana Tracy's table. The change was more than troubling. "We have some Brandusian coffee if you'd like some," he said, to appease the gnawing feeling in the pit of his stomach.

"Ah," Carson said with a smile that looked uncomfortable on his face, "I haven't had any of that in years. Yes, that would be very nice."

As he got up to instaperk the coffee, Gerard said, "You still owe us a little more information about who you are, Carson, and why . . ."

"Why I didn't want anyone else investigating the colonies. Yes, I know." Carson looked almost embarrassed. "But as I told you on the ride in, I'm merely an educated man who hated playing the role of an educated man. Before Amsrita arrived I was content to pass for a farmer, stock handler, and jack of minor trades. Then after she came, well, not only did she make me ashamed of hiding my education, she tried to show me how to put it to work for all of us."

"And you fell in love with her," ShRil said softly.

"That I did, ShRil. That I did."

"When did you find out she was prescient?"

"Later. Much later. She called it precognition—and it didn't work for her all the time, but it was certainly something that I wasn't prepared for."

"Why do you think it has something to do with the flowers?" Gerard asked, as he set the steaming mugs of coffee in front of them. "Did she tell you it did?"

"Yes, and no. Not directly she didn't. But after she first made contact with them, the visions or whatever you want to call them started coming all the time. She said she knew what would happen the next time she went to see them."

"Was she always right?"

39

"No. But most of the time she was. Later it was hard to tell. We argued."

Carson paused and looked down into his mug as though trying to find answers there. Gerard wanted some answers of his own. He had possessed some prescient ability once, an ability which the Federation's mindwipers had all but destroyed. The only fragments which remained were tense, gut-level feelings he would get when something was about to happen. The feeling in the pit of his stomach had not been caused by hunger.

"They were ruining her mind," Carson continued suddenly. "I tried to convince her of that, tried to talk her out of the experiments—the 'dialogue' as she called it—but she wouldn't quit. So, we argued. We argued a lot. But we kept working together because I couldn't let her do it alone. Then . . . then she . . . well, then there was no way for her to do it alone."

He paused with a brief shake of his head. "Her mind started wandering. She changed. She needed help, help that I couldn't give her. I didn't know how. Then the visions and the visits to the colonies all blurred together for her. She'd talk about things which hadn't happened yet, and I'd take notes. Then the next day they would happen and she'd talk about them again."

ShRil laid a hand on his arm. "Wasn't there anyone here who could help her?"

For a moment Carson looked startled, then a different, darker look crossed his face. "I'm tired. Junathun is going to put me up for the night. We'll talk about this later. I'll be back early in the morning." He emptied his mug and stood up. "Thanks for the coffee. And thanks for listening. I hope I'm wrong about your daughter." Without another word he left.

Gerard sighed heavily after the door closed and looked at ShRil. Concern was written plainly on her face. "What do you make of all this?" he asked.

"I am afraid to make anything of it."

"So am I." For a long time they sat in silence until the sounds of CrRina stirring sent them both into the sleeping room to look at their daughter with new and troubled eyes.

Gel and his wife had fed Chizen and Hap well and made them as comfortable as possible in their small house. After a long monologue during which Gel had extolled the virtues of Brisbidine, Essenne had finally insisted that their guests be allowed to get some rest.

Chizen waited until Hap's breathing evened out in the healthy rhythms of adolescent sleep and the sounds from the other rooms had stilled. Then she turned on the small glowlamp beside her bed and stared at her personal locker.

Resting securely near the bottom was the directive. She had been too busy to think about it since they had landed. Then the shock of seeing someone who looked like Hap's father had pushed the directive further from her mind. Now she couldn't stop thinking about it.

She slipped quietly out of bed, wrapped the blanket around herself against the chill, and sat on the floor in front of the locker. Its dark, travel-worn surface looked somehow warm and reassuring to her in the dim light, but she hesitated to open it. As much as she wanted to know what the directive contained, she didn't want to know. Finally, after several false starts, she centered her thumb over the lock-plate and pressed.

Moments later she had the directive in her hands. She closed the locker and climbed back into bed. Lying on her stomach, she broke the seal on the thin box and slowly opened it. With a shiver she pulled the blanket tight around her and read the message she had carried halfway across the universe.

The directive was written on the inside of the box itself. Disbelief, anger, and confusion fanned the fires of her memory as she read the words, then watched them slowly fade as some self-destructive mechanism in the box destroyed the message. Nothing could destroy it in her mind. It would always be burned there in the indelible fire of emotion.

Sister,
Gerard Manley lives. He who betrayed Ribble Galaxy survives. He is said to be going to the planet Brisbidine. If you would restore your good name and honor, you will kill him. We await verification of his death.

41

7

Spinnertel smiled with satisfaction. His message had been acknowledged positively. Whatever happened to the Verporchting could not be linked to him. That much had been taken care of.

The remnants of the smile still lingered on his face when he made communications contact with Gatou-Drin. "Greetings!" he said to her image on the screen. The pleasure he felt was evident in his voice, too.

"To what do I owe this interruption of my duties, Spinnertel?"

He heard no pleasure in her voice, but ignored that. "I only wanted you to know that I am looking forward to our trip," he said. "And to tell you that I plan to apologize to the Constant for my loss of temper."

"Why are you telling me this?"

"Because I think I owe you an apology first." He paused and waited for her response. When none came, he continued. "I was rude to you, my dear Drin, and I am sorry for that. If I have interrupted your duties, then I owe you a double apology."

"I accept," she said curtly. "Is that all?"

"Why, yes, I suppose it is."

"Then I shall see you aboard Askavenhar's ship. Goodbye, Spinnertel." The screen went blank.

"That wasn't all, my dear Drin," he said to the empty screen. "That was not nearly all. But the rest you will have to learn for yourself, you and the rest of the Constant when the real questions come out from behind your precious flowers and show themselves for all to see."

He had planned to put the male to another use on Cosvetz,

a use he would have found most amusing, but which would not have seriously disrupted Drin's idea. Now that the Verporchting was there also, and the Constant was having a senile fit about it, his plans had been modified. That the boy and the Verporchting were linked had been a wonderful stroke of luck.

Or had it? he wondered suddenly. How had the two come together so conveniently? Was some other member of the Constant playing a game he knew nothing about? Suddenly the picture changed, and Spinnertel was again worried about his vulnerability, this time from a threat he couldn't identify.

The Guardian stood tall in the night, its anthers warmly shrouded by the pale sepals which had folded up around its blossoms. Life for Brightseed was slowly changing, but the Guardian was only aware of the distant night eaters, the swelling seeds in its ovary, and the faint dreams transmitted by the groundsel from kinous Sirreena.

The time of spreading would soon be upon the colonies. Pollen would fly from flower to flower and colony to colony until the air would be alive with the blessings of the One. Carriers would come forth, Guardians heavy in their fecundity, ready to pull up their roots and take the slow, painful walk which would take the fertile seeds to the new meadow chosen the season before. The carriers would pull the seeds down into their new home with their tendril roots, then stand guard over them for a full season as the new colony established its own roots and organized its thoughts.

Then the carriers would die. The chemicals from their systems would feed the young colony. The blessing would be reaffirmed. And the One would again prove itself whole.

Such is the way it had always been. Even the coming of the alien colonies had not disrupted that. The alien colonies stayed far away while the blessing was being spread, as though they respected what was happening.

The Guardian received a faint stirring of mind and listened. Kinous Sirreena was awake. Following Brightseed's decision, he called to her. *Peace, Sirreena. Joy, Sirreena. The One is here and everywhere.*

See the One, her response came back.

Yes, Sirreena, come see the One. The One is here and

everywhere, the Guardian responded. Then it sent her another image of Brightseed.

Hazy dreams crowded Gerard's mind. Wild circles of flowers whirled before him, then spun away. A face appeared, then melted behind a swirl of colors. Another face took its place.

Gerard knew he was dreaming, knew in some faint way that nothing he saw was real. But he also knew from long experience that there was no way for him to escape until the dream settled into the pattern which Self was working on. An odd mixture of discomfort and acceptance settled around his thoughts like a salty, viscous fluid whose stinging kept him alert.

The whirl of flowers slowed and stopped with spasmodic grace. The face shimmered in their center. The wrinkles around her eyes were darkly radiant. Dull fire burned in her eyes. A faint smile tugged her sad lips upward. Her voice grated softly like sand swept across a rough floor.

"Traitor," it said. "Traitor."

"No!" a hollow echo of his own voice screamed in denial.

"Traitor," she repeated.

"No, Fairy Peg. No," the echo said more quietly.

Her harsh laugh swept the flowers away and started the colors whirling again. "Traitor . . . traitor . . . traitor," the grating voice called as it faded to a ringing silence.

"No," Gerard heard himself say aloud. He was fully awake now, and he knew that Self had been trying to tell him something. But what? What message was there in this dream that hadn't been in all the others?

As he stared into the darkness Gerard knew there were no answers, yet. But more than he ever had, he felt that someday there would be answers to the mystery of his past and the ten years he had lost in Ribble Galaxy. Yet that knowledge gave him no comfort.

Across the room he heard CrRina burble quietly in her sleep. Then he wondered about her, and the flowers, and Carson, and Amsrita, and what it all meant, and how it all fit together.

The question of sentient flowers had started out as an interesting research assignment which would take him and his family far away from the reaches of Ribble Galaxy and its hired assassins. Now it was no longer interesting and simple. It was personal, and complex, and threatening.

Threatening in more ways than one.

Questions tumbled and fell over one another in his thoughts. Were the flowers a threat to CrRina? Was Carson a threat? Was Carson mentally unstable? Had the flowers caused that? Or had the loss of Amsrita? Or both? Or neither?

And what had happened to Shttz? First he had warned them of danger. Then he had disappeared. Where was he? And what did he have to fear from the flowers?

It was a long time before Gerard fell asleep again.

Geljoespiy accepted the acknowledgment of his message and shut down his transceiver. Staring out the window at the first streaks of another cold dawn, he wondered what Letrenn was so worried about and why his mentor was acting so secretly. Annoyance prickled his speculations. The pair had been located and Gel was sure he could draw the woman into his plans. There was no reason for anyone to suspect that he was acting on outside orders. So why was Letrenn's acknowledgment worded with such harsh cautions?

Gel tried to shrug off the feelings of annoyance and clear his mind for what he would have to do this day. But still the annoyance lingered. Then he realized what was at the heart of it. Letrenn was afraid of something. Or someone. Geljoespiy had no way of knowing which or what, yet the idea that his mentor could be afraid of *anything* caused him to shudder slightly and pull his heavy morning jacket tighter around his chest.

If Letrenn was afraid...of *anything*...then Geljoespiy knew he also had reason to be afraid.

He refused to speculate further. Letrenn had saved his life, pulled him from the collapsing mine on Tschudi, healed his wounds, and brought him to Brisbidine. Gel owed him everything. If helping Letrenn now meant risking everything, that was a price Gel was willing to pay...almost.

Perhaps it wouldn't come to that. Perhaps the best way to protect himself was to do what Letrenn asked as quickly and efficiently as possible. According to Letrenn, Chizen had cause to hate Gerard Manley. Gel would encourage that hate and help her in whatever method she chose to get rid of him. She would be the perfect tool, an outside agent with an

45

outside motive, and when the task was finished, Gel was sure that Letrenn would take care of her in the same way he had taken care of Gel.

With a brighter feeling he rose and began preparations for breakfast. It was going to be a full day, and now he was ready to face it with the proper attitude. As if in response to his mood the first rays of morning sun broke through his windows and scattered on the wall.

Hap awoke with a start. He shook his head to clear it of the images which had haunted his dreams. They made no sense to him, and worse, they frightened him. He had seen swirling colors and a gross distortion of his mother's face slashed by daggers of light. Other faces had joined hers, faces crazed by darkness like the cracked finish on old wood.

He shook his head again. This was not the first time he had suffered such a bad dream, but none of those before had so thoroughly shaken his youthful assurance. None of those before had struck at the heart of his only true security—his mother. Was he being punished for something he had done to her? Was that voice of conscience which had so recently come to plague him now chastising him in his sleep?

Hap shivered with fear and wrapped himself tighter in the heavy blankets of his bed. He listened for his mother's breathing from across the narrow room as though the sound of her presence would still the restless darkness inside him. Nothing.

With a quick jerk he pulled the covers from his head and turned to look toward her bed. In the grey light of dawn which filtered through the window he could see her sitting in the bed with her back against the wall. Even though her eyes were hooded in shadow, he knew she was awake.

"Mother?" Her head moved slightly, but she said nothing. "Mother? Are you all right?" When she didn't answer this time, Hap threw back the blankets and made his way quickly to her side.

"Mother? Mother? What's the matter?" Cold bit into his bare feet as he laid one hand gently on her arm. When she spoke, it was in an emotionless whisper.

"Go back to bed, my son."

"Not until you tell me what is wrong with you. Shall I get help? Are you sick?"

Chizen shook her head slowly and sadly. "Nothing is wrong. Now go back to bed and don't worry about me."

Hap didn't know what to do. It was obvious that his mother was not all right. It was just as obvious that she did not want his help. Two years before back on Sun's March he had come home from a work party and found her sitting still beside the window, unwilling or unable to talk to him. He never knew which.

The numbing cold crept up his legs. "I'll be right here if you need me," he said quietly. After giving her arm a gentle squeeze, he stepped quickly across the room and climbed back into his bed. Surprisingly, it had retained some of its previous warmth, and he snuggled deeply into the blankets with his knees drawn tightly up as he waited for his shivering to stop.

He remembered that other time only too clearly. His mother had waved off his offers of help then, too, and he had finally contented himself with sitting across from her and waiting to see what would happen. His first impulse had been to run for assistance. His second had been to cry. Then a sense of forlornness had overtaken him and he had sat on the hard plasteel bench across the room from her and waited, waited with a patience that was foreign and frightening to him.

Now he waited again, unsure if he was dealing with the same kind of problem, afraid that something was truly wrong with his mother, and surrounded by the residue of uncertainty left by his dreams.

Yet the blankets were warm, and his mind was fatigued. Drowsy fingers of sleep crept heavily across his eyelids. He knew he should stay awake, knew that he shouldn't abandon his mother, but the faith of youth told him that when he awoke everything would be all right again. He smiled ever so slightly as he fell asleep, but the corners of that smile kept twitching down and away.

Then he dreamed again, hearing more than he saw. Strange voices in singsong patterns lulled him to rest under the shadows of giant flowers. But the shadows darkened. The voices crackled with harsh static. And the whirling nightmare returned.

8

ShRil thought she should have questioned CrRina under Carson's guidance, but he had insisted on doing it himself.

"I'm afraid you might unintentionally influence her answers," he had said, "and I want her to react to me, not you."

Now ShRil was sure Carson had made the wrong decision. CrRina had been stubbornly uncooperative, limiting her responses to shakes and nods of her head. And with each response she had looked to ShRil and Gerard for approval.

As Gerard emptied the pot of Brandusian coffee into their mugs, he felt a growing sense of frustration. Carson's line of questioning had been too indirect as far as he was concerned, almost as though Carson were seeking answers to something besides indications that she might be receptive to the telepathic broadcasts from the flower colonies. Gerard wished that Carson would leave. But at the same time, he was fascinated by Carson's oddly detached attitude.

"I don't think you really have anything to worry about," Carson said quietly as he accepted the coffee from Gerard. "It seems to me...that is, she seems all right to me."

"Based on your questions?" Gerard asked. He tried to keep his tone as neutral as possible.

"Or on something else?" ShRil added almost before Carson could answer.

"I don't know. Call it informed intuition. Call it experience. It just seems to me that your daughter doesn't show signs of communication with the flowers."

CrRina looked up from the floor where she was playing with her blocks. Flowers. The man with the ooky face said "flowers." She knew what flowers were. She knew he was

48

mean. Ooky face, she thought. Ooky man. Mummum and Dedo told her to talk to ooky man. He talked funny. He was mean. CrRina didn't like him. "No," she said suddenly.

The three of them looked at her in surprise as she stared straight at Carson.

"No," she repeated with a mischievous smile. Then she started shuffling her blocks around on the floor.

"What do you suppose that meant?" Gerard asked with a look of amusement.

"I suspect your daughter doesn't like me."

"Perhaps," ShRil said quietly, "perhaps she did not like your questions."

"You think I asked the wrong things, don't you?"

"I think we both do," Gerard said.

"And you think I should try again?"

"No." ShRil did not want Carson questioning CrRina again—not now—not ever. Carson's actions and attitude had forced her to reevaluate her first impression of him, and she now believed that the cold distance she had felt behind his exterior was far closer to the real Carson than any of the positive impressions he had made on her. A shiver rippled almost imperceptibly up her spine.

"Maybe I should leave then," Carson said in an oddly defensive tone.

Gerard had to restrain himself from agreeing immediately. "It might be a good idea, for now," he said finally. "That will give us a chance to talk about all this. And talk to CrRina, too. Will you be staying with Junathun? Or will you be going back—"

"I'll go back. Nothing for me to do here. You can call me if you want to talk about this some more. But I still don't think you have anything to worry about." He rose as he said that and took his rough morning jacket off the back of the chair.

"Please don't misunderstand us, Carson," Gerard said as he rose also. "We do appreciate your interest and concern."

"Most certainly," ShRil added.

"But I'm afraid we're still a little confused by all this."

Carson stood at the door for a moment as he sealed the front of his jacket. "My fault. My fault. Shouldn't have alarmed you that way." When neither of them responded to that, he quickly said goodbye and left.

Gerard looked from the door to ShRil to CrRina, and was

suddenly aware of a hard knot in the pit of his stomach. "There's something wrong here," he said as he watched CrRina play, "something wrong with this whole thing."

ShRil picked CrRina up off the floor and cuddled her in her arms. CrRina immediately nestled her head between two of ShRil's three breasts as ShRil stroked her hair. "We love our CrRina," she whispered.

Love our Sirreena, echoed in her head. "Love Mummum. Love Dedo. Love Seets," CrRina mumbled. Mummum rocked her. The pictures came back soft and warm. *Sleep*, a voice whispered. CrRina slept.

The affection Gerard felt for his mate and daughter at that moment was something he could not have put into words. Of all the images he carried of them, the image of CrRina sleeping peacefully in ShRil's arms was one of his favorites. For a brief instant he remembered the day of CrRina's birth, and the joy they had shared with all their friends of Reyyer Delled. Then he thought of how hard physmedicant KtRiny had worked while treating CrRina, doing everything he could to ensure that one day she, too, would be capable of having children of her own.

The treatments had finally succeeded, but not without cost to Gerard and ShRil as well as CrRina. But their costs of mental anguish had been small in the face of CrRina's delayed development. Yet somehow CrRina had grown stronger much faster than anyone had expected she would after the treatments were completed. She had grown physically and mentally at a seemingly accelerated pace, as though trying to make up for the time she had lost. Only her speech patterns had remained immature, and Gerard was sure that, too, was a temporary problem.

"What shall we do?"

ShRil's question startled him out of his momentary reverie. "I don't know. Carson's questions seemed odd and off-center to me."

"To me also, my love. And I do not wish for him to question her again."

The tone of her voice told him as much as her words. "Why?"

"He frightens her. And he frightens me. Would be far better if you were to question her, I think."

"Why not both of us? I mean, why me?"

"Because, my love, you are the one who had the prescience, not I. How should I know what to look for?"

"I don't think we're talking about prescience here."

"Perhaps not. But if CrRina has some talent, some ability to listen to the flowers, I think you better capable of recognizing it than I. Does that seem unreasonable to you?"

It did, but Gerard wasn't about to say so. ShRil's voice carried a hard tone of commitment, and he had learned early in their relationship that when she used that tone she was very difficult to influence.

"I suppose not," he said carefully, "but I think we need to talk about what we're going to ask her before I do it. I thought she was a little frightened, too, and if she was frightened by the questions rather than Carson, I don't want to scare her any more."

ShRil stood up slowly, holding CrRina firmly against her. Had CrRina been reacting to the questions as well as Carson? She did not know, and she was not sure she wanted to know. Yet there was no way to avoid the problem. "I shall put her to bed, and then we shall talk."

Brightseed sensed the approaching kinous and recognized it. The silent companion to Amsrita had been a mystery to them while Amsrita was with them, and had remained a mystery after Amsrita had left. But Brightseed feared the silent kinous. Its muddled thoughts always echoed violence and a fear of its own which came through the barriers it erected against their probing.

Now, however, it stopped above them at the top of the meadow and Brightseed's Guardians sensed a new element in its thoughts. But this new element was something Brightseed could not define. It flowed out of the silent kinous in slow turbulent waves of dark emotion. Beneath the waves a steady undercurrent of revulsion tore at Brightseed's thoughts like the night eaters had torn at its roots.

Brightseed acted. First it sent a buffering wave of love through the groundsel to kinous Sirreena. Then it focused all its energy on one dark concept and sent that picture to the silent colony.

Carson saw death.

Gaping chasms opened in his thoughts and howling winds sucked at his soul from their depths. He stumbled and reeled, screaming with fury and pain. Nightmare images blinded him. Darkness opened up behind him and pulled him down, down, down into a whirlpool of insanity.

"Noooo!" he screamed in a voice that echoed like thunder through his mind. "Nooooo!"

The pain paused for one endless second as Amsrita's face hovered above him. "Amsrita!" he cried. "Nooo-o-o . . ."

Brightseed was stunned by the image. The concept of death rebounded from the kinous with numbing force. Death and Amsrita, locked in eternal embrace, turned in a narrowing gyre which bored into the center of all that Brightseed held sacred. Then the cold, deadly truth touched Brightseed's understanding, blocking out all other thoughts and all other feelings.

Kinous Amsrita was dead.

In the moment of that realization Brightseed recognized its own mortality. That death had come to other colonies was an understood fact. That it might one day come to Brightseed was a rational thought. But the idea that it was near at hand, as close as the silent kinous itself, and that Brightseed could in fact die at any moment, brought an upsurge of emotional truth which could not be denied.

Against all the teachings of Our-Gatou, Brightseed broadcast an impassioned denial of death laced with fear and contradiction.

Carson reeled again, buffeted by winds of confusion and anger, but freed for the moment from the agonizing pain. As quickly as he could he ran away from the patch, and with each step his aching heart pumped a newer and more poisonous hatred into his brain.

The flowers had gone too far. First they had tampered with the mind of the child. Then they had dared try to crush him with Amsrita's death. He would have his revenge. He would find a way. He would. He would. He would.

As though sensing the silent kinous's new resolution, Brightseed's thoughts suddenly stilled. In the harsh peace which followed there came a new image of itself, an image tainted by death and shame.

The One is all and always, came a weak thought. But the refrain was not taken up, and the subtle stirrings of Brightseed's thoughts were shaded by a kind of misery it had never known before.

Tears sprang uncontrollably from Hap's eyes. He sat in the late morning sun on a hill overlooking the settlement station and cried without knowing why.

Then for the briefest instant he knew why. Yet he was still too young to understand, too tender to recognize what he saw. In his confusion he thought the dark image in his brain was connected somehow with his mother's moody silence. But as he probed at that thought with the irrepressible curiosity of youth he knew that something else was happening to him.

Hap was suddenly afraid. He wanted to be held in his mother's arms. He wanted to be comforted. At the same time he knew in his heart that there would be no comfort there, no shelter from the blackness which invaded his thoughts. This pain did not come from his mother's mysterious mood. Nor did it come from inside him. Without understanding why, Hap knew that whatever was causing him to cry was coming from outside his thoughts, and fears, and dreams.

Like small streams after a heavy storm his tears increased. He hugged his knees in desperation, seeking some solace in the feel of his own body. But nothing helped. Nothing stemmed the tide. Nothing brought him the peace he sought.

Then totally without warning his tears subsided and a strange, blank stillness came over him. It was as though some unseen force had laid its presence upon his mind and brought him the peace he could not find on his own. He looked up, almost expecting to see someone or something which would explain what had happened to him. He was alone.

Then he heard the voices, distant and foreign, voices in a strange chanting rhythm which brought melancholy along with his newborn sense of peace. Hap rested his head on his knees and drew his legs tighter against his chest. The empty hollow in the pit of his stomach added to his sense of isolation.

This is the end, he thought. I am going to die.

Even as that idea coursed through his brain, a quiet voice inside him laughed at it. He wasn't going to die. He was just unhappy because his mother was unhappy. It was the trip, and the flight down on the shuttle, and the strange dreams which were causing this. It was the air in this new place which made him feel like a little boy again.

Hap growled with youthful determination. This was their new home, and nothing, nothing was going to ruin it for him. He would go to his mother and help her as best he could. But he would not let the dreams and the trip spoil this place.

As he looked up he realized that this small hill offered him a dramatic view of their new home. Brisbidine was beautiful. To his left a high range of hills mounted above the horizon. To his right flowers grew in wild profusion. He caught a glimpse of a man running down the hill toward the settlement station, but he could not guess why the man was running.

Exercise, he thought suddenly. With an odd shift of emotion he felt the need to run also. He stood up quickly and let out a little whoop of joy. Then he ran, letting his momentum carry him faster and faster down the path and back to his mother. He could cheer her up. He knew he could. And when he did, they would be a team again, ready to face their new challenges.

9

"I do not understand, my love. Why do you think moving close to one of the flower colonies is going to help us? If CrRina is vulnerable to them, would that not place her at much greater risk?"

Gerard reached for ShRil in the darkness of their bed and pulled her close to him. "Yes, perhaps it would," he said softly, "but Windy could also be used to shield her. And maybe, just maybe we can use Windy's computers and detection equipment to determine what the colony is actually broadcasting."

ShRil squeezed him gently and nestled her head on his shoulder. "I had not thought about Windy protecting her. Do you suppose we would have any trouble with the move?"

"What do you mean?"

"Well, it seems to me that the settlement council is not going to be very pleased when you tell them what you want to do. They were very particular about where we set her in the first place. I cannot imagine how they will react when you say we want to move our spaceship out into the bush. I suspect, however, that they will not be pleased."

"Suppose we don't ask them? There's nothing going on out there, no farming or anything. How could they object?"

ShRil sighed. "My love, my love, how innocent you seem sometimes. People do not need rational reasons to object. All they need is the thought of someone doing something they have not done or would not do themselves."

Gerard absently traced his fingers along her naked ribs in light little circles which edged along the sides of her breast. She was right, of course. The settlement council would probably object just for the sake of objecting. Still, he didn't think those kinds of objections would be too difficult to handle.

"Look, we don't have much time. According to Amsrita's reports, or Carson's reports, or whosever they are, once the colonies start freeing their pollen we won't be able to do anything out there. And according to Junathun we only have about fifteen days at best until that starts. The least we can do is try to gather as much information as possible during that time."

"I agree."

"Then why are you resisting the idea of moving Windy?"

"I am not resisting your idea. First I wished to understand your reason for wanting to move her. And then I hoped to help you see that the problem was not as simple as you seemed to think. If you do not care for my help, I am sure I can find other things to do."

She tried to pull away from him, but Gerard held onto her. "What are you so touchy about?"

"I am not touchy. However, there are times when you treat me as though I were your adversary rather than your mate—and a stupid adversary at that."

"And what is that supposed to mean?" The irritation he heard in his own voice only served to annoy him further.

"It means, Gerard Manley, that you should practice that sensitivity which so attracted me to you in the first place. There have been times of late when I do believe you take me for granted. Faithful ShRil, always here when you need her, but not to be considered otherwise."

"Kravor in Krick," he said. "Isn't it bad enough that we have to cope with the problems at hand without you starting an argument about how I feel about you? We've been through this before. I accept you as an equal, and assume that you want to be treated as one. But when I treat you too much like an equal and refuse to pamper your—"

"Pamper?"

"Yes, pamper. When I refuse to pamper your intellect by drawing a picture for you, *you* claim I'm being insensitive."

"Not so loud. You will wake CrRina."

"Let her wake up. She's in the middle of this thing. Or have you forgotten that?"

"No, I have not."

Silence filled the room. They had indeed had this argument before and ShRil always came out of it feeling as though Gerard had not understood what she had said. He listened. He sympathized with her complaints. But always, always he had a calm, rational way of taking the heat out of them and leading her into agreement with him that she was making too much out of the problem. Yet that was at the heart of the problem. Gerard never took it as seriously as she did.

He stared at the dark ceiling, grateful that ShRil had not turned away from him, but unable or unwilling to make the first gesture of reconciliation. There was no person in the universe he respected more than ShRil. She was intelligent, logical, quick-witted, and sensitive. But there were times when she frustrated him totally. One remark made in the course of a discussion could put him in trouble with her for days. That was one of the enigmas of their relationship which he had yet to learn to cope with.

"ShRil," he said finally, "I'm sorry. I meant no disrespect to you."

She waited to see if he was going to say more before responding. When it was obvious he was not, she said, "I know that, my love."

56

Gerard wrapped his arms around her and gave her a long, firm hug. "Forgive me?"

"Of course." Her fingers searched out the soft flesh at his waist where he was the most ticklish.

"Watch that stuff," he said, drumming his fingertips lightly on her ribs.

"Watch what?" she asked with a well-placed little poke that caused him to jerk with a stifled giggle.

"That." He dug his fingers gently into his favorite sensitive spot on her ribs. She tensed with a muffled gasp.

Instantly they twisted together, each seeking advantage, each trying to defend against fingers, then toes, then lips. ShRil pulled out from under him and straddled his body, attempting to pin his arms with her knees. He got one hand free and pulled her toward him until he could draw her middle breast into his mouth. She resisted for a moment longer, then adjusted her hips to pin him another way.

Gerard moaned. ShRil tensed her muscles. He moved against her seeking a closeness they had found many times before. Their argument was forgotten for the moment, and so was the question of moving *Windhover* to a site near the flower colony.

Later as they snuggled together in the warmth of their love, they talked of that and many other things which were troubling them. Just before they mumbled off to sleep Gerard wondered briefly where all this was leading and if it might not just be smarter to report failure to Alvin and head back to Jelvo U.

Essenne and Hap had both gone to bed. Chizen and Geljoespiy were alone for the first time since they had met and she felt uncomfortable. It had been a bad day, a day full of questions which had no answers, and memories from which there was no reprieve. She wasn't sure why she hadn't gone to bed yet. She had barely slept the night before. Nor was she sure why Geljoespiy had been so interested in sitting up with her.

"Have you thought about what I asked you?"

His voice registered oddly in her ear. Its tone carried an emotional undercurrent she couldn't identify. "I have," she answered quietly, "but we know too little about our options to make a choice yet."

"So what is it you want to know?"

57

"I am not sure, Geljoespiy. I am not sure that we even know enough to ask the proper questions yet."

"Then perhaps I can give you another option," Gel said. He wanted to explore her feelings about the boy's father first, but at the same time he felt a sense of urgency about making his proposal to her.

"What would that be, Geljoespiy?"

"You can call me Gel. Most folks do."

"Thank you. When we know each other better perhaps." She paused a moment. "The other option?"

Gel looked away from her, afraid she would see something in his eyes he was not yet ready to reveal. "I may be rushing this," he said as evenly as he could, "and you'll forgive me for butting against your personal affairs, but I think we might have a great deal in common, you and me—a great deal indeed."

Was he about to proposition her? Chizen couldn't believe it. Who did this man think he was?

Who was he? That was a better question. And what was he talking about? "I am not sure I understand you."

Gel looked at her, then away again. He had started it all wrong. He could tell that by the look on her face. "Don't get me wrong, Mis Chizen. I'm not leading up to anything personal, if you know what I mean."

"No, I don't know what you mean. And I am not sure I want to know. Goodnight, Geljoespiy," she said as she stood up.

"Please, mis. Don't go yet. Let me explain to you what I'm talking about."

Chizen stared at him for a long moment. The questions repeated themselves. Reluctantly she sat back down, unwilling to give up this chance for some answers. "Very well, then. But please be as direct as you can."

Gel let out a heavy sigh. "I'll try, mis, indeed I will. But you'll have to hear a bit of history first that can't be avoided. Do ya mind?"

"As I said, Geljoespiy, please be as direct as you can. If the history is necessary, I will listen, but I will expect you to tell me only that which is necessary."

Gel wished he could start over. He knew she was interested. Yet he could also hear her impatience and sense her suspicion. With another deep sigh he began.

"I have a friend, a very powerful friend who saved my life once. Don't ask his name," he said, holding up his hand. "I can't tell you that. And it's for your own protection. Anyway, this friend of mine knew you were coming here and—"

"How? And who is this friend?" Fear laid a cool hand on her neck as she wondered if her sister . . . She let the thought fade as Geljoespiy answered. But the fear remained, an almost tactile presence which raised the hairs at the base of her skull.

"I told you I can't tell you his name. And I don't know how he knows what he knows. He's powerful, that's all. And he's got connections. He made sure you landed in our sector and told me to watch out for you. He's a good friend to have, Mis Chizen. You do little things for him and he'll do big ones for you."

"What possible interest could I have in this friend of yours?"

"Gerard Manley."

Chizen felt frozen in place. She fought an impulse to gasp, and another one to jump out of the chair. The last thing she needed was another link to Gerard.

"He's here, Mis Chizen, not five kilometers from where we sit. And my friend tells me you have reason to want him dead."

"Goodnight, Geljoespiy," Chizen said curtly as she rose from her chair. The hand of fear had turned cold and tightened its grip. "There is no need for us to talk about this further."

Gel knew he had failed. She wasn't going to listen, and he had no idea how to make her.

Before he could say anything else Chizen left the room. She closed the door to their room as quietly as she could so as not to awaken Hap. Then she leaned back against the door with her arms folded tightly across her chest and tried to understand what she had just heard. A surprising flow of tears rolled quietly down her face.

Who was Geljoespiy's friend? Targ Alpluakka? Fianne Tackona? One of the Holstens? Squo Lyle? The list of men in Ribble Galaxy who might have gained knowledge about her emigration to Brisbidine was too extensive to pursue. But whoever it was owned Geljoespiy. She could tell that. So, if she failed to do what the directive asked of her, if she failed to kill Hap's father, Geljoespiy's friend would know.

And what would he do? Order Geljoespiy to kill her for failing? She sniffed and shuddered at the same time and rubbed her nose on the sleeve of her shirt. She felt as though she had been robbed of something she had never owned, something precious which had almost been hers, but which had been suddenly pulled beyond her grasp.

That something was freedom. She had not been free when she existed under her sister's oppressive hand in Ribble Galaxy. She certainly had not been very free on Sun's March. But freedom was why she had applied for emigration to Brisbidine, and the magnetic lure of that freedom had allowed her to accept the sealed directive without hesitation.

Now that was all gone, swept away by the combined power of the directive and Geljoespiy's mysterious friend. Like a delicate flower shriveling under the heat of a relentless sun Chizen slowly slid down the door into a tightly curled ball.

Her tears had stopped and a tight, dry pain replaced them. Was there no end to what she must suffer? Was there no peace for her anywhere in the whole universe? The answer blew through her mind like a dustdevil carving a tortuous path through the parched desert of her hopes and dreams.

She would do as directed. She would kill Gerard Manley. His seductive presence in Ribble Galaxy had ruined her life. Now she would take his life and be free of him and all the grief he had brought her—forever. She had no idea how she would do it, but she was sure Geljoespiy did.

Her lips twisted into a grim smile which died almost immediately at the sudden thought of Hap. What if he found out? What would she do? How could she explain that . . . that . . . that it had been necessary to kill his father?

Tears flowed again, bitter, angry tears. There was no stopping them and Chizen did not try. She would suffer for whatever she chose to do, and she would find no peace, no freedom, no release from the dark shadows which hovered constantly over her life.

10

Cosvetz circled its sun once every four hundred fifty-four local days. Its seven moons returned to their most spectacular arrangement in the sky once every sixteen years and sixty-two days. The conjunction of the approaching lunar spectacle and the arrival of the Constant above Cosvetz was an unfortunate one. The pioneers would be watching the skies in anticipation, and the Constant would have to use great caution to shield its presence from Cosvetz's inhabitants.

Only Gatou-Drin and Spinnertel were unconcerned by this—Gatou-Drin because she would be the only member of the Constant allowed to escape that shield and set foot on Cosvetz—and Spinnertel because he had intentions of visiting the planet quite without the Constant's permission.

Another conjunction worried Spinnertel much more. That the alleged Verporchting and its offspring had come to this out-of-the-way planet from opposite ends of the universe smacked of outside intervention, intervention which he had to assume came from some member of the Constant.

Consequently, a middling infraction of the Constant's rules concerned him far less than what he observed after arriving early at the rendezvous behind Cosvetz's fourth moon. His plan for the Verporchting was not going well at all. Spinnertel had limited his observations to the most surreptitious kind, but what he had seen and heard left little doubt in his mind that he would have to take a personal hand in the matter.

Yet he knew that personal attention would also have to be surreptitious, and very, very subtle. If he were caught, the consequences could be extremely painful. But that risk excited him more than it frightened him. In fact, he acknowl-

61

edged to himself, he had not been so excited in a long, long time.

That worried him. He wasn't used to being excited. The strange thought had entered his mind that it was just as dangerous to be excited as it was to thwart the Constant's rules. And despite several serious attempts to dismiss that thought, it refused to go away.

With a shrug of his hairy shoulders he accepted the mix of responses and decided to focus his monitoring equipment on the alleged Verporchting. It was time he knew more about this individual Gracietta was so impressed with, time to prepare for any contingencies which might arise, and time to decide for himself whether this was the true Verporchting or not.

Hap had awakened the night before to the sounds of his mother crying. He had tried to comfort her as she had comforted him, holding her in his arms, telling her everything would be all right, and trying to soothe her mysterious grief by stroking her hair. The whole time he had been frightened and uncomfortable. But when she had finally quieted and fallen asleep in his aching arms he had felt a new sense of strength and resolve.

It's the move from Sun's March, he thought, as he wandered into the hills above the settlement station the next day. Or, his young mind suggested, maybe it was leaving Ribble Galaxy which made her so sad. That had to be it. He had been born on Sun's March, and from a very early age had understood that their struggle to survive in that hostile environment was something which had been forced on them.

Hap knew very little about his mother's past, but simple observation had shown him she was different in many ways from the mothers of his friends. When he was very small she had told him enchanting stories about princesses and battles and the famous Tania Houn Draytonmab.

But as he got older and asked for repetitions of those stories it seemed to him that she shortened them. Then finally when he was nine or ten years old she had refused to tell the stories any more. "You are too old for stories like that," she had said. "It is time you learned to live in the real universe instead of a make-believe one."

Yet Hap always suspected that the stories were real, that

she had lived in that magical place she described so clearly. He had never dared confront her with that idea, but now, in the face of her inexplicable tears and grief he was convinced that part of what she was crying for was a world she would never see again. He could understand that. He had left some friends behind on Sun's March, friends he really liked, so maybe—

A soft, distant voice buzzed in his ear and cut his thoughts short. Hap turned his head quickly from side to side trying to see who was out here with him. There was no one around. But he still heard the voice. It sang or chanted in words he couldn't quite understand to an odd, buzzing tune that sounded vaguely familiar.

He turned more slowly this time, looking for signs of movement or a spot of color which would help him locate the singer. All he saw were the hills, and the grass, and the low trees and bushes, and off in the distance below him, a huge circle of flowers. He remembered the nightmare with the flowers and his mother's face and for a moment he was frightened.

The voice changed pitch, rose in a long trilling sound, and then fell silent. Hap shook his head. He had heard that voice before. He was sure of it. But he couldn't remember where.

Then he heard another sound, a low mumbling mix of voices which seemed to be carried up the slope on the faint breeze. Someone was down there. He knew it.

Hap never asked himself if he should investigate who was talking. He just headed down the hill toward the distant flowers. Then a sudden memory made him blush and hesitate. Once on Sun's March he had followed the sound of voices to a small shed behind the work school. When he had peeked inside he had seen a boy and a girl wrestling with each other without their clothes on. He ran away without getting caught, but he had wondered about them for a long time. After he finally asked his friends if they had ever seen anything like that, he didn't believe what they told him. So he asked his mother.

She told him more that night than he ever wanted to know about boys and girls and what they did when they wrestled naked. And why they did it. For months after that whenever he was with a girl he thought was nice, he would suddenly feel himself blushing and wanting to run away. Suppose something like that was going on down near the flowers?

That possibility drew Hap like the scent of pollen draws heatherflies. There was no way he could have resisted. Without thinking, he moved quickly into the line of low trees and bushes and made his way quietly down the hill, impelled by an overwhelming curiosity and a healthy stirring in his glands.

The One is here and everywhere, the voice said quietly.

Hap stopped in midstep, trembling with confusion, his mouth dry, and his heart pounding.

Welcome, kinous Hap.

"Uuune!" he gasped. Then he lost his balance and fell down.

Peace, the voice said quietly. *Do not be afraid.*

It was in his head! The voice was in his head! Hap grabbed at the bushes as he tried to get to his feet. The voice was in his head.

We are Brightseed. You are Hopeman-known-as-Hap. The One is whole. Be not afraid.

Hap was very afraid. Whoever was talking knew his name. As he got to his feet he looked wildly around. Panic pumped through his veins.

Peace, the voice said soothingly. *Please do not leave us. We welcome your presence.*

"Where . . . where are you?" he asked in a voice which quavered between high and low registers. He still didn't see anyone.

We are . . .

The rest of what they said came to Hap as images rather than words, images of flowers which filled his brain, then flowed through his eyes until they matched what he saw before him. The flowers? He didn't understand.

Yes, kinous Hap. We are what you call flowers. *Come talk to us and share our thoughts.*

For the second time that afternoon Hap moved down the hill drawn by an attraction that stirred warmly within him. None of this made sense. Flowers couldn't talk. It was silly. It was crazy.

It is the One as Our-Gatou has told us, the voice said.

The one what? That didn't make any sense either.

The One which is everything and nothing.

Hap broke through the last of the bushes and stared at the

meadow below him. A huge circle packed with knee-high flowers almost filled the space. Around the edges there were funny-looking plants shaped like—

The Guardians.

Without thinking Hap sat down. He felt numb and alive at the same time. If this was real, it was crazy. And if it wasn't real, he must be crazy.

You are not crazy, Hopeman-called-Hap. You are in the High-Fertile-Meadow, and Brightseed is graced by your presence.

"That's your name? Brightseed?"

That is how we are called. As you are called Hap, we are called Brightseed.

"How can you hear me?"

The One provides a way.

"Are you reading my mind?"

Our friend, the kinous called Amsrita, described it so.

"Who's Amsrita? What's a kinous?" Hap had forgotten his fear. He was so fascinated by what was happening that for the moment nothing else in the world existed for him.

Amsrita is gone.

Hap saw the image of a woman and felt a deep sense of sorrow he couldn't explain. But he knew in some instinctive way that this Brightseed had loved Amsrita.

Yes, Brightseed said. *You understand. Amsrita was kinous as you are kinous.*

He saw a hazy image of himself as though distorted in a bad mirror. Beside his image was a clearer one of the woman. Then his image sharpened and focused until it looked like the picture his mother carried of him.

Better? Brightseed asked.

"Yes, but how . . ."

We see you as you see yourself, Brightseed replied.

Hap thought about that for a moment. He was still confused and a little skeptical, but he was also excited. "How did you know my name?" They read my mind, he thought. "Well, how did you get here, I mean . . ."

Before Brightseed could answer Hap heard a new voice singing in the distance. "Who? What?"

Kinous Sirreena.

The image of a little girl filled Hap's mind. "Can she talk to you?"

Kinous Sirreena is young and open. Her heart is with the One, Brightseed said. *Listen as we talk to her.*

Hap listened as Brightseed and this kinous Sirreena exchanged little chants about the One. It seemed silly to him, a waste of time. Yet as he listened he realized that he was listening to a field of flowers talking to a little girl far away. A sense of wonder grew in him until it surpassed anything he had ever experienced.

The flowers were *talking* to the girl, and he was *listening!* He couldn't wait to tell his mother about this.

The chanting stopped abruptly. *No, kinous Hap, you must tell no one.*

"Not even Mother? But why?"

The time is not right. Share with us first as we will share with you. When the time is right to tell others, we will know.

When Hap wandered back into Gel's house shortly before dusk he felt as if he had interrupted something. No one seemed particularly concerned about where he had been, and his mind was too distracted by all that had happened to pay much attention to them. As he lay snuggled down in his blankets after eating a huge supper, he thought he heard Brightseed and Sirreena chanting again. Their songs filled his head, blocking out the low conversation from the other rooms.

When his mother came in much later she saw Hap's face bathed in the soft light of Brisbidine's seven moons and wearing an innocent smile. At least one of them had found some peace here.

Carson held Liana tenderly in his arms. "I've got to go," he said quietly.

"You've always got to go. And you always expect me to be here when you get back."

"But you always are. That's one of the reasons I'm so fond of you."

Liana pulled gently away from him and rolled on her side. "Well, don't be surprised if you come back this time and I'm gone. Maybe it's time I wandered, too."

"Where would you go?"

"I don't know. Just away somewhere. Maybe I'll meet some man who can be more than fond of me."

"Don't, Liana. Please? We've been through this before. I

give you all the affection I have to give. What more do you want from me?"

Liana didn't answer. She lay still, and stiff, and quiet, her only response to his question a long-drawn-out breath which signalled her disappointment.

11

Gerard had marked and cleared the landing spot carefully and placed the homing beacon at its northernmost edge so that Windy had no trouble at all setting herself down directly in the center of her new berth. ShRil had been right about the settlement council's eagerness to object to moving Windy out near the flowers. However, when Junathun surprised everyone by recommending approval of the move, their objections lost what little momentum they had gained, and the issue was settled in less than an hour.

It had taken them a full day to locate, mark, and clear the place he thought would serve them best, and almost another day to pack their gear back aboard Windy and make all the other arrangements necessary to placate the council.

Now as he waited patiently for Windy to level herself, Gerard stared at the flowers down the hill from them and wondered if this would really help resolve anything. Sitting there on the hilltop he realized that it was only the vague hope that Windy might do them some good which had impelled him to suggest that they move in the first place. He had no specific ideas in mind about what they were

"Seets! Where is Seets?" CrRina demanded as she appeared beside him suddenly.

"I don't know, CrRina. Maybe Shttz took a trip to see the rest of Brisbidine."

"Hap. Where is Hap?"

Gerard picked her up and sat her in his lap, marveling at how much her speech seemed to be improving. "Who is Hap, darling?"

"You know, Dedo," she said in a singsong voice. "Hap is that bo-ey."

With a smile he said, "I don't know who you're talking about. Did you meet a boy at the center?" She had spent most of the two days it took them to prepare for the move being cared for by Essenne at the community nursery center.

"No, Dedo, not *that* boy. The *other* boy. The boy with the flowers in his hair."

Gerard laughed. He certainly hadn't seen any boy with flowers in his hair. "You show him to me next time, okay?"

CrRina tilted her head at an odd angle and scrunched up her face. "Oh, Dedo, you know, the Boy!" Without warning she squirmed out of his lap and headed for the ladder. "Come on, Dedo. Play."

"In a minute, darling. You go see Mummum. Tell her I'm hungry." He watched her climb carefully down the ladder and smiled again. What a daughter, he thought. As he turned back to Windy's controls with an amused shake of his head, another thought struck him. It was more an image than a thought and it lasted barely long enough for him to recognize it.

That was enough. It was the image of Fairy Peg surrounded by the whirling flowers.

Whatever humor he felt was gone. Was that what CrRina had meant? Had she seen an image like that? But who was this Hap? He didn't recall any child on Reyyer Delled or Alvin's Place called Hap. But maybe she remembered some child he hadn't met. He would have to ask ShRil. Maybe she would remember.

The image of Fairy Peg had caused a darkening of his mood. He tried to shrug it off and finish giving Windy her status instructions. I'll cope with it later, he thought.

Now, Gerard, Self answered. Cope with it now.

"Talking to myself again," he mumbled, "won't do any good."

Yes, it will.

With a sigh he leaned back in the pilot's chair and switched on his journal recorder. Self wasn't very good at being put off, so if he was going to have to cope with it now, he might as well make notes he could refer to later.

"Okay, let's look at the facts. CrRina says she saw a boy with flowers in his hair, a boy named Hap. That name doesn't ring any bells with me, and we don't know where she saw him. If she got the image through the flowers, that means we're just going to have to be that much more careful. And if she really did see a boy with flowers in his hair, then we're getting excited about nothing. There, Self. Satisfied?"

When he got no response, he switched off the journal and finished his shipkeeping chores as quickly as he could, knowing all the while that Self would not let this problem rest until they came to some greater understanding of it.

As he worked Windy seemed to sense his impatience and set the routine up ahead of him without having to be prompted. "Thanks, girl," he said to her as he rose from his chair and pressed the last button. "Keep an eye on us. And on that patch of Wheezer's Bane down there. I want to know if anyone else comes out our way. Not that I'm worried or anything, you understand. I just want to be careful."

Windy gave him an affirmative beep. With that he hit the ladder with his hands and the arches of his feet and with a practiced slide dropped down to the main deck. He was startled to see ShRil waiting for him there. "You ready to eat?"

"The food is prepared and CrRina is eating. I was just coming to get you."

The look on her face told him something was bothering her. "What's wrong?" he asked, as he drew her into his arms and gave her a gentle hug. Fara, he loved the feel of her.

She pulled back from him a little but kept her hands around his waist. "CrRina is talking about the One again."

"And about some boy named Hap," he added.

"Yes. Do you know who she means?"

"I was going to ask you that very question. I thought it might have been some child she remembered from Reyyer Delled or Alvin's Place."

"I remember no child by that name." ShRil looked at him carefully and could tell by the set of his eyes that he had been thinking about this. "What did she say to you?"

"First she asked where Shttz was. Then she asked where

69

Hap was. When I asked her *who* Hap was, she said, 'The boy, Dedo! The boy,' like I should know who she meant."

"She said the same thing to me."

Gerard squeezed her. "We'll figure it out one way or the other," he said as reassuringly as he could. "But we can't let CrRina know how concerned we are."

"Agreed, my love."

As they went to join CrRina for the meal, neither of them felt very reassured.

The content of Letrenn's latest message was a surprise to Gel. Letrenn was coming to Brisbidine. The message gave no indication of when, just that Letrenn was coming and that he would tell Gel when and where to meet him. Gel was not surprised that Letrenn insisted on complete secrecy for the visit, but he was both surprised and concerned that Letrenn was coming.

In spite of all the persuasion he could muster, Gel didn't think he was any closer to persuading Chizen to do anything. She was a puzzle he might never work out. She asked intelligent questions and seemed interested enough in what he told her. But she staunchly maintained a detachment from him that he just did not understand.

Gel had tried to be circumspect. He had talked about the advantages of doing favors for Letrenn and how well Letrenn had taken care of him. Of course, he never mentioned Letrenn by name, and that might have been part of his problem with her. He, too, would have a hard time placing his trust in some unknown stranger pressed upon him by still another stranger.

He had also kept Gerard Manley's name out of the conversation, waiting for her to mention it, for her to ask the questions which would allow him to tell her more. She steadfastly refused to take advantage of that opening, preferring to let him take the lead and guide the conversation. It was as though she were being entertained by his attempts to win her confidence, but refused to acknowledge the link which connected their interests.

The boy was another problem altogether. He usually wandered off every day right after breakfast and didn't return until sundown or later. Gel didn't mind not having the boy underfoot, but he wanted to win his confidence also. Gel had seen far too little of his own sons and their families since they had married and gone out to the distant settlements, and he missed them. Hap seemed like a nice enough boy, and Gel wanted to take a fatherly attitude toward him.

His fatherly instinct said that the boy was too much of a dreamer, too wrapped up in his own thoughts to be concerned enough with the demands of life. Gel had held his tongue about that, too, not wanting to alienate the boy, and certainly not wanting to give Chizen more reasons to maintain her detachment.

"You sleeping in there?" Essenne asked as she rapped on the door of his tiny office.

"No. Come on in." As soon as he saw the look on her face he was sorry. She was working on some problem, something she had been stewing over for a while. After twenty-three years with her he could almost tell whether it was a problem about things or one about people. Problems about things wrinkled her brow. Problems about people almost always puckered the skin between her eyes into deep ridges. This looked like a people problem. "What's bothering you?"

She sat in his lap and nestled for a moment until she got her bony frame comfortable. When she put her arms around his neck, that was almost positive confirmation that she was struggling with a people problem.

"You looked close at that boy?" she asked. "I mean, have you looked at him real close? 'Course you haven't. You never did look close at kids. Somethin' about him's bothered me since the moment they set foot in the door."

"He hasn't given you any trouble, has he?"

"Not that kind of bother," she said in a tone which implied he should have known what she meant. "I mean the 'look' of him bothers me. Couldn't figure it out until this morning at the nursery. Then it all . . . well, I don't know what all it did."

"It got you to talk to me about it," he offered.

"True enough, Gel. But I still can't put my finger on what it is—about the way he looks, I mean."

"He remind you of someone?" Gel regretted the question as soon as he asked it. No sense in her having to deal with all the complexities he was already involved in. She always had her own to worry about, what with coping with the nursery staff, dealing with problem kids—and parents—and somehow always being there when anyone needed a little extra help.

71

"That's the part of it that doesn't make any sense. He looks like CrRina."

"CrRina?"

"Oh, you know. Belongs to Gerard and ShRil. I know you know who ShRil is. Her three juggles have been the talk of the settlement since they got here."

Gel laughed, trying to hide everything that he did know. "You mean since her juggles got here? Or since she got here?"

"Don't you make fun of me, Geljoespiy. You're just like every other man around here, wondering what you couldn't do with a third one."

"Now, Essy—"

"And don't you now Essy me, either. I came in here with a problem and I expect you to help me solve it."

"So what's your problem?"

"I want to know why that boy's looks bother me so much. I've seen lots of kids that looked like other people's kids before—especially around here where half the folks seem to be getting related to one another—but it's more than that."

"And it's really bothering you?"

She moved her hands from his neck to his shoulders and tightened her grip. "No, Gel. I just came in here to sit on your lap and let you make fun of me."

He knew she was angry, and sighed heavily. "All right, Essy. I'm going to tell you something. But you've got to promise me, absolutely and totally promise me, that you won't tell another soul." He knew that if he didn't tell her the truth, she would worry it to death until she figured it out for herself, or drive him crazy trying to. Might as well save her the trouble, and prevent the possibility of her saying something about it to the wrong person.

"You know something, don't you?"

"Yes, Essy, I know something. But you've got to promise before I tell you."

"Now you don't trust your own wife, is that it?"

"That's not it at all. It's just that Letrenn—"

"Letrenn? Is he back? I thought you said he wasn't—"

"*He* said he wasn't ever coming back here again. But he needs my help, and what he needs has to do with your problem."

She leaned back and looked at him suspiciously. "You know

72

I never did like him, even if he did save your life. Too hairy and strange . . . but . . . all right. I promise."

"I know you don't like Letrenn, and I know you're not going to like what I'm about to tell you, but you're going to have to accept the whole situation. We owe more than my life to Letrenn. If it hadn't been for him, I'd have never made it to Brisbidine. Then I wouldn't have met you, and we wouldn't have had three fine sons and twenty-three happy years together."

"You never told me—"

"There was no reason. I just want you to understand why I feel so strongly indebted to him. Over the years he's never given me much of an opportunity to repay that debt, and the little favors he did ask were easy enough to do. Now he wants something bigger, much bigger, something that will just about make us even."

For the first time Gel realized how heavily his obligation to Letrenn had been weighing on him, but he continued with only the slightest hesitation. "Gerard Manley was a diplomat before he became a researcher for that Jelvo Universal Institute. And while he was a diplomat he did two things which are important for you to know. He fathered the boy, Hap, and he caused the deaths of thousands of innocent people on two different occasions."

"Him? He seems like such a nice—"

"He may be now, but he wasn't then. The people who died were Chizen's people, so she has two reasons to hate him. I don't know what Letrenn's interest in him is. All I know is that Letrenn wants him dead, and he wants Chizen to kill him. He asked me to make sure that happened, and I said I would."

"It's horrible, Gel. Just horrible."

"It's life, Essy, and justice. The man has to pay for his crimes. That's all you have to think about. I'm going to help see that justice is done. And you're going—"

"But, Gel—"

"And you're going to help me do it," he insisted, "by keeping all this tight inside you. All right?"

After a long pause she whispered, "All right."

12

Brightseed feared the strange presence at the top of the hill. Whatever it was had destroyed hundreds of groundsel and sent death images through the colony on high voltage jolts of pain. It belonged to the kinous—Brightseed was sure of that. But what kinous? And why was it there?

Compounding Brightseed's concern was that with the coming of the killing thing to the top of the hill kinous Hap had failed to return. Surely kinous Hap had not been killed by the strange presence. Brightseed was sure it would have known if that had happened.

Low-Riverside-Bend and East-Slope and three or four other colonies had heard Brightseed's cry of anguish when the thing had killed the groundsel. But they could offer no help, and little consolation. Rolling-Field-with-Thorns had even gone so far as to suggest that Brightseed's use of the groundsel to communicate with kinous Sirreena had caused this misfortune. Brightseed had not believed that, but it was worried about kinous Sirreena also. She seemed to have disappeared. In an effort to quiet its own fears as well as answer Rolling-Field's accusation, Brightseed had responded with a refrain from the Accumulated Words.

The One is all things which happen, whether by day or by night. The One abides in all events, and all things, and all times. The One is.

None of the colonies had answered that, and Brightseed had withdrawn into its own thoughts, attempting to heal the wounds which traveled from the aching crown of its dead and dying groundsel.

Then a new pain struck. But it was followed almost immediately by the thoughts of kinous Sirreena. She was happy. She was well. She was there on the top of the hill with the strange presence.

There?

There? Had kinous Sirreena brought death to the groundsel? Brightseed gently probed her thoughts. Sirreena had come with the presence of death. But she knew no death.

A momentary stillness filled Brightseed's mind. The implication was all too clear. *Our-Gatou walks with death, but does not die.* So said the Accumulated Words. Could kinous Sirreena be Our-Gatou come again to bless them with . . . No. Kinous Sirreena was an innocent, a young colony unknowing in the ways of the world. Some outside force had brought her into Brightseed's presence, some outside force with no understanding of what it had done.

Again stillness filled Brightseed's mind, followed by one word which would ever rule its actions: *patience.* So it lay quiet under the shadow of the hill, and waited, and listened with growing wonder to what it heard.

"See the flowers, Dedo? They're my flowers. Let's go see my flowers?"

She looked up at him in such sweet innocence that Gerard almost said yes. But the memory of his encounter with the flowers plus the tangled story of Amsrita and Carson made it easy for him to be firm with her. "Maybe tomorrow, CrRina," he said softly as he squatted down beside her.

"Why, Dedo?"

"Because we have some things we have to do first."

"What?"

"Just some things your Mummum and I have to do."

"I'll go."

She almost pulled away from him, but Gerard quickly grabbed her and hugged her to his chest. "Oh no you don't, you little spacer. When you go, we'll all go."

"Hap can go. Why can't I?"

Hap. That name again. Gerard was more than ready to find out who this mysterious Hap was. "You'll have to ask Hap," he said lamely. "Now it's time to get back aboard."

"Aw, Dedo. The flowers are fun."

"Back aboard," he said as he picked her up. "Tomorrow we can have fun." There was no conviction in his voice when he said that, and he was more than glad that CrRina was too young to detect such things.

(Dedo told a fibber), CrRina thought as Gerard carried her back aboard *Windhover*. (But I'll see you tomorrow.)

Hap sat in the dark talking to Brightseed. It had warned him not to come too close, trying to explain the strange presence on the hill, but he didn't really understand until the first three of Brisbidine's seven moons had broken the darkness and cast their silvery light onto the distant hilltop. There was a spaceship sitting there.

It had taken Hap more than a little while to explain to Brightseed exactly what the spaceship was. But when it finally gathered enough images from his mind and sent them back to him for confirmation, it added another image, the image of that little girl, the one Brightseed called kinous Sirreena.

"You mean she's aboard the spaceship?"

Yes.

"Can we talk to her?"

Yes, but only with great difficulty. There are barriers we do not understand between her and us. But the kinous called Dedo has promised to bring her to us when the sun shines again. We shall talk to her then. Now we must rest, Hap. We will be glad when you return.

Hap recognized Brightseed's form of goodbye. He thought about the good feelings he got talking to Brightseed, felt that feeling acknowledged, and headed back toward Geljoespiy's house.

As he walked he wished he had someone to share all this with. Brightseed had told him there would come a time when he could share what had passed between them, and Brightseed had also said that he would know when that time was. For now he would have to exercise the patience he had learned so slowly during his life on Sun's March.

He would wait before he told anyone. He would talk to Brightseed as much as he could, and perhaps the girl, Sirreena, and he would watch for some sign that—

"Whoa, boy."

Hap almost jumped out of his skin. A man was standing in the path not three meters in front of him.

"Got to watch where you're going, boy. Can't be wandering around in the dark without paying attention. I thought you were going to run right into me."

"Stuh-duh, um. I'm sorry, uh—"

"That's all right, boy. Say, what you been doing up the hill there? Hunting murples?"

Hap had no idea what murples were. He had no idea who this man was. Suddenly he was sorry he had stayed out so late, and more sorry that he hadn't been paying attention to where he was going. "No, sir. I was just—"

"Wanderin' around, huh, boy? Well, you better get that outa your system in the next few days. Pretty soon the damn Wheezer's Bane's gonna start spreading, and you won't be able to walk around like you owned the place."

"Yes, sir." Hap didn't like this skinny man. He wasn't afraid of him, yet, but he certainly didn't like him. "Uh, I have to get back, sir. I'm late already." As quickly as he could he walked around the man and down the path toward the lights of the settlement station.

Carson watched him go with a grim smile. The boy fit the description Gel had given him of the greenie with the attractive mother. Seemed a little odd for a greenie to be out in the hills after dark, but Carson didn't spend much time worrying about it. There were other things too heavy on his mind to let himself worry about a stray boy. With a shrug he turned and started back the way the boy had come.

It was only when he got to the low rise which allowed him to see *Windhover* sitting on the hill overlooking the patch that Carson paused and thought again about the boy. Had he been up here? Had he been too close to the flowers? Was that why he seemed so disoriented?

Or was it something worse than that? Suddenly the boy became much more interesting. What *had* he been doing up here? Getting old, Carson thought, and slow, too. If that boy had been up here talking to one of the patches of Wheezer's Bane, then there was something far more serious going on than Carson had first suspected. But he would have to find out for sure before he did anything. It wouldn't do to get all worked up over a stray kid if that's all he was. But it also wouldn't do to ignore the other possibility.

He moved under the shadow of an estoma tree and sat with his back against its narrow trunk. He wasn't sure why he had decided to come up here in the dark, but somehow he hoped the serenity of the night might help him find a way to sort out the problem he faced and help him find a solution. And he wanted to be near a patch when he did it so that he had that constant reminder of what he faced and the difficulties which were involved.

The Guardians sensed his presence, but they also sensed that he was a fixed distance away. With practiced patience they woke the groundsel instead of the colony, then tried to filter out all the background emanations of the night and listen to their enemy, the silent kinous of death.

Burning has to be the answer, Carson thought. But it might be too late to get things organized before the pollination. Have to wait until they've spread their seeds and sprouted the new patches. Then we can burn the old patches first and fire the new ones as we locate them. Fire will do the trick, fire to burn this part of our world clean for...

The Guardians caught an image of a colony consumed by fire. Immediately it sent the first message of warning into the heart of Brightseed. *Danger. The kinous of death brings danger.*

The back of Carson's neck prickled. Almost immediately he recognized the sensation. It was the same one he had gotten every time he had listened to a patch with Amsrita. But he was too far away from a patch now. Or was he?

As quickly as he could he got out from under the estoma tree and stared through the moonlight to where the patch sprawled in shadow up the hill. Maybe it was time to burn a patch for practice, he thought. Maybe it was time to... His thought turned to action as he pulled his heavy work knife out of its sheath on his hip and hacked off a limb of the estoma tree. Green estoma branches were local favorites for starting fires because their sap burned so steadily and so well. He would just light this one and throw it into that patch up there. Give it a taste of the death it had shown him.

By the time Carson had covered half the distance to Brightseed, it had come fully awake. With the same energy it had used before on the silent kinous, Brightseed focused on the image of death and broadcast it with the full force of its energy.

Carson fell to the ground clutching his head, the estoma branch and his vision of fires forgotten.

Hap screamed, then flailed at the invisible menace and fainted, dragging his dinner onto the floor with him.

Windy beeped her warning of someone approaching. CrRina burst into tears. And a dull, pressing pain forced Gerard to squeeze his eyes shut and press the heels of his hands against his temples.

Around Brightseed all was still. The kinous of death stumbled away through the growing light of the moons, tracked by the groundsel upon which he stepped.

Chizen sat on the floor with Hap in her arms as she wiped the stew off his face and listened without understanding to the strange words he mumbled.

CrRina continued to cry. Windy silenced her warning signal when the stranger moved away. And the pain in Gerard's head eased but did not go away.

Spinnertel raked his talons through his long beard and smiled grimly, pleased that he had been monitoring at exactly the right moment to detect one of Drin's group minds in action. He was too far away, and the emanations were too weak to tell exactly what had happened, but—

"Greetings, immortal," a squeaky voice said.

"Ahwhou!" Spinnertel gasped.

"And pardon our intrusion," the squeaky voice continued.

For the first time in centuries Spinnertel was truly frightened. Some intruder had—

"Allow me to introduce myself and my companions."

Faint images floated in front of Spinnertel. He blinked his eyes and small corneal lenses slipped into place and greatly reduced the infrared light by which he normally saw.

"I am Shttz Pylynnkimbeth. My companions are Ronda Loner War Crow—"

The middle shadow image tilted its head slightly.

"Bertilina—"

A luminescent ball glowed then dimmed.

"And Woltol."

The tallest of the images made no sign. "Ghosts!" Spinnertel said suddenly. "You're ghosts!"

"But of course, immortal," the middle shadow said. "Surely you have seen our kind before?"

"Yes. Of course." Spinnertel had seen ghosts like these before, and he hadn't much liked it. They had frightened him then also. He would just as soon never have seen any more of them. "You may leave now," he said dismissively.

"We have no intentions of leaving quite yet." She, it

seemed to be a she, spoke without hesitation. "We would ask some questions of you."

"Get off my ship. All of you. Now. I do not talk to ghosts." The tall one shifted position slightly so that there was nothing between it and Spinnertel and he could see it had four arms, the two lower ones ending in hooks. An image flashed into his mind of his last encounter with ghosts and a small shiver went up his furry back. "I said, get off my ship."

"Not until you tell us what you are doing," Ronda Loner War Crow said calmly. "We are curious."

Spinnertel did not know what to do. He had tried to bully the ghosts in his previous encounter and they had made life miserable for him for three years. That had been centuries ago, but he hadn't forgotten it. Nor had he forgotten how powerless he had been to stop their nerve-racking appearances. For the first time in a long, long time he remembered the seven Weverian females he had coaxed aboard his ship, and how when the moment of his mass seduction had almost reached its glory ten or twenty ghosts had materialized making terrible noises. And that had not been the worst of what they'd done.

"All right," he said finally, "what do you want to know?"

"What youse are doing," four-arms said, speaking for the first time.

"Waiting for some friends," Spinnertel lied.

"Why?"

"Because I want to. What are you all doing here?"

"Who are these friends?" Ronda asked.

"Just friends." He frowned at them. This was ridiculous. "Look," he said, "I haven't done anything to you. Why are you bothering me like this?"

"We suspect you," Shttz squeaked.

"Unlike you, our friend Shttz is incapable of lying. What are you doing here?"

Spinnertel stared from the little blue triangle with its floppy hat to the female thing to four-arms, and finally down at the silent, luminescent lump on the floor. "I'm spying on Cosvetz," he said simply.

"It is confirmed." The statement came from the luminescent lump. "Why are you spying?"

Spinnertel had hoped that by giving them an honest answer they would go away. He could feel his fur matting along his spine as it soaked up perspiration. The moisture caused a chill which added to his discomfort. "I need information on a project of mine . . . but I don't want the personnel involved to know I am watching them. Is that all right with you?"

There was a long moment of silence during which the air seemed charged with electricity.

"Yes, that is quite all right," Ronda said finally, "but we think we will stay and watch you awhile. We will dematerialize so as not to disturb you, but we will be watching all the same. Thank you very much, immortal."

"But I'm going to leave . . . soon," Spinnertel said to empty air. The four apparitions had disappeared. He almost wished they had stayed visible. It was bad enough to have them on his ship, but it would be worse not being able to see them.

No matter what he did he would always feel like they were watching over his shoulder. It had taken him decades to get over that feeling after the last time. But he knew—as surely as he knew that he would have to leave soon so that he could come back after Askavenhar arrived—that it would probably take another decade or two before he shook that feeling of presence again.

"By the dung of the power!" he cursed. "How dare you pop in here and do this to me? How dare you?"

Only silence answered him. With a sigh of resignation he reached into a recessed cabinet and took out his liquor. So they wanted to watch him, did they? Well, let them watch him get drunk.

13

Burning waves of anger washed over Gerard and scorched his soul. He tried to cry out, but his voice died in the desert of his throat. Violence slashed at him from the lasers of a thousand ships. Hordes of armed figures overwhelmed him and threw him to the resilient ground of his nightmare.

Hovering above it all was the face of Fairy Peg, mocking him, deriding his affection, scorning his weakness—and cursing his betrayal.

Gerard struggled to awaken, using every trick Chief Headfoot had taught him to pull himself out of the pit of his dream. Strong hands pulled him back down. For an eternal moment he was sure that if he did not escape he would die.

His lungs gasped for air. His brain screamed for oxygen. Something splashed. Gerard turned in panic toward the sound and saw a deep, dark pool, a refuge which begged him to seek its comfort. He had been there before. He didn't know when, but he knew that within that pool lay safety. At the moment of realization a heavy mist rose up and obscured the pool. But he knew where it was, and what he had to do. With a scream of triumph he leapt into the darkness.

"Gerard! Gerard!"

Pilot.

Someone shook him.

"Gerard! Wake up!"

Pilot . . . Pilot . . . Pilot . . .

He was afraid.

"Gerard," the voice begged, "please, wake up."

Wake up. "Wake up."

It was all right. It was ShRil. Gerard let go of the darkness and felt himself rise to the surface. It was all right.

But it wasn't all right. Even after he awoke and ShRil took him into her arms and tried to comfort him it wasn't all right. Somewhere in his dream he had confused ShRil's voice with Fairy Peg's voice. That brought him a darker pain than the dream itself. No one could take ShRil's place in his life. No one.

Yet Self had betrayed him, had made him confuse the two of them in the ugliest way. He shuddered and ShRil pulled him closer. He cried from guilt and shame, and she soothed him with her hands and her kisses, cradling him against the softness of her breasts until finally he lay still.

"I'm sorry," he whispered.

"There is nothing to be sorry about."

"I know. But I wish you didn't have to go through all this torture with me."

"Is there someone else you would rather share it with?"

Her voice was light and teasing, but his thoughts fell into its shadow. Fairy Peg, he thought. She should have to put up with it because she caused it.

That thought startled him. How could Fairy Peg have caused those nightmares? He was the one who had been accused of betrayal. He was the one who had done something so terrible back in Ribble Galaxy that they had put a bounty on his head and sent assassins out to kill him.

"Well?" ShRil asked with a gentle poke in his ribs. "Is there someone else you would rather share your life with?"

"No, my love," he said as he curled tighter into her arms. "There's no one else in the whole universe I'd rather share my life with." He nibbled lightly on her neck, trying to distract himself from the turmoil inside.

ShRil kissed his ear. "Are you sure?"

"Positive." He let his fingers run in feathery circles down her hips and into the folds of her loins. "Positive."

"Perhaps you should prove it, then."

His turmoil was diverted into widening channels of passion as he did everything he knew how to give ShRil maximum physical pleasure. It was more than a well-practiced ritual for him. Every time they made love he felt an additional sense of wonder and discovery as their bodies responded to each other in new ways. Slight changes of position brought them magnificent levels of interaction. A long, searching kiss along a lower rib, or a different rhythm of massaging fingers only heightened their eagerness.

But they had learned that their finest responses came when they slowed the final tempo, forced themselves to prolong the exquisite fire in their nerves until the last possible moment. Then the rhythms of their love swept them up to a living crescendo of flesh and spirit.

Later, after ShRil mumbled a contented, "Goodnight," Gerard lay close beside her. He was vaguely aware of Self working deep in his brain, circling their problems with silent, invisible determination. He tried the self-hypnotic relaxation techniques which often worked for him, hoping to sink into the annealing darkness. When they failed he tried counting backward from one hundred to zero.

Three, two, one, zero, he thought despondently. Then he remembered part of the dream, the part about the dark pool where he had tried to escape. What did that mean? Had Self dredged up a new fragment from his past for him to cope with? The pool had seemed very familiar, as though he had sought refuge in that kind of mind trick before. But when? And why? And how did it all connect back, back, back to Ribble Galaxy and the omnipresent Fairy Peg?

Torture.

Self's answer startled Gerard. Torture? Had he been tortured? Was that part of the mindwipers' techniques?

Suddenly a new image formed in his mind, an image of a stark room lined with odd equipment and dominated by a sadistic laugh. Gerard knew that room. He would have recognized it as soon as he saw it—but he had no idea where it was. Yet nothing could make him doubt its reality.

So he had been tortured. By Fed? Or in Ribble? Somehow it didn't matter. To know he had been tortured and had survived was enough. What impressed him was the sense of resiliency he felt. That was more important, far more important than who had tortured him and where.

Then just as he started to drift off to sleep he realized that Self had not betrayed him. Self had mixed Fairy Peg's voice with ShRil's, but he had misinterpreted the message. Self was trying to tell him that he had indeed loved Fairy Peg, perhaps loved her as much as he now loved ShRil. But Fairy Peg, Fairy Peg had betrayed . . . had betrayed him . . . and his love. There would be no sleep for him now.

Gerard slipped out of bed as quietly as he could and went to the galley. Hours later the morning chime found him still sitting there thinking about what Self had revealed, and wondering, wondering if it could indeed be true.

Geljoespiy and Chizen sat across the table from each other after Essenne had left for the nursery. Hap was still asleep.

"How is he?"

Chizen looked down into her cup, then up at Geljoespiy. "He seems to be fine. I woke up several times during the night and checked on him, but he slept peacefully."

"That's good. Has anything like this ever happened before?"

"No. Never."

"Perhaps he was just tired from running around in the hills all day? Do you suppose?"

"I thank you for your concern, Geljoespiy, but I do not know what to suppose. Is there a physmedicant here who could examine him?" Despite the fact that Hap's spell had been brief, and that he had insisted on eating afterward, Chizen was still worried.

"A physmedicant? What is that?"

"A qualified medical person. A healer."

"Oh, yes, the station has a medtech. Davidem's her name. A good woman, too. Competent. But I thought you said the boy was all right?"

"I do not know that! Houn in heaven, man! If he were your son would you not be worried?"

"I would, Mis Chizen. I certainly would. But I can't say as I'd be ready to rush him off to the medtech just 'cause of this one time. If it happened again, I might, but I'm not much in favor of Davidem or anyone else poking around on folks when there's no obvious need." Gel didn't want her upset, but neither did he want to involve Davidem with this pair. Like most of the pioneering medtechs he knew, Davidem liked to ask too many questions about things which didn't concern her.

Chizen sighed and finished the mug of bitter tea. "What would you do, then?"

"Watch him. See how he acts. If he doesn't do it again or act like he's sick, I wouldn't worry about him. We had three sons, me and Essy, and all of them acted strange at one time or another. But that's just the way kids are. Especially at his age. He's changing and growing, Mis Chizen, and his body has to be a little confused by that. Then bring him to a new planet, and well, it just seems to me that he's adjusting."

"You call screaming and fainting like that 'adjusting'?"

Gel refilled her mug and his own from the stayhot kettle on the table. "Trust me," he said finally. "The boy's going to be all right."

"You keep coming back to trust, Geljoespiy," she said as she stirred a spoonful of thick syrup into her tea. "You keep telling me I should trust you, that I should let you help me, that I should trust your mysterious friend. Yet you give me no evidence to base that trust on. Why is that? Why can you not give me some substantial reason to place my trust—our trust—in you? Why?"

"Suppose we took Hap to Davidem and had him examined? Would that make you feel better?"

"Yes, it would. But it would not answer my question."

"Perhaps not, Mis Chizen, but understand that I would be doing it because I have your best interests in mind, yours and Hap's. I'd be doing it—"

"To give me a reason to trust you? That is not very substantial, Geljoespiy. I could find this medtech Davidem and take Hap to her on my own."

"True enough," Gel said with a sigh. "True enough. Yet I have little else to offer you beyond that and all that I've said before. Except, perhaps, one other thing. I could tell you my friend's name. It would mean breaking a small trust with him, but I think he would understand." He waited, trying to gauge her reaction to that offer, trying to read in her eyes what was hidden behind her motionless expression.

Suddenly Chizen wasn't sure she wanted to know who Geljoespiy's mysterious friend was. The name would tell her who in Ribble Galaxy besides her sister had laid plans to use her as a weapon of justice. But it could also render her even more powerless than she already was. The name would carry with it a host of questions she doubted Geljoespiy could answer, questions about the current power structure in Ribble which she did not want to have nagging away at the back of her mind and confusing her even further about what she should do.

Then another thought struck her. Knowing his name would give her a certain power over him. If he were someone acting outside of her sister's direction, Chizen might be able to use that knowledge to her own advantage—and Hap's. "Tell me."

"Very well. But his name must not pass beyond the walls of this house."

"On my honor."

"His name is Letrenn."

Chizen blinked. That name meant nothing to her. "Letrenn what?" she asked, hoping for some familiar family name which would give her the tie to Ribble.

"Just Letrenn. It is the only name I know him by," Gel lied. He had sworn on penalty of death never to reveal Letrenn's true name to anyone. Better that he fail in this task than run that risk. "You look disappointed," he said.

She was disappointed, more than disappointed. Letrenn, Letrenn . . . nothing. A meaningless name. She looked steadily at Geljoespiy. "That is not enough."

"That is all I can give you. I was not even supposed to give you that. You asked for a reason to trust me. I gave you one by sharing that confidence with you. Now you tell me it's not enough? Beg pardon, Mis Chizen, but that is all you will get."

For the first time Chizen heard anger in Geljoespiy's voice. Whether it was indignant anger or frustrated anger, she did not care. The anger itself was enough. If she pushed him now, she might learn more than he intended for her to. "Why do you want him dead?" she asked quickly.

"What?"

"Why do you want Gerard Manley dead?"

Gel forced himself to pause. The sudden change in her approach had caught him off balance. "For the same reasons you do," he said carefully.

"And why do I want him dead?"

"Because... because of what he did to you and your people." There was a fire in Chizen's eyes that was new to him.

"And? And? Be specific."

The aggressiveness of her tone startled him even more. "I only know what Letrenn told me—that you had been personally betrayed, and that your people had been betrayed. He said that Manley had caused the deaths of thousands of innocents in your galaxy. If revenge and justice were your only reasons, that would be enough."

It rang false to Chizen. Even in the remote isolation of Sun's March there had been questions about what had happened in Dinsey space when Ribble's fleet and the Federation's had met for the signing of the reconciliation treaty. The blame was placed on Gerard Manley, Consort to the Throne, and Fize of the Gabriel Ratchets. He was branded a traitor. His name was ordered expunged from the public records. And after the sensational gossip died down, he became a nonperson.

But political treachery was part of life in Ribble Galaxy as Chizen knew almost as well as anyone. She had her own doubts about the official version of the story, doubts which had nothing to do with her attraction to Gerard the man, and she would not have been surprised to learn that he had merely been an instrument used by one of the powerful political forces to accomplish its own ends.

Yet behind all those doubts lay something darker which the directive had brought to the fore and Geljoespiy had reinforced with his constant harping on the subject. There had been a part of her, a small part but a strong one, which had indeed wished to see Gerard Manley dead. He had rejected her. He had rudely spurned her offers of affection. With his studied ingenuousness he had made her feel less of a woman—less of a person.

What frightened her now was that, once released, that small part had grown larger and larger, filling her with an irrational desire to accept Geljoespiy's offer of assistance and kill the father of her son.

But that was what stopped her. He was the father of her son, acknowledged or not, and if she killed him, or helped to kill him, Chizen was not sure she could ever look at Hap again without guilt. And if Hap ever found out... Chizen shuddered.

"Are you all right, Mis Chizen?"

"Uh, yes. You have given me much to think about, Geljoespiy, and I must do so. If we—"

"Mother?"

Hap's call from their room interrupted her. "Please see if medtech Davidem is available," she said as she rose quickly from the table and left the kitchen.

Gel shook his head sadly. He had almost convinced her. He was sure of that, and just as sure that the boy's interruption had pushed her decision back again. As he rinsed the mugs and hung them to dry he shook his head and wondered again how and if he would ever succeed.

Junathun had been startled the night before when Carson had stumbled into his house and collapsed on the floor. When he mumbled something about Amsrita and Wheezer's Bane, Junathun had known exactly what to do. He had given Carson a sedative and helped him onto the low couch in the kitchen, knowing that nothing but blank sleep could calm the demons which plagued his friend and rival.

The sun was well up, and Junathun had chores he should have been doing. Instead, he sat and sipped blend, and thought about how many times he had watched over Carson on nights like this. And for what? To watch Carson dissipate? To listen to him curse Amsrita, then moan about missing her? To have Carson tell him that he was too stupid and slow to... to impress Liana? Was that why he stood by Carson?

Junathun got up, refilled his mug of blend from the tap,

and stood leaning against the counter. After a long sigh he took two or three deep swallows of the blend and refilled his mug again. He knew he shouldn't drink this much, especially this early, but some angry force inside him pushed back the warning. So what if he got a little drunk? What did it matter? Carson wouldn't care. He'd probably sleep another five or six hours.

On a sudden impulse he set down the blend and moved over to the radio phone. He had to wait a long time before Liana answered. "It's me, Junathun."

"Hallo, Junathun. Carson's not here."

He almost told her where Carson was, then thought better of it. "I didn't call to talk to Carson. I called to talk to you. Actually, I want to come out and talk to you."

There was a long pause before Liana answered. "About what?"

"I, uh, don't want to say on the air. May I come? Please?"

"Of course, Junathun. When will you be here?"

"Whenever it's convenient for you."

"If you're willing to do some chores with me, you can come out today."

"I'll be there in an hour."

"You in that much of a hurry? What's the matter?"

"Nothing's the matter, Liana. Absolutely nothing." He was surprised at how happy he sounded. "Listen, you save the heavy work for me, and I'll see you in an hour or so."

"Skim carefully."

"I will. Junathun out."

"Liana out."

Junathun wrote Carson a quick note telling him there was food in the cooler and the blend tap was full. Then as an afterthought he added that Carson shouldn't worry if he didn't come back that night.

That he had dared think Liana might ask him to spend the night was a bold and irrational thought, but Junathun was too busy stuffing a change of clothes into his kit to worry about that. He would need the clean clothes after doing the chores anyway, so it didn't really mean anything.

He took one last look at Carson, then went out the door with a smile. Minutes later his skimmer was flying through the hills toward Liana's place.

14

Spinnertel waited for the ghosts to reappear after he woke up, but they didn't. That made him angry and uncomfortable. If they were going to inhabit his ship for a while, the least they could do was stay out in the open where he could see them. The more he thought about it, the angrier he got.

"Let me see you, dammit! I have a right to see you. This is my ship!"

His words echoed back to him from the bulkheads, but no ghosts materialized in front of him.

"I hope you're all ready to go for a little ride," he said loudly, "because I'm going to warp out of here in a little while."

"No, you're not," the squeaky voice answered.

Spinnertel turned around and saw the blue triangle standing in the companionway. "What's your name? Shoots?"

"Shttz. Sheeetz. Sheeetz. And I must tell you that you are not going to warp anywhere. Bertilina doesn't like warps."

"I don't give a wasted idea in the void what Bertilina likes. This is my ship. *My* ship. And I'll warp any time I damn well please."

"No," a voice behind him added. "That would make youse very unhappy."

He spun around and saw four-arms. "Make me unhappy!?!" he screamed. "You've already made me unhappy! Your presence makes me unhappy! Get out of here! LEAVE ME ALONE!"

"He does that rather nicely, don't you think?" Shttz asked.

"Too loud. No modulation."

"Shut up! Both of you, shut up!" Spinnertel backed away

from them and braced his back against the bulkhead. They had already done the one thing he had sworn he would not let them do. They had made him lose control.

Spinnertel slowed his breathing and prepared to defend himself as four-arms approached. Then he remembered how difficult defense against a ghost could be. A low growl of fear and anger mixed in his throat.

"Afraid," four-arms said.

"Better leave him, then."

Two hands grabbed for Spinnertel. Two hooks whistled in the air. A deep laugh echoed through the empty cabin. They had disappeared. No. Yes, it was a different one who stood in front of him now, the one who had spoken for them. She laughed again and motioned for him to sit down.

"Be still, immortal," she said quietly.

He let his wet back slide down the wall until he settled into a defensive crouch.

"Be still. Be still."

"How can I be still when you and your friends pop up at me like that? What do you want from me?"

"Energy," she said simply. "We rushed to get here and burned up far too much energy to be comfortable. It was your energy emanations which attracted us. But your spying made us curious. We have friends on Brisbidine and do not like having them spied upon."

"What friends? More ghosts?"

Before she answered she sat cross-legged on the deck in front of him. "Perhaps," she said with a strange lilt in her voice. "And other friends as well. We do not respect you for spying on any of them."

"So just tell me who they are and I won't spy on them. I'm only interested in my people anyway."

"Oh, no. That would be too easy. Perhaps you should just stop spying altogether."

Spinnertel wanted to strike out at someone. Instead he dropped his defensive posture and sat heavily on the deck. "What if I don't?" he asked.

"Then we shall continue to bother you."

"What if I offer to leave?"

"As soon as we are ready to leave, you may leave also."

"Look, whoever you—"

"Ronda Loner War Crow."

91

"Look, Ronda Loner War Crow, why don't you and your friends take as much energy as you want and just get out of here?"

"That is exactly what we are doing. But it takes time, immortal, and you will have to be patient with us."

"How much time?"

"Two more days. Maybe three."

"I don't have that much time. I have to leave before then." Askavenhar's ship was due in three days. "Can't you hurry?"

"Yes. But we choose not to. It disturbs our, well, for the use of a word you might understand, it disturbs our auras."

"All right, Ronda Loner War Crow, if that's—"

"You may call me Ronda."

"All right, Ronda, if that's the way it has to be, that's the way it has to be. But would you all mind terribly if I moved my ship to the other side of the sun?"

In an instant she shifted from sitting in front of him to standing. "Why?"

He wanted to lie, but could not think of anything he could tell her that he might get away with. "Because I don't want to be here. Too much electromagnetic interference on this side of the sun and—"

"There is less on the other side?"

"I hope so."

"That should be interesting. I shall tell the others we are going to..." She faded away with the sound of her voice.

Well, he thought, at least I won't be sitting *here* when Askavenhar and the Constant arrive. His message that he would meet them had already been acknowledged. Now he could only hope they wouldn't detect him hanging out in a far orbit.

With a sigh Spinnertel pulled himself to his feet and headed for the flight deck. As he walked down the companionway he looked involuntarily over his shoulder, expecting to see one of them following him. Damn ghosts, he thought. Damn rotten ghosts. Why did they have to show up now? Why did...they—of course! Someone had sent them. Some member of the Constant, the same member whose meddling was already evident.

He would bet on Gracietta. It would be just like her. Or maybe even Askavenhar herself. The game taking place behind his back was beginning to worry him more than anything. And the damned Verporchting was the cause of it all.

Spinnertel knew he would have to find his hidden opponents and turn their efforts to his advantage. That naïvely vague plan brought a small smile to his lips. But it faded quickly as he looked over his shoulder again for the ghosts. There was nothing naïve about the fact that he was operating at a distinct disadvantage.

No matter. He had operated at disadvantages before. Once the Verporchting was dead everything else would work itself out, and he would make sure it worked out the right way. He hadn't lived this long without learning a few tricks about survival which he could put to good use here. With a low growl of determination he climbed up to the flight deck.

Dedo held her hand as they walked slowly down the hill. CrRina was confused. The flowers wouldn't talk to her. Please, she thought, tell me the One. Sing me a song. Please.

The One is with us even now.

Dedo stopped and jerked her arm. "Dedo! That hurts!"

"I'm sorry, CrRina," he said, as he stooped down beside her and looked in her eyes. "Dedo didn't mean to hurt you. Did you hear something?"

"The flowers talked," she said simply.

Gerard thought he had prepared himself for this revelation, but CrRina said it with such casual pride that he was stunned. "Can you talk to them?" he asked carefully.

"Of course, Dedo. So can you."

"I don't think Dedo can." He sat down beside her and pulled her into his lap so that they both faced down the hill. "What did the flowers say to you?"

"They said the One is here. Didn't you hear them?"

"I heard something—"

"Listen, Dedo. I'll sing to them and they'll sing back."

Gerard tensed as CrRina hummed a little tune. Its rhythm tugged at a memory in the back of his mind. Was she really talking to the Wheezer's Bane? His answer came a moment later.

Faith is the love which gathers us all into the heart of the One. This is the faith we share with you, delicate kinous Sirreena.

"See, Dedo?"

Gerard had almost heard words beneath the melodic buzzing. Almost. He was afraid and excited at the same time.

Gentle zz-buzz peace of luzzz.

"Gentle is the peace of love," CrRina sang aloud, "living in the wondrous time..."

...zz-buzz-zz bzzz promizzz.

Each buzz was an ache in his head. He wanted to retreat back aboard Windy. Yet he was riveted with fascination by what CrRina was doing.

"Because of the One two things exist, forever separate and joined. Ten thousand colonies of faith do not offend the sense of One where..."

...zz-zz finz zz thoughts are truzz. Zzz-buz.

"You try it, Dedo."

It was all Gerard could do to keep from screaming with pain before a soothing hum filled his mind. He felt dizzy and weak and slowly let himself lie back on the grass. "Go get Mummum."

"But, Dedo—"

"Now, CrRina. Please."

Brightseed's reactions were a mixture of concern and elation. It had caused pain in the kinous called Dedo. But it had also made contact and soothed that pain. Brightseed was afraid to push the contact, afraid that kinous Dedo might be repelled by its efforts, and more afraid that kinous Dedo would take Sirreena away from them. It was the kind of problem Brightseed had been trying to cope with since the departure of Amsrita. But Brightseed knew that whatever it did would have to be done slowly. That much it had learned.

Sirreena's thoughts came clearly through the groundsel. Why is Dedo on the ground? Why does he want Mummum? She can talk to the flowers, too.

"Hello, mate," Gerard said quietly.

Why does he call Mummum *mate*?

"Hello yourself. CrRina said you—"

"I know. I think I'm all right, but I wanted you to be here just in case. Did she tell you—"

"That she talked to the flowers? Yes." Her smile stopped when she saw the lines of pain on Gerard's face. "Did you talk to them, too?" she asked as she sat down beside him.

"No. I only listened a little... to something... oh, I don't know how to explain it. But I want to try it again."

"Now, Dedo? Can we talk to the flowers now?"

"In a minute. Sit here beside me." He gave ShRil a look of amazement. "See what's going on? CrRina thinks we should be able to *talk* to them like she...like she seems to."

ShRil looked away from him and down the hill. This whole experiment frightened her. It had no controls. Suppose something went wrong? Suppose..."I think perhaps you have both had enough for one day. Why do we not all go back aboard Windy and talk about it."

"No, Mummum. You can talk to..." Her voice trailed off as she cocked her head.

Brightseed. You are kinous Sirreena, and we are colony Brightseed.

"Brightseed!" she exclaimed. "Their name is Brightseed! Hi, Brightseed. Say HI!"

Her greeting echoed back from Brightseed in a soft, deep tone. Gerard heard it. "It answered her," he said as ShRil helped pull him up into a sitting position.

"I did not hear anything."

"Listen, Mummum. Just listen."

ShRil looked quickly from CrRina to Gerard. He seemed to be listening also. She felt cut off from both of them, frightened by dangers she could not understand, and worried for all the correct, rational reasons.

Greetzzz, Zherard-callzz-Dedo.

"Gerard, I think—"

"Not now, ShRil. They're talking again."

"I think this is too dangerous for us to attempt—"

Greetzzz, Zharill-callzz-Mummuz.

"...some help."

Gerard gave her a quick look and saw the worry in her eyes. "Please, ShRil. They're almost clear to me."

"Then why is your face wrinkled with pain?"

Go now in peace, for now we must rest.

"'Bye, Brightseed," CrRina said as she scrambled to her feet and waved toward the colony. "'Bye."

ShRil almost expected to see the flowers move. Her second reaction was to stand up and make sure CrRina did not try to go down the hill. Gerard extended his hand and she helped him up beside her. "Why is she saying goodbye?"

"'Cause they said goodbye, Mummum. Didn't you hear them?"

"No."

"I heard something," Gerard said as he stared at the whirl of colors, "but it was too low for me to make it out. Why did they say goodbye, CrRina?"

"Rest time, Dedo." With that she turned around and started running toward *Windhover*. If Brightseed was resting, she would rest, too. Then they could sing and talk. Talk quietly, she thought. Loud talk scares Mummum and Dedo.

"Rest time for both of you," ShRil said as she took Gerard's arm. "You look terrible."

"Just a little headache. But I'll tell you what, ShRil, if you think you're scared, you should be inside my head right now. I'm scared as Krick." As they walked back to Windy the fear rumbled in his mind. "She could be hurt by all this," he said as they reached the boarding ramp.

ShRil held him back and turned him to face her. "I know. And so could you, my love."

"So what—"

"That I do not know. Can Windy shield you two?"

"Maybe me. But I don't know about her." He wrapped his arm around ShRil's shoulders.

"You are trembling."

"Come on. Let's get aboard. We can talk about this after we've eaten."

"While CrRina is taking her nap."

"Absolutely. The less said in front of her for now, the better. Don't you think?"

"More than you know." His fear had mixed with her own to form a bubbling pot of questions. Their possible answers frightened her even more.

Hap went calmly through the whole examination. He thought it was silly. But he knew he couldn't tell his mother why. And he surely couldn't tell this physmedicant, or medtech, or whatever she was. First of all, who would believe him? Brightseed had only been protecting itself. He let out an amused grunt. Then he would have to tell them about Brightseed.

"Be still, child. I'm almost—"

"I'm not a child."

"True enough. But you're not a man yet either."

As she moved back in front of him she slipped a shiny, palm-sized instrument into the pocket of her long grey coat.

Her pale brown eyes sparkled from webs of wrinkles which ran into her blond-and-silver hair. Hap decided she must have been very pretty once. "You can call me Hap," he said.

"That seems fair enough, Hap. You can call me Davidem. Where I come from girls are named after their fathers, and boys are named after their mothers. My father was David, and since I was his first daughter, I became Davidem. Who were you named after?"

"I don't know. My real name is Hopeman—but my mother and everyone else always calls me Hap."

Davidem smiled. "Would you like to be called Hopeman?"

"No. I don't think so. Sounds too formal." He paused for a second then said, "There's nothing wrong with me, is there." It wasn't a question, it was a statement.

"Not that I can tell. You can put the rest of your clothes back on now. And then you can answer a question for me."

Something in her tone made Hap immediately suspicious. As he pulled his firstshirt over his head he asked, "What questions?"

"Just one question," she said from the little standing desk where she was making notes. "Why won't you tell us what caused you to faint yesterday?"

Hap hesitated too long. "Because I don't know why—"

"Yes, you do, Hap. Listen to me for a . . ."

Another lecture, he thought. Just like Mother.

"I'm a medtech, not a psych specialist. We've got one of those if you want to talk to her, but I suspect you won't." She waited for him to respond, then continued. "Anyway, like I said, I'm just an old woman who's been practicing genmed for fifty years. And one of the things I've learned to do pretty well during that time is spot a lie from a patient, especially from—"

"Children," he said, offering the word and hoping she'd get to the point.

"I was going to say young men—young men who are hiding something from their parents. You've got that look about you, young man, a look that says you've found a girl, or just figured out how much fun masturbation is . . ." She paused and smiled as Hap blushed. "Or some secret they don't think they can share."

Hap wished the heat would leave his face. And he wished she would just shut up and let him go.

"I'm not prying. I want you to understand that. But I also want you to know that if you just have to talk to somebody about it, you can talk to me. That's like telling your secret to that wall over there. It can't repeat anything, and I won't."

She seemed to be waiting for an answer as Hap stood there putting on his jacket. He remembered his manners. "Thank you, Davidem," he said in a voice which trembled a little, "but, uh—"

"I didn't say you had to tell me now. I just wanted you to know these old ears are available if you need them. Now get out of here and send your mother in. I'm going to tell her there's nothing wrong with you and she should quit worrying so much."

"Thank you."

"You're welcome, young man."

Hap had a good feeling inside when he left her. While he waited for his mother he wondered if he really could tell Davidem about Brightseed. No, not yet anyway. Besides, he really didn't *need* to tell anyone.

As soon as they got back to Geljoespiy's house Hap wanted to go see Brightseed. Chizen made him eat, then told him he was to get back well before dark.

"I do not care what that medtech said. I still think there's something wrong with you."

"But, Mother..."

"Before dark," she said. "An hour before dark."

"Oh, all right." Hap gave her his best smile. "I love you, Mother."

"Of course you do. And you will love me even more when you get back on time."

He gave her a quick kiss on the cheek and left on the run, eager to talk to Brightseed and unwilling to waste any time.

15

Carson stretched his arms and shook his head, trying to clear the fog which rested on his brain. He knew Junathun had drugged him again. I must have been... what? Carson couldn't remember. Oh, he remembered his encounter with the Wheezer's Bane. And he remembered the fire.

Fire? What happened to the fire? Then he remembered that, too. Simple fire might not be the answer to getting rid of that patch after all. He could do it that way if he had to, the same way he burned out the patches on Liana's place. Put on his psi-damper, spread the estoma oil, and burn this one out like all the rest. Maybe.

Something held him back from that idea, something which loomed larger than one patch of Wheezer's Bane, something which sent shivers through his drugged body. Either his sensitivity to their thoughts had greatly increased, or... or they were able to project much farther than they used to. And if they could now *project* farther, how much farther could they... listen? Was that the right word for what they did? Did they listen to him? Is that how—

Of course! How stupid he had been. He should have recognized that when they struck out at him with images of Amsrita's death. They had known he was there by listening to his thoughts. Something had happened to him—or them. Amsrita had told him they couldn't hear his thoughts.

A thickness filled his throat. Amsrita. How he had loved her, and maybe hated her at the same time. She had asked too much from him, more than he had ever been able to give anyone else. But she had gotten it—gotten it all—love,

99

affection, loyalty, devotion, and finally, some part of his soul. He hated her for that.

Amsrita had come to mean more to him than any other person had ever meant. His parents—losers, both of them—hadn't meant much, hadn't been there often enough to mean anything. Years ago he had realized that he couldn't even remember their faces. And Fillebuil? She had been the wife of his . . . of his lust. Her death had taught him the final lesson against giving to others.

So, when he had fallen in with Liana he maintained his distance from her, refusing to rely on her—or to allow her to rely on him. They had taken what each had to give when they could give it, and that had been that. Until Amsrita came into their lives.

Carson stood at the sink washing his face and arms and wished that warm water and a little cleanser could wash away memories as easily as they washed away grime. No, not the memories, he thought, just the pain. That would be enough. Just let him forget how much it had hurt when Amsrita refused to give up her research, even after she knew it was killing her. Just let him forget how she had ridiculed his selfishness. Just let him forget those months of agony as she slowly slipped away from him—and the years of grief after she died.

He dried his face and rubbed his arms briskly with Junathun's fine murplehair towel. Now the Wheezer's Bane was threatening a child, not with its debilitating pollen—with its killing thoughts.

Or corrupting thoughts.

That new idea bolted through his mind. Suppose the Wheezer's Bane was corrupting CrRina? Suppose it was making her its agent in some way? He saw a brief image of a patch surrounded by a ring of armed children. Then they charged outward and the image shattered.

Wheezer's Bane enslaving the children and controlling Brisbidine? No!

He threw the towel at the counter. A wisp of paper slipped off its edge and fluttered to the floor. In his anger he almost ignored it, but on second thought he picked it up.

It was Junathun's note. ". . . gone for a day, maybe two. Use what you need." Typical Junathun, he thought, as he wadded it up and threw it at the crumpled towel, just does whatever he damn well pleases.

Well, he didn't need Junathun, not yet anyway. Pieces of a plan were already stacking up in the back of his mind, but it would take some time to work out the details before he started enlisting help. Liana wouldn't do. She was too soft.

Carson smiled bitterly. Tried to make me soft, too. No, he would need Junathun then, because Junathun was the only one he could trust enough to help coordinate everything when the time came. And to take over if I don't make it, he thought with a second bitter smile.

He dressed in a rush, suddenly eager to work out the details. But he wanted to take another hard, daylight look at the terrain around the killer patch before he did anything else. He wanted something special for that patch, something that smelled like slow, burning revenge.

Hap left the path and followed the faint yellow-green line through the brush. He knew what the groundsel were, now, and was careful not to step on them. He was just as careful to keep the hill between himself and the spaceship.

You are close enough, Brightseed said quietly.

"Why are you so worried?" Hap barely mouthed the words, but he knew that Brightseed could hear him.

Death and confusion sit on the hill guarding kinous Sirreena. Rest with us and listen.

"Okay. Wait a minute." Hap picked a spot between two bushes where their exposed roots wrapped around a low rock and formed a weblike seat. Brightseed started talking even before he sat down and found the most comfortable position.

It is better to be in the Seeking-Heart-of-One than to wait at dusk for the morning light. The roots hold the answers that night would hide, but they are—

"Brightseed? All this confuses me. What is it supposed to mean? What does it have to do with me?"

Do not seek meaning, and meaning will come.

"That still doesn't make any sense. Are you trying to teach me some kind of religion?"

Religion?

Hap thought about the worship of Houn and quietly chanted part of the litany he had learned from his mother. He hoped Brightseed would understand.

No, this is not like that. The Accumulated Words of Our-Gatou are reflections of the One. The One is all things, but has no division. The One gives life in the threefold way.

"It still doesn't mean anything to me," Hap said with a frustrated shake of his head. "Why don't you tell me about that spaceship? I can understand that."

It, too, is part of the One.

"Can we talk with Sirreena?"

We can hear her faintly. Yet we would not alarm the kinous Dedo by calling her to us.

"Who's this Dedo?"

A kinous whose thoughts are shrouded in pain. The scars of burning have injured him. The Not-One has gnawed at the roots of his mind.

"But who is he? Sirreena's father?"

Your word is as good as ours. Kinous Sirreena grew from his seed. Yet he is not the silent Guardian who carried her.

"There you go again." Hap saw images of a man and a woman and knew immediately that Brightseed had picked them up from Sirreena. "But I think I know what you mean. You can't talk to her mother, can you?"

Her Guardian is silent, as we said.

The image of the woman flashed through his mind a second time and Hap was startled to realize that she had three breasts. He had seen that woman. Surely there weren't two women like *that* on Brisbidine. A faint sexual stirring accompanied the image.

Do you know this Guardian?

"No. Uh, no, I don't. But I know who she is. She and her husband are here— Wait a minute! They're here to investigate you. At least that's what one of the station hands said."

We are not surprised. The One returns to the One.

"Doesn't that worry you?" Hap had raised his voice without realizing it.

Carson heard him and paused twenty meters away on the path.

Be still! Danger approaches. Brightseed sent a buffering message of love through the groundsel surrounding Hap. Then it shrieked at the kinous of death.

The pain struck Carson between his eyes, then trailed off down his spine in miserable little spasms. He slapped the psi-damper switch on his helmet. Pain lanced through his hand. For a long moment he held it in front of him, staring at the stub of the switch sticking from his palm. Then he reached up and jerked the stub out. Blood spurted from the hole. A harsh, sucking noise escaped through his clenched teeth.

"I think he's hurt," Hap whispered.

Be still, Brightseed responded.

Damn, Carson thought. An artery. As quickly as he could he rummaged through his pockets until he found his facecloth and wrapped it around his hand. He cursed again. How long had it been since he'd had his last coagulant shot? Too long. His third curse was for the legacy of bleeding his faceless parents had left him.

He sighed and turned back toward the station. The scouting trip would have to wait. But despite that he had learned something. The boy, Hap, was talking to the Wheezer's Bane, too. Carson had recognized his distinctive accent.

That brought new evidence to support his suspicion. And new power to his earlier fears. The patches were contacting the children. But why the offworld children? he wondered as he pressed the already bloodsoaked bandage tighter against his palm. Were they susceptible because they hadn't gone through a season which gave the Wheezer's Bane its name? Was that it?

"He's leaving. I can hear him."

We will wait until you are sure he is gone.

Hap sat patiently and listened to the retreating footsteps.

New questions nagged Carson. Would the patch's deadly pollen destroy the children's contact with them? Or would it just make their contact stronger? He looked up in the stillness and realized one of the station hands was in front of him. Then he pulled off his helmet so that he could hear what the man was saying. For the moment, the questions would have to wait.

Hap counted to three hundred after the footsteps faded away. "He's gone. I'm sure of it now," he said almost without moving his lips. "What happened? Who was that?"

The kinous of death.

Brightseed's mental tone carried a harsh sting. Hap flinched and squeezed his eyes shut. "Don't!"

Immediately Brightseed sent him a buffering message of love. *Peace. Be still. The One is whole.*

Small tears seeped from the corners of Hap's eyes. "You scared me, Brightseed. What happened to that man?"

The One closed in on him. He is Not-One.

Before Hap could respond he heard a new message in his mind. Then he saw the image of the flowers from above. Sirreena had left the spaceship. He opened his eyes and the image was gone. Then he shut them again and thought, (Hi, Sirreena.)

(Where is Hap?) he heard her ask.

He is near, Brightseed answered in a tone as soft as the breeze which chilled the tears on Hap's face. *He is near.*

(I want to see him.)

"Hi, Sirreena," Hap whispered. Then he thought of his picture.

(Hi, Hap. Come see me.)

Where is kinous Dedo?

(Asleep. Nap time.)

The rest of the message Sirreena sent was jumbled too fast through his mind for him to sort it out, but the overall imagery made him smile. Sirreena was happy with her parents. He could tell that much.

You should stay up there. Dedo might worry.

(That's okay. He said we could come later.)

Brightseed passed on to Hap Sirreena's image of the flowers. He decided it was time to meet this little girl who talked in his head. There was still a tinge of uncertainty in his mind aroused by all this telepathic communication, and he hoped that if he saw her he could put that to rest. He stood up, brushed off the seat of his pants, and headed toward the crest of the hill.

Brightseed was busy crooning rhymes to Sirreena and apparently wasn't paying any attention to him. Resentment pricked his thoughts as first the spaceship and then Brightseed came into view. It took him a moment to spot Sirreena, but when he did see her sitting a short distance from the ship, he waved and called, "Sirreena!"

She waved back. (Hap!) "Hap!" Her call came faintly in an annoying echo after her thought. (Don't talk, Sirreena. Just think.)

(Hap!) "Hap!" she echoed again.

"Hap!" a new voice called.

A man was standing behind Sirreena. Hap didn't know

104

what to do. Should he run? Should he hide? Brightseed was strangely silent. (Brightseed? What—)

Kinous Dedo, Brightseed whispered. *Go to him*.

"Hap!" the man called again. "Come here. Please?"

(Hap!) "Hap!" (Hap!). "Hap!"

Sirreena's echo was going to drive him crazy. Hap wanted to run, but Brightseed had said to go. Almost reluctantly he started walking toward Sirreena and her father. (Help me, Brightseed), he thought.

This is the threefold way of growth, Brightseed whispered.

"Not that," he said in frustration. "Stay with me."

The One is here and everywhere. The One sees and hears all.

Hap barely heard the last phrase and knew Brightseed was retreating. Because of Sirreena's father?

Brightseed's affirmation was no more than a positive feeling in Hap's mind. As he skirted one of the Guardians he reached up and let his hand brush its pink flowers. (Then listen), he thought. (I need you.) Again the affirmation was only a feeling, but stronger and more reassuring.

With dark determination he took long, deliberate strides up the hill, eager to meet Sirreena, but anxious about the man whose mind Brightseed said had been damaged.

"Speak your mind, Junathun. You've been twisting around something since you got here."

Despite the amused look he saw on her face Junathun knew he was trying Liana's patience. "Hard to do that," he said finally. "Specially since I don't know how things stand with you and Carson."

"Carson? Is that what—wait a minute. You said you weren't coming out here to see him."

"Came to see you." He hoped he could head off her anger. "And to talk to you. But maybe I ought to finish those chores you set out for me."

"You sit right back down," she said as he started to rise. "The chores can wait."

"Can I get myself some more blend?" he asked with a small smile.

Liana took his mug. "I'll get it for you."

"Don't trust me to stand up? Afraid I'll run out and start working again?"

"No," she said over her shoulder as she stood at the tap. "Then again, maybe yes. As strange as you've been acting, I'm not sure what I expect." She wiped the outside of the mug and then set it carefully in front of him. "Nurse it. The tap's almost dry."

"Should've told me. I could have brought you some." He took a long sip with his eyes closed, unwilling to look at her. But as he put the mug down he found Liana leaning across the table staring at him. "What's that look for?"

"Curiosity," she said quietly. "Sometimes I feel like I hardly know you."

"Is that all you feel about me? That you hardly know me?"

Liana leaned back and laughed. "Sakes, man. Is that what you skimmed all the way out here for? To find out how I feel about you? I thought you . . ."

He looked at her steadily as her voice trailed off. For no reason he felt a sense of confidence. "Might be," he said, "might be I just wanted to know that—what with Carson going crazy again, and—"

"Going crazy? What's he done this time?"

Junathun hesitated before answering. He had never tried to spend so much time understanding things as he had . . . "Like before," he said quietly. "Just like before."

Liana closed her eyes and tensed for a moment. Then she let her breath out in a long sigh and looked over at him. "So, that's what it is. I wondered. But I should have guessed. Just about time for the Wheezer's Bane to spread its pollen. Should have known. Where is he?"

"My place." Junathun took another long sip of blend and gave her a chance to comment. When she didn't he said, "That's why I came out here."

"To tell me that?" Disbelief rang in her voice.

"And more. To ask you foolish questions, questions I got no right asking you." Her reaction to the news about Carson had weakened any notions he had about—

"Like what foolish questions?" she asked.

"Like the one you already answered about how you felt about me." He looked down into his mug, then quickly lifted it up and finished the remaining blend in three long swallows.

"I didn't answer it," she said in an odd tone of voice.

"Came close enough," he said, as he put the empty mug down and looked at her.

"No, I didn't, Junathun Wyatt. You just jumped to your usual conclusions about me and what I think."

"You said—"

"I said that sometimes I feel like I hardly know you. What's so wrong with that?"

"Nothing. I just wish you knew me, that's all." As soon as he said that Junathun wished he could suck the words back into his mouth. Liana's silence made him wish it all the more.

"Junathun," she said finally, "why do you think I tease you all the time?"

There was a warmth in her voice which surprised him and made him uncomfortable. "Didn't know that you did."

"All right, then," she continued with a touch of amusement added to the warmth, "why do you think I always give you such a hard time?"

"'Cause I don't measure up to..."

"To what? Of course you measure up. What's the matter with you? Do you think I'm cruel? If you didn't measure up I wouldn't tease you so. I just do it because... well, because it's the only way I know how to draw you out."

After a long pause he looked steadily into her clear eyes. "Can't say as I understand that."

She looked back at him without blinking. "I guess not. But think a minute, Junathun. And answer this. Have you ever known me to hold my tongue when I didn't like something? Or someone? Well, have you?"

A smile cracked the firm set of his lips. "No."

"Then do you think I'd have put up with you all these years if I didn't like you?"

"Maybe."

"Why? Because of Carson? I didn't put up with Amsrita, did I? I made him—"

"But that was different."

"No, it wasn't."

She paused and glanced away, but only for a second. When she looked at him again her eyes seemed clearer than he had ever seen them.

"Not in the beginning anyway. I just didn't like her. Told her so. Told him, too. You should remember. You were there."

Junathun remembered only too well. He hadn't liked Amsrita all that much either, too impressed with herself—and

107

Carson too impressed with her. "So? What's that got to do with me?"

"Everything," she said simply. "And nothing. Dammit, Junathun, I've always thought of you as my friend—not just Carson's friend. Didn't you ever see that?"

Her words and her tone revived the strange hope which had brought him out to see her. A nervous twitch in his stomach made him wish he had nursed the blend like she suggested. "Maybe I didn't dare. You were always Carson's."

"But that's just it," she said, as she reached unexpectedly across the table and put her hand over his, "I never was Carson's woman. Amsrita was the only woman he ever really cared about. If you'll think about that for a minute, you'll know it's true."

"So? You cared about him. And you still do. I can tell it every time you say his name." He pulled his hand out from under hers and crossed his arms over his chest. This wasn't going the way he had hoped after all. Yet as he looked at her he thought he saw a warm light in the paleness of her eyes.

"Does that mean I can't care about you, too?"

"Don't want to be your second-best friend." Junathun blurted out the words and surprised himself.

She gave him a smile he had never seen before. "Then why not be my best friend?"

"For how long?" His voice trembled.

"For as long as you can put up with me."

Her voice had trembled also. Or at least he thought it did. "What about Carson?"

"Carson's gone. For good. I told him if he left this time he wasn't coming back."

"He's still my friend," Junathun said quietly.

"That's between you and Carson. But you can't bring him here. I never want to see him again."

There was no coldness in her voice, just a flat statement of fact. Junathun sighed, then smiled. He didn't want to think about what he felt. He just wanted to enjoy it. "Maybe I better get those chores done now."

"I'll help you."

They walked out the door together.

16

ShRil looked at Hap in wonder. His broad forehead, the wide set of his eyes, the slight crook in his nose, all echoed Gerard's features. They could almost be father and son.

"Please, Hap," Gerard said, "we only want to try to understand what's been happening."

Hap was sorry he had agreed to board the ship. This man made him nervous—not frightened, just nervous. "It's, uh, hard to explain, sir, but—"

"We talk, Dedo," CrRina said, interrupting them for the tenth time. "We talk through Brightseed."

Gerard leaned intently toward the boy. "Is that it, Hap? Do you talk *through* the flowers?"

Why won't he call Brightseed by name? Hap wondered.

"Can you hear CrRina's thoughts now?"

He could, but just barely. "Not exactly, sir. I think we both need Brightseed and the groundsel to—"

"The groundsel? I am sorry," ShRil said softly, "I should not have interrupted."

Hap was glad she had. It gave him a reason to look directly at her. He tried not to stare at the distinct outline of her breasts so visible through her thin garment, tried to look at her face when he spoke, but fascination kept dragging his eyes downward. "The groundsel help Brightseed listen, and, uh, talk, too, I guess." Hap forced himself to raise his eyes to hers, acutely aware of the growing knot in his groin. "Brightseed's not very clear about things like that."

"The One hears us all," CrRina offered.

"That's another thing," Gerard said. There was something about Hap's posture, something about the look of the boy

109

which bothered him. He didn't want to pressure Hap, but Gerard felt a close sense of urgency he couldn't shake. "What can you tell us about the One?"

Turning his attention back to CrRina's father did not ease Hap's aching groin. "It's like it's everything. But it's more than that. I asked if it was like religion, but Brightseed didn't seem to think so. It gets pretty confusing—"

"One, one, all is the One. The One is here and everywhere," CrRina chanted.

"Please, CrRina, Dedo is trying to talk to Hap."

"Talk to me, too," she demanded.

"Yes, darling, we'll talk to you, too. But first we want to hear what Hap has to say. Is that all right? Can we listen to Hap first? Will you help us with that?"

CrRina didn't answer, but instead held out her arms to ShRil. A small pout puckered her lips.

"Mummum will hold you," ShRil said lovingly. Holding CrRina made her feel better also. It also allowed her to be more of an observer and less of a participant in the conversation. Again she was struck by how similar Gerard and the boy looked.

"You said it was pretty confusing. It's pretty confusing for us as well. Have you told your parents about this?"

"No, sir," Hap said immediately. "Brightseed said to wait— said I would know when it was time to tell my mother."

"What about your father?"

"I don't have one, sir." Hap didn't like talking about that. Even though there had been many other children on Sun's March without fathers, most of them knew what had happened to their fathers. He didn't. All his mother would say was that his father had been killed in a battle with the Federation.

"I'm sorry to hear that." Gerard almost asked more, but the oddly familiar look of unhappiness on Hap's face made him decide not to. "Don't you think you should tell your mother?"

Hap waited before answering. His nervousness had ebbed and the knot had relaxed a little, but he was not prepared to tell this stranger about his life. "She has enough to worry about, sir. I think the trip from Sun's March was harder on her than she is willing to admit—at least to me."

"Is that where you're from? Sun's March?" The name rang

a distant bell in Gerard's mind. "Is that part of the Federation?"

Hap made a face. "No, sir," he said forcefully. "It's part of Ribble Galaxy."

The bell rang louder. A chill shocked Gerard's thoughts. Why would— "What brought you here?" His voice was steady, but his emotions were not.

He's from the Federation, Hap thought. I should have known that. "A chance for a new life, sir," he answered carefully. "A chance for a place of our own." Anyone from the Federation could be dangerous to him and his mother just because they were from Ribble Galaxy.

Gerard sensed the boy's caution and understood it. He wanted to know more about this boy and his mother, and he wanted to know it immediately. Yet he knew without thinking about it that he would have to be patient, very patient, or Hap might refuse to tell him anything.

"Uh, sir, mis," Hap said quietly, "I think I ought to leave now. I don't want Mother to worry about me."

"But you've only been here—"

"We understand, Hap," ShRil interrupted. "But we would like it very much if you would come back tomorrow. Can you do that?"

"Uh, I think so." He wouldn't mind seeing her again.

"Good. And, Hap?"

"Yessir?"

"If you want to tell your mother, this might be the time. Then you could bring her with you."

Hap just shook his head and stood up. Brightseed had said he would know the right time, and this wasn't it. They all escorted him to the exit ramp and said goodbye to him there. He was confused as he walked back toward Brightseed, but no more confused than they were.

"I don't think he'll come," Gerard said as he took CrRina from ShRil.

"I do, my love. But he will not bring his mother."

"Hap come back?"

"Yes, CrRina. Hap will come back." He's already come halfway across the universe, Gerard thought, straight from the rotten heart of my past. "Let's get back aboard."

"Talk to Brightseed," CrRina demanded.

"Tomorrow, darling. Tomorrow."

*　*　*

Gel was surprised to see Carson standing at his door. Carson was surprised to see Chizen sitting inside. And Chizen was immediately fascinated by this strange-looking man with the bandage on his hand and the wild light in his eyes.

"I must speak with you, Geljoespiy," Carson said formally.

"In the office, then. Will you pardon us, Mis Chizen?"

"Certainly."

As she watched them enter the tiny office and close the door behind them Chizen was tempted to move closer and try to listen. She had no idea who the gaunt man was, but she wanted to know. However, instead of moving closer to the door she took the dishes off the table, moved them to the sink, and started washing them vigorously and noisily.

"There is a problem."

Geljoespiy's voice startled her and she almost dropped the mug she was hanging on the rack. When she turned to face him both he and the stranger were pulling chairs up to the table.

"This is Carson," Geljoespiy said simply. "He is a friend and can be trusted."

The man nodded toward her and Chizen returned his nod. She did not know what to say to him—or to Geljoespiy—so she stood with her back to the sink drying her hands and waiting.

"Carson has just come down from the hills above the station. While he was up there he heard your son communicating with the Wheezer's Bane."

"Hap? Wheezer's Bane? What are you talking about?"

"You don't know, then?"

She looked at him uncertainly, then at Geljoespiy. "No, I do not know what you are talking about. What is this Wheezer's Bane? And what does it have to do with Hap?"

"You should have told her."

"There were other things—"

"Tell me now." Chizen was angry. "And you, Carson, tell me why you were spying on my son."

The tone of her voice startled them both, but Carson was the first to speak. "I wasn't spying on your son. I went up

112

here to see, uh, how close the Wheezer's Bane is to pollinating time. That's when I heard him talking to them."

"Pollinating time? Talking to whom?" Confusion blocked out her anger. Yet she also sensed a lie in Carson's statement.

"Wheezer's Bane is a kind of flower, Mis Chizen, that grows in big groups all—"

"Colonies."

"Yes, colonies, all over Brisbidine. Aren't no trouble most of the time, but when they are spreading pollen—"

"They're killers," Carson finished for him. "And they think. Sometimes they communicate telepathically. And your son was talking to them."

Chizen shook her head. "Are you a telepath? How do you know he was talking to them? And what if he was?" The idea of Hap talking to flowers would have struck her as silly if Carson and Geljoespiy had not seemed so concerned about it.

"Because he was talking out loud, like Amsrita used to—"

"Amsrita?"

"She's the woman who discovered they could think—at least that's what she said."

"I heard them, too, Gel."

"I know that. But none of the rest of us—"

"Will you stop it!" They both looked at her. "I want one of you to explain to me exactly what you are talking about from beginning to end," she said in her most commanding tone. "And I do not want the other to interrupt."

Geljoespiy and Carson looked at her with new respect. Then Carson rose from his chair and said, "You tell her, Gel. I have some things I have to do. But I'll be back later."

"All right."

Carson stood there for a moment looking down at his bandaged hand and rubbing it. When he raised his head he stared straight at Chizen with those strangely lit eyes. "And you listen to him, Mis Chizen. You listen to him good." A moment later he was out the door.

"Well," Chizen said as she sat across the table from Geljoespiy, "perhaps you had better tell me who that man is, and why he is so rude, and what all this talk about flowers and telepathy has to do with my son."

Gel sighed. "I had not anticipated this, Mis Chizen. You must believe that. Carson is . . . well, Carson is Carson. It

113

would take more time than you wish to listen and I wish to talk to explain about Carson. But he can be trusted. I—"

"Do not babble so, Geljoespiy. Just tell me the facts. I will sort them out for myself."

"Very well. The facts are these. Amsrita was a researcher who worked here eight or nine years ago. She believed the Wheezer's Bane were intelligent. Carson became her helper and her . . . her lover. He believed it, too. He also believed that the Wheezer's Bane killed her."

"How? That is an absurd idea."

"No it's not—not for Carson. He said their thoughts drove her crazy and—"

"But that is not killing."

"It can be. You said you wanted the facts. I'm trying to give them to you."

"I'm sorry, Geljoespiy. Continue, please." The story got more confusing as he tried to explain it, and Chizen sensed an ugly pattern behind what he called the facts.

"Anyway, after she died Carson sort of went crazy himself. We all tried to help him, especially Junathun and Liana, but we couldn't. He left Brisbidine for a couple of years. Wouldn't talk about where he'd been when he got back, but he seemed, well, resigned I guess. But he became a kind of specialist at burning out patches of Wheezer's Bane from farms and stations."

"Revenge."

"Yes, mis, revenge. Then I saw him the other day and he was all upset because the girl, Manley's daughter—well, Carson was convinced that she had been in contact with the Wheezer's Bane."

Gerard's daughter? "A child?" Chizen asked. Jealous anger flashed through her thoughts, but was darkened by her concern about Hap. "What made him—"

"I don't know. But he was angry and upset. Then he found your boy talking to them this morning, and he says the Wheezer's Bane attacked him."

"Hap? It attacked—"

"No, sorry." Gel waved his hand. "Attacked *Carson* with its thoughts. Sent him images of death, he said. He thinks they're trying to take over the children's minds."

Geljoespiy paused and Chizen did not know what to say. Plants, flowers taking over the minds of children? It was an nsane idea. At least it should have been. But Geljoespiy and Carson weren't treating it that way. "So what does all this mean?" she asked finally.

"I don't know, Mis Chizen. Carson's working on some plan," e said, and he wants my help. I told him you might be villing to help, too."

That angered her. "Why did you tell him that?"

"Because, because I thought you'd want to help protect our boy. And because it might give you a chance to do what ve've been talking about."

"Kill Gerard Manley," she said flatly just as the door opened.

Hap wasn't sure what he'd heard, but the looks on their aces made him wish he hadn't heard anything. "Uh, Mother, —"

"Come here, Hap."

Reluctantly he came in and shut the door behind him. He ook a few steps toward the table, then stopped.

"Did you hear what I said, Hap?"

He took three more steps which brought him to the edge of the table and stood there with his head down as though he had been caught doing something wrong. *Kill Gerard Manley.* Her words echoed in a whirlwind of thoughts.

"I asked you a question." She knew he had heard, but she wanted him to admit it.

"Yes, Mother," he whispered.

"Wait in our room and we will talk about it in a minute."

As soon as Hap shut the door to their room behind him he looked frantically around. He didn't understand what was happening, and he didn't know what to do. (Brightseed) he thought.

We hear you, Hap.

(I need you.)

Come.

Five minutes later the only thing which greeted Chizen when she walked into the room was the scent of fresh air blowing in through the open window. Hap was gone.

"We have come to say goodbye, immortal."

Spinnertel jumped and spun around. "Damn!" he said aloud. "Do you have to frighten me like that?"

"We did not mean to frighten you," Shttz squeaked.

"Well, you did. Now get out of here."

"If you insist on being rude, we can stay awhile longer."

It was the she-ghost, Ronda. Spinnertel shuddered at the thought of having to put up with them any longer. "You disturb me," he said. "I can't help that. You got your energy. Now why don't you just leave?"

"I think we should stay," four-arms said gruffly. "He could be fun to play with."

"No," the luminescent blob said, speaking for the first time in Spinnertel's presence. "The immortal has done nothing to deserve that—yet."

As if its words were a prearranged signal, they all disappeared with a harsh *pop*. A bitter odor clung to the air in the cabin and settled into Spinnertel's fur. It made him angry and uneasy. He wasn't sure if they had really gone. And he might never be sure.

"Damn ghosts," he whispered under his breath. With a sudden burst of energy he left the cabin and went down the companionway to the maintenance controls. After turning up the air filtration system to its maximum level he decided to bathe.

Spinnertel hated water, but he hated the ghost-smell worse. He would have to deodorize everything to get rid of it, starting with himself. But he knew he couldn't get comfortable again on his own ship as long as the slightest trace of that smell lingered to remind him of them.

As he lathered his fur with the oil-rich shampoo he used on those rare occasions when dry brushing wouldn't get him clean, the real-time message bell started dinging insistently. He turned the water jets to full power and furiously tried to squeeze the lather from his body. Then he stopped and a puzzled frown changed the flow of water down his forehead.

A real-time message could only be from Askavenhar or—

He decided to let it ding. If it was Askavenhar, he did not want her and the Constant to know he was already here. If it was from Cosvetz, it was a mistake. Spinnertel had told him never to use real-time messages unless there was an emergency. And no mortal's emergency could be important enough to make Spinnertel answer while he was soaking wet.

Spinnertel forced himself to relax and make sure the lather was thoroughly rinsed from his fur. Then he turned off the water and turned on the airstream. As he brushed himself in the warm rush of air the bell finally stopped dinging. Spinnertel smiled with satisfaction, then realized it was the

116

first time he had smiled since the ghosts had popped in on him.

After carefully powdering and then brushing out his armpits and crotch he took a liter of alcohol from the cabinet and headed up to the flight deck, stopping on the way to turn the air filtration system back to normal. He sniffed several times and the odor seemed to be gone.

He made himself comfortable in his pilot's chair, drank half the liter of alcohol, then casually turned on the message console to see if his insistent caller had left an identity. What he found didn't surprise him, but it did disturb him.

Geljoespiy had panicked. The message said that between the lines. But it didn't say what Geljoespiy was doing. It didn't say how the boy had found out, or if he had managed to warn the Verporchting. And it didn't say what the woman intended to do. The omissions bothered Spinnertel as much as the information.

His answer was brief. Restrain the boy. Force the woman to make a decision. Coerce her if necessary. Then prepare a plan to take effect no sooner than three local days from now.

He sent the message and sat back with a sigh. As he finished off the alcohol he cursed the Verporchting, Geljoespiy, the Constant, and the situation in general. Then he went to get another liter.

The ghosts were waiting for him in his cabin. "I thought you'd left?" Quiet despair tinged his voice.

"We changed our minds," Shttz squeaked quietly.

"Actually, Bertilina changed our minds."

The luminescent lump purred.

"We want to apologize for causing you distress."

"You don't have to apologize," Spinnertel said through clenched teeth. "All you have to do is leave and stay gone."

"But we apologize anyway."

"All of us," four-arms added.

"Yes, all of us," Shttz squeaked.

He could smell it. They were fading, and he could smell it. "Please," he said as steadily as he could, "just leave. I accept your apologies. I appreciate your concern. But if you keep popping back on me, you only . . . distress me more," he finished to the walls of the empty cabin.

The bitter odor clung to the air and settled heavily on Spinnertel's fluffy fur. His roar of frustration echoed through the empty ship.

117

17

Hap sat under a small rock ledge on the side of the hill. He could see Brightseed, but not the spaceship *Windhover*. "I can't come any closer," he whispered. "If I do they'll see me."

What causes your fear?

"I told you. Mother was talking about killing CrRina's father. She was serious. I know she was."

How do you know?

As Hap tried to explain to Brightseed what he felt and why he had run away, the whole thing got more confusing. He was hungry and tired, and he wanted more than anything else to eat something and go to sleep. He wanted release from his churning emotions, an escape—

You should tell kinous Gerard. He can help you understand what troubles you.

"You don't understand. You really don't! What am I supposed to do, Brightseed? Run up the hill and tell CrRina's father that my mother is planning to kill him? Is that what I'm supposed to do?"

Brightseed tried to soothe Hap with a loving message.

"And don't send me all that One-is-wonderful stuff. That's not going to do any good. Not now." Hap wrapped his arms around his legs and pulled his knees up. "Oh, never mind," he sighed, "just leave me alone for a while."

He rested his forehead on his knees and tried to think. Instead, he cried. There was nothing to think about. The dark sea of confusion washed over all his thoughts, drowning them in irrational tides he could not contain. Yet while he wept he was aware of Brightseed chanting faintly in rhythm with the ebb and flow of his emotions.

Let others who will speak ill of us. Let others deny our faith in the One. The sky will burn with empty torches. The night will fill with falling stars. The roaring wind . . .

Somewhere in the middle of the chanting and the tears Hap slumped against the rocks. Pulled down by the relentless currents which swirled around his soul, and eased by Brightseed's hypnotic chants, he fell into a black sleep.

The quiet *pop* startled Gerard when the four ghosts appeared in the galley.

"I brought help," Shttz said simply.

"Ronda? Bertilina? And . . ." Gerard looked carefully at the four-armed ghost.

"It is Woltol, my Fize."

Woltol! Pieces of memory tumbled through Gerard's mind like rocks and boulders in an avalanche, colliding and bouncing off each other, blurred visions illuminated by the harsh light of pain. He collapsed in the chair, aware of the pounding in the back of his head. "Woltol? Is it really you?"

"Yes," Woltol said proudly. "It is good to see my Fize again. Youse look good."

"But how? Why?" Gerard pressed his fingers against his temples as the pounding moved forward.

Ronda laughed, the same hollow laugh he remembered from years ago on Quadra, and answered for all of them. "Shttz came to Bertilina for help. I was bored and agreed to come. Not much excitement since you left, just too many corporeals."

"And you, Woltol?" Gerard still couldn't believe his eyes. The tumbling memories slowed momentarily and the pain steadied. There were a hundred questions he wanted to ask, needed to ask, was afraid to ask.

"Spirit news travels fast, Fize. I heard youse were in need, so I decided to join them."

"But how did you die? What happened to the rest of the string? What can you—"

"Too fast, Fize. Too fast. There will be time enough to tell youse everything."

When Woltol smiled Gerard could see the bulkhead through it. It was somehow disconcerting to think of a ridlow as being a ghost. But it was more disconcerting to realize that he was finally faced with someone who could answer his questions, fit the pieces of his puzzle together for him, someone from Ribble Galaxy who obviously didn't think . . . or did he?

"You have to answer a few things now, Woltol."

"As my Fize commands."

The title made Gerard uncomfortable. But the pain in his head swelled again and he knew he would have to hurry. "How did you die?"

Woltol's smile disappeared. "When the Fedships attacked us in Dinsey space."

Dinsey space. Woltol. Fairy Peg, Orees, Fianne, Targ.

Memories broke and slid. Then they jumbled together in a roar and crashed unbearably through his brain. Gerard wanted to scream and cry and curse and laugh all in the same instant, but the scream was the only thing which made it out.

Pain rushed along dark pathways lined with shadowy faces. It hissed past a series of distorted scenes, lit the burning darkness with flashes of laser fire, and burst from the center of his mind in a brilliant explosion of blinding agony.

Brightseed's thoughts were seared by the message of pain. It recoiled, but not before Hap felt it, too, and cried aloud at the nightmare in his hypnotic sleep.

CrRina screamed in echo to her father.

ShRil rushed to CrRina's side, then almost fell backward when Shttz appeared in front of her.

"Hurry," he said. "Gerard . . ."

ShRil grabbed CrRina to her bosom and tried to comfort her terrified daughter as they made their way to the galley. What she saw there made her gasp. Gerard was lying on the floor covered by three ghosts.

CrRina screamed again.

Brightseed listened in shock, trying to calm itself, still the questions which poured in from the surrounding colonies, and calm Hap's dreams all at the same time.

"He is alive," Bertilina said as she shifted her shining presence over his chest.

"Shh, shh, CrRina. It is all right. It is all right." ShRil knelt beside Gerard and rested CrRina on one knee. The ghosts made way for her. "It is going to be all right." Her voice trembled with fear. "What happened, Shttz?"

"I don't know. Woltol was talking—"

"Woltol?" ShRil looked at the ghosts and for the first time

120

recognized Ronda Loner War Crow and Bertilina. The four-armed ghost must be Woltol.

"I am Woltol," he said as if reading her thoughts. "My Fize asked when I died. When I told him it was in Dinsey space, he shuddered and screamed, clutching his head as though it were filled with demons."

"Shh, CrRina, shhhhh." As she felt the pulse in Gerard's neck she suddenly realized what Woltol had said. "Are you from Ribble Galaxy? Did you call him Fize?"

"Yes to both of those. I was from Ribble Galaxy and Gerard Manley was my Fize."

"Fize of the Gabriel Ratchets?" ShRil asked as though unwilling to believe her ears.

"There is no other Fize."

She knew what had happened. Woltol had triggered memories, and the blocks left behind by the mindwipers had triggered Gerard's pain. It was not the first time she had seen this happen. "CrRina," she said softly, as she set her daughter on the floor and wiped her running nose with a facecloth, "you have to help Mummum."

CrRina clung to her arm and snuffled.

"Dedo is sick. Mummum has to carry him to the rejuvhosp cell. You can come, too, but Mummum cannot carry you. Do you understand that?"

CrRina snuffled again, but loosened her grip on ShRil's arm.

"Look. Here's Shttz. You can walk with Shttz while Mummum carries Dedo. All right?"

With a drier snuffle CrRina nodded her head.

"Can you all help?"

"A little," Woltol said, with a look ShRil took for sadness.

"Good. I'll lift him and you do what you can." She moved around until she was kneeling over him with his head almost between her knees. Then she slipped her arms under his, locked her hands together over his chest, and lifted. Ronda and Woltol pressed in upon Gerard's still form, and suddenly ShRil felt less of a strain as she struggled to her feet. Still, she dragged him more than carried him out of the galley and down the companionway to the rejuvhosp cell.

CrRina stayed right beside her the whole time, but was careful not to get in the way, and even tried to help get

Gerard's feet up on the thin mattress. "Is Dedo hurt, Mummum?" The tremor in her voice threatened to crack.

"No, dear. Dedo's just sick. He'll be all right in a little while." As she activated the cell and adjusted its monitors, she prayed to HnSa that was true. Gerard had never had a shock like this one before, and there was no way of knowing if he actually would be all right. Yet she refused to let herself believe anything else.

"It was my fault?"

"No, Woltol," ShRil said, as she made the last of the adjustments. "It was not your fault." She pulled the one chair in the tiny cabin up beside the cell and let CrRina climb into her lap and nestle against her.

"We don't understand," Shttz squeaked.

"I do," Bertilina purred.

ShRil had not even realized that Bertilina had come with them and was surprised to see her beside Gerard in the cell.

"You should understand also, Shttz. It is part of the same confusion we discovered in his mind when he was stranded."

"The mindblocks."

"Yes, I think so."

Ronda moved closer and looked down on Gerard. "What can we do for him?"

"Nothing. We can only wait." ShRil remembered the first time years before when she had found Gerard driven to unconsciousness by the pain of memories. She shuddered. CrRina whimpered and pulled herself closer to ShRil's breast.

"What can we do for *you*?" Woltol asked.

ShRil's bladder demanded relief. As CrRina pressed against her, the discomfort became acute. "Watch over him. I will return in a few minutes. CrRina? Will you stay here and help watch Dedo? Please?"

CrRina nodded and reluctantly climbed off ShRil's lap. "Seets, too, Mummum?"

"Yes, I will stay with you," Shttz squeaked.

"I will be right back." ShRil walked quickly to their cabin. She could have used the small head beside the rejuvhosp cell, but she needed a moment of total privacy. As she sat down her nose started running uncontrollably. She yanked out a facecloth with an angry motion that set off a shudder, then a sob, then a series of rolling spasms as her body released its tension.

Long after her bladder was empty she used the last dry corner of her facecloth to wipe her nose a final time. She had to get back to Gerard...and CrRina. She knew that. But the cold pressure of fear kept her from moving. What if this had been too much of a shock? Would he be all right? And what would she do if...

There was no time for those thoughts. ShRil shook off the fear, cleansed herself, and prepared to go back and face the truth, whatever that truth might be.

"It's getting too dark to see." Geljoespiy cursed himself for not bringing a nightlight.

Chizen shivered. "We cannot stop looking. The moons will be up soon, will they not?"

"Not for another couple of hours. Let's go back and get something to eat and some warmer clothes. I think Junathun has a heatscope we can borrow. Then we can come back with that and a nightlight and we're sure to find him."

"I will wait here for you."

"Please, Mis Chizen. You can't do any good here. Besides, the boy could already have—"

"His name is Hap!"

"I'm sorry. Hap could already be back at the house. Then you'd be standing up here in the cold for nothing."

The thought that Hap might have returned was enough to make Chizen change her mind. She doubted he would be there when they got back, but if he was...Geljoespiy's arguments made sense. "Very well. But if he is not there, I want to start looking again immediately."

"Soon as we grab something to eat and get the heatscope from Junathun. That will make it a lot easier to find him."

As she followed Geljoespiy down the path she had an idea. "Could we not call Gerard Manley's ship? Perhaps they have seen Hap? Perhaps they could help us—"

"No! I'm sorry, but no. We'll call the communications center and ask them to call Manley. But you know we can't—"

"Of course." Chizen shivered again and wrapped her arms around herself. He was right, of course. There was no way she could ask for Gerard's help.

Her foot twisted. She stumbled and gasped before catching her balance.

"You all right?"

"Yes." But she was not all right. She had finally admitted to herself that she was ready and willing to kill Gerard. Chizen tried to concentrate on the path, a lighter shadow among the darker ones which mounted around her. Willing? Was she really willing to kill him? Once she questioned that willingness she was no longer sure of it. But she recognized a danger she had not anticipated. The final decision could come without warning.

Denial surged through her. She could not let that happen. She must make the decision consciously, deliberately, then be prepared to live with it. Or die with it.

Ghoulish figures charged through the darkness to devour him. Faceless voices screamed his name. Scenes of confrontation, pain, and horror rose and fell through his dreams like giant waves in an ocean of memories. But through it all Gerard felt detached, remote, withdrawn from what he knew were phantoms from his shrouded past.

A faint humming sound pulled at him. At first its rhythms matched the waves. Then slowly, ever so slowly, it beat them down, calmed the swells, and left him rocking gently in an empty twilight sea. Only the humming remained, quiet, insistent, drawing him up through the dimness into the light.

He blinked and looked around. ShRil was sitting in a chair next to the rejuvhosp. CrRina was curled in her lap humming to herself. "Hello," he said weakly.

"Dedo!"

"Gerard! Oh, thank HnSa!" She set CrRina on the floor and knelt beside him. "How do you feel?"

"Lightheaded. Tired." His hand trembled as he reached for hers. "Weak," he added with a faint smile. "Where are—"

"We are here, Fize," Woltol said, as the ghosts moved into his field of view.

"How long . . ."

ShRil gently squeezed his hand and glanced at the monitors. "The better part of ten Standard hours. Do you—"

"I love you, Dedo."

"I love you, too, CrRina." He smiled as she noisily kissed his cheek.

"Do you remember what happened?" ShRil asked.

Gerard sighed wearily and closed his eyes. "Yes."

"Was it like before?"

"No. It was better."

"Better? That is an odd description. I do not think you truly remember."

"But I do. It was better." He opened his eyes and looked steadily into hers. "The pain wasn't . . . wasn't nearly so bad. I almost felt like it was happening to someone else."

"Rest," she said quietly. "I will turn on the soother."

"No. Please. I would rather just . . . just sleep." The weariness pulled his eyes closed again. "Just sleep and I'll be all right. So tired."

"Yes, my love," she said as she laid his hand beside him and stroked it softly. "You sleep now."

"Why is Dedo going to sleep again?"

"Because he is tired."

"But he just woke up!"

ShRil pulled CrRina into her arms and gave her a big hug. "Yes, he did, CrRina. But now he is going to sleep some more. I think we ought to do the same thing."

"I'm not sleepy!"

"Then you play with Shttz and let Mummum sleep. All right?"

Minutes later as she settled the blankets around her and closed her eyes a peaceful smile settled on her lips. Shttz was playing with CrRina. Ronda, Woltol, and Bertilina were watching over Gerard. And HnSa had been kind. In the middle of her prayer of thanks ShRil fell asleep.

Hap was safe. Kinous Gerard had escaped his pain. Brightseed was satisfied that the sacrifices had been worth it. Over two hundred individual plants had given up their life energy during the night to make those two things possible. Such was the balance of the One. *When pain blocks the way to the Heart-of-One, sweep it away with pain of your own. There are no songs for the shadow of pain. There is no pain for the singer of songs.*

Petals folded tightly over chilled anthers. Sepals sealed themselves around the petals with waxy secretions. All but four of the twenty Guardians closed their flowers and joined in Brightseed's rest. Those four stood tired, but vigilant, aware of the setting moons and the coming dawn and the groundsel which monitored Hap. Their rest would come later.

18

"I told you not to come back here," Liana said defiantly.

Her voice rang coldly in Carson's ear. He looked from her to Junathun, and back to her again. "I was looking for Junathun. I did not come to see you."

"Please, Liana," Junathun said softly.

She tilted her head and started to say something, then turned silently and went back into the house. Junathun watched her with open admiration.

"I looked for you . . ."

"What do you want?"

"Not her. We're finished. But I don't suppose I need to tell you that, do I?"

"You can tell me whatever you want."

"I was looking for you because I'm going to need your help. The patches have gotten totally out of control, and I think it's time—"

"What do you mean, 'gotten out of control'?" Junathun saw the cycle of the past repeating itself, and hated Carson for it. His night with Liana opened the way to a future filled with—

"They're talking to the children—only the offworld children as far as I can tell—but they're talking to them the way they used to talk to Amsrita."

"So?"

"Dammit, Junathun. The patches are *talking* to them. I made calls to some of the other stations to see if they had noticed the same thing. So far there's no evidence, but I think it's time we burned a lot of patches."

Junathun saw the wildness in Carson's eyes and heard the excitement in his voice more clearly than he wanted to.

Carson had lost control again, gotten himself hyped up, and was ready to do Fara only knew what to feed the dark fires of revenge which burned in him. "So what do you need me for?"

"I need backup, someone I can rely on, someone who will follow through on my plans in case anything goes wrong." Carson glanced toward the house.

"Why me?" Junathun followed Carson's glance and saw Liana watching through the window. If he had to choose between the two of them, there was no choice. Liana outclassed Carson.

"Because," Carson said slowly, "you're the only one I know I can rely on."

"And if I say no? What will you do then?"

It had not occurred to Carson that Junathun might refuse to help. "I don't know. Find somebody else, I guess. Gel maybe. Or Davidem."

"Davidem? You think she would help you? Why?"

Carson gave him a malicious grin. "Because she owes me."

Then Junathun remembered. On one of those nights after Amsrita's death when Carson had been drunk and drugged he had babbled on about Davidem and how he had helped save her medtech's license by making sure that certain records conveniently disappeared. Junathun had dismissed the babbling as part of Carson's usual bragging about what he had done for others. Now he wasn't so sure. "Why don't you just get her, then?"

"I want you."

"I don't know, Carson. It seems to me like you're going off the cliff with this one. If you had more—"

"More evidence?" Carson sneered. "What's the matter? You afraid that if you help me you'll miss your chance with Liana?"

"That doesn't have anything—"

"Of course it does! Dammit, Junathun, I need you. You want Liana? That's fine. She want you? That's fine, too. I'm not asking you to choose. I just need your help for a little while. Then you can come back here and lifebond if you want to."

Junathun refused to look at Carson. He wanted to help, but another part of him didn't want to have anything to do with—

"Well? Can I count on you?"

"I don't know. I just don't know. You'll have to let me think about it for a while."

"Tomorrow. I need to know tomorrow." He turned away and climbed aboard his utility skimmer. "I need you, Junathun," he said as the skimmer whined to life. "I need you to—"

"Stay at my place. I'll call you there."

"Tomorrow."

Before Junathun could answer, Carson spun the skimmer around and headed north out of the valley. Not going back to the station, Junathun thought, as he stood there watching the skimmer disappear. He sighed, wondering if—

"What did he want?"

Liana was almost beside him when she spoke, but Junathun was not surprised. "My help in burning out some patches," he said as he turned to face her. "Seems to think they're talking to the children—the greenie children, anyway."

"So what are you going to do?"

A hard implication underlying her soft tone told him what she wanted him to say. "I told him I'd think about it."

"That's no answer. Are you going to help him or not? I'd bet a year's crops you've already made up your mind."

"No."

"No you haven't made up your mind? Or no you're not going to help him?"

"I'm not going to help him."

"Why? Isn't he your friend?"

"Dammit, Liana, what do you want from me?"

"I want you to be sure you know what you're doing and why."

"That's all? You sure that's all?"

She turned away from him and looked up the valley where the skimmer had disappeared. "No. I guess not." Suddenly she stepped close and grabbed his arms. Anger burned bright in her eyes. "Junathun, I never promised you anything yesterday. But I'll promise you something now. Two things, in fact.

"First, I promise you that helping Carson will be a big mistake. He's headed for trouble. You know that as well as I do. You can see it in his eyes. Second, I'm willing to make you a personal promise."

"There's no need—"

"Just let me finish." She took a deep breath and blinked rapidly. "You stay with me, and I'll make sure you . . . well, I'll make you as happy as I can for the rest of my life."

"Liana . . ." She slumped against him and he held her tightly against his chest. He might be getting her on the rebound from Carson, and he might have to cope with that later, but Liana was the most honest person he had ever known. If he accepted her promise, she would keep it. "Liana, I don't know what to say. There's no need to make promises like that. Neither of us can guess what the future—"

"I'll take my chances," she said through her tears.

"I'm not worth—"

"You are." She pushed him back and looked up at him with wet red eyes. "Do I have to beg you? Is that what you want?"

"No, Liana, no." He pulled her back against him and stroked her hair. "I just want you to be sure—"

"I'm sure."

Junathun tilted her chin up and looked into the liquid depths of her eyes. The promise he saw there was almost more than he knew how to cope with. "I'll stay," he said quietly. "I'll stay."

Gerard looked up at ShRil's smiling face. "Hello, mate," he said softly.

"Hello yourself. How do you feel?"

"Fine. I feel just fine. Where are the ghosts? I mean, I didn't dream them up, did I?"

"No," she said as she squeezed his hand, "you did not dream that they were here. Do you remember what happened?"

He frowned. "Only too clearly. Lots of memories. And lots of pain. But a different pain this time. Passed out again, didn't I?"

"You did, love. But what do you remember?"

"Fragments, mostly. Strange fragments. I want to talk to Woltol first. He can help me sort it out."

"When you are stronger."

"No. As soon as possible. I want to talk to him before it all slips away from me."

"Very well. I will get him."

As Gerard climbed from the rejuvhosp cell a faint voice whispered past his inner ear, a voice that had nothing to do with the fragments and memories. Then it was gone. Despite the swell of images which swept behind it, a dry rustling lingered in his thoughts.

Later as he sat across the galley table from Woltol, Gerard didn't know where to start or what to ask. Woltol seemed perfectly content to sit and wait.

"Listen, Woltol," Gerard said finally, "your appearance brought back a lot of memories, memories I didn't know I had. After the mindwipers got through with me—"

"Mindwipers, Fize? Your mind was, was..."

"Adjusted, Woltol. Adjusted to block everything that happened to me while I was in Ribble Galaxy." Woltol's face narrowed as he puckered his lips. Gerard thought it was a look of sadness. "I've remembered part of it since then, but only bits and pieces, just enough to confuse me. Can you help me remember? Will you?"

"As my Fize commands. But I do not understand how youse could not remember. Do youse not remember Brunnel's string?"

"Only vaguely.... I'm sorry, but it's like I've been looking through a fog back at shadows in my past. You were in Brunnel's string... and so was I. And we did something on one of the moons, an exercise, I think?"

"Youse saved my life, Fize."

Gerard remembered with pain. "When the wall collapsed," he said suddenly. "In a ravine." The pain crept under his scalp.

"Yes. Then youse fought Commander Alpluakka and became our Fize. And Brunnel's string was you personal string."

As the ache seeped into his skull, Gerard thought Woltol looked more pained than he felt. Reluctantly he washed down the pain capsule ShRil had given him with a mug of Brandusian coffee. "I want to talk about that, about you and the string. But more importantly, I want to know what happened in Dinsey space."

"I do not know, Fize. Knip and I boarded the guard ship as soon as you ship started spinning. We stayed there when youse recovered, prepared to join and guard youse. Then we died."

"Knip? Did he become..."

"No, Fize. Knip did not remain. He disintegrated."

For a long moment there was silence in the galley. The

disappointment Gerard felt mixed darkly with the pain and he prayed for the painkiller to take effect. Woltol had answered the question as best he could and was waiting for the next one.

"What happened then?"

Woltol's form shimmered. "I found myself in the company of several other spirits moving away from Dinsey space, drawn by some unseen force which controlled us. At first I was frightened, but my fright soon disappeared as I felt a freedom I had never known."

Gerard was ready to cry. "So you don't know what happened back there?"

"No, Fize. I left them all behind."

"And Fairy, uh, Princess Peg? Can you tell me about her?" Tears moistened his eyes. The pill was not working.

"As much as I know, Fize. But perhaps..."

"Yes, Woltol," Gerard said, as he rose unsteadily from his chair, "perhaps we... should... wait." The galley spun away as he did a slow pirouette down into twilight.

"Haaap!" Chizen called hoarsely. "Haaap!" She sat under a tree at the top of a low rise, knowing as she called that her voice was not carrying very far. With a dry swallow she whispered his name over and over. "Hap, Hap, Hap." The quiver in her breast brought no tears. The ache under her heart marked the dry well which had been emptied of tears early in the morning when Geljoespiy had finally forced her to come back to the house.

It was her fault. It was all her fault. If Hap hadn't overheard her, if she had explained rather than ordering him to their room, he wouldn't be gone. But he was gone. And she would find him. She had to. Then, after he was safe, she would beat him to within a millimeter of his life for scaring her so.

That thought refilled her well of tears. She could never beat him. Would never beat him. Only wanted to hold him and hug him and cry over him. Only wanted to have him back. To know he was all right. Safe.

Geljoespiy saw her hugging her knees with her head down, and even from the bottom of the hill knew she was crying. With a sigh of resignation he trudged up the hill. "Mis Chizen," he said softly when he reached her side, "I've

131

alerted the station guards. They're getting some volunteers with skimmers and hikebikes to help us look."

When she didn't lift her head or reply, he continued. "If you could just get a little rest before they get to my place, you might be able to help them more."

Chizen did not want to listen to him. He made too much sense. She snuffled and spat, despising herself for that filthy habit. But it was the least of the residue left in her by the years of exile. After clearing her throat and spitting again she smiled weakly at Geljoespiy. "You have been very good to me." Her voice rasped painfully.

"Then please come back with me."

"Very well. When will they be—"

"As soon as they can. Probably in a couple of hours. It'll take some time to round up enough people. You can rest until they come."

Reluctantly she let him help her to her feet. But she refused to lean on his offered arm as they walked down the hill. She still had her pride. It was bad enough that she had cried in front of him. It would not do at all to appear any weaker than she already had.

When she walked in the door of Geljoespiy's house, the first thing she saw was Carson sitting at the table. The second thing she saw was Hap tied in the chair beside him.

"Hap!" She rushed to his side. "What? How?"

"Found him asleep up near the big patch I told you about," Carson said. "He didn't want to come, but I convinced him."

Chizen saw the bruise on the side of Hap's face. "You hit him!" she screamed, as she worked frantically to untie the tight knots which bound him to the chair.

"He hit me, too," Carson said with a smile.

Hap sat with his head bowed, unwilling to speak. He was ashamed and angry and frightened. "He grabbed me," he said finally. "And lied to me."

"I only told him that you had been hurt looking for him. Your feelings were hurt, weren't they?" The expression on his face was half-smile, half-leer.

"Silence!"

Carson's expression froze for an instant, then disappeared from view as he lowered his head. Chizen released the final knot and pulled Hap to his feet. "If I ask you to wait in our room," she said, looking straight into his eyes, "do you promise to stay there?"

"Yes, Mother," Hap said sullenly.

"Thank you. I will join you shortly."

Hap went into the room and shut the door. He had an odd feeling in the pit of his stomach. He wanted to climb out the window and run again, but he also just wanted to curl up under the covers and shut out the world. As quickly as he could he undressed, climbed beneath the covers, and pulled out the small diary he had started keeping when they left Sun's March.

The last entries were mostly what he remembered of what Brightseed had told him. As he read the entries he thought of Brightseed's love, the kind of love an older brother might have given him. Or a father.

He could hear his mother berating the man who had dragged him back. (Brightseed), he thought, (I need your help.)

"There was no need," Chizen said through clenched teeth. "You had no right to hit him."

"That may be true. But would you rather I'd left him there? I thought you wanted him back."

"I did, but not that way."

"It was the only way he would come. Look, offworlder, your son has been in contact with the Wheezer's Bane. I don't know what they've done to him, or what they're planning to do. But they killed someone I loved once and I didn't think—"

"Exactly. You did not think. Had you thought, had you had your wits about you, you would not have dragged him away. You would have noted his location and informed me. I am his—" Carson's laugh interrupted her, and made her wonder exactly what kind of man he was. And what kind of man Gel was for sitting there so quietly this whole time.

"Forgive my humor, your uppityness, but I only thought to save the boy. You would have had me leave him in the greatest danger for reasons I do not understand."

"Then listen," Chizen snapped, "and maybe you will discover some understanding. You made a grave mistake. If what you say about the flowers is true, you alerted your enemy. And your enemy no doubt alerted my enemy. Thus you took the advantage from both of us."

As much as he hated to admit it, Carson knew she had made a logical point. But he didn't care. Alerted or not, the Wheezer's Bane would burn, even if he had to do everything himself. "There are other advantages," he said quietly.

"Discuss them with Geljoespiy. I am going to attend to my son." Chizen looked hard at both of them. "And you, Geljoespiy, if you want my cooperation, you will guide your friend's thinking." Before either of them responded she went into her room and closed the door quietly behind her.

19

By the time ShRil came back with Woltol, Gerard was sitting at the galley table nursing his aching head with another cup of Brandusian coffee. "I'm all right," he said as soon as she walked in the door.

"Woltol said—"

"I know. But I think he was wrong. I didn't really pass out. Just went dizzy for a second or two."

ShRil moved behind him and rubbed his shoulders. "You were talking about Ribble," she said flatly.

"Of course. I told you we were—"

"Dedo! Mummum! It's Hap! It's Hap!" CrRina ran straight to ShRil and desperately clutched her legs.

"Here, here," ShRil said, as she reached down and pulled CrRina up into her arms. "What is the matter? Where is Hap?"

"Hurts, Mummum," CrRina cried. "Hap hurts." A series of sobs shook her body.

It took Gerard and ShRil several minutes to calm her down. When she finally quieted, Shttz and Bertilina joined them in the galley. "Tell Mummum about it," ShRil said as CrRina nestled against her.

"It is ooky," she said with a slight tremor in her voice. "The ooky man hurt Hap."

"What ooky man?" Gerard asked.

"*That* ooky man. That man who doesn't like Brightseed."

"Carson?" He glanced at ShRil with raised eyebrows. "Was it the man who asked you the questions?"

"Yes. . . . Mummum, he hurt Hap."

"How do you know? Did—"

"Brightseed told me."

Gerard leaned back with a frown. The dry rustling which had hung in his mind since he had gotten up grew louder.

"Danger," Shttz squeaked.

"Why?" ShRil asked. "You said that before you disappeared, but you did not say why."

"Too much confusion. Ronda and I tried to go to this Brightseed. The group mind is dangerous. It enslaves and confuses all single minds. We must leave this place."

"Then go!" Gerard's sudden anger subdued the dry rustling. "If you don't like what we found here, why did you come back?"

"To help you if we can, as you helped us on Quadra."

A flush of shame followed his anger. "I'm sorry," Gerard said quickly. "I know you want to help. But running away from this isn't the answer."

"CrRina has a special talent," ShRil said quietly. "We cannot ignore that, Shttz. We must try to understand it here and now if we can . . . and help her understand it."

"Or we'll leave her vulnerable in the future," Gerard added.

"Help Hap, Mummum. Please?"

"How can we help him, darling?"

"Brightseed." CrRina looked up and gave her a self-assured smile. "Brightseed knows how."

"Does Brightseed know where Hap is?"

Ronda suddenly materialized in front of them. "The boy is in one of the domes down there."

"In the settlement station? How do you know that?"

"Because, friend ShRil, I followed a man dragging a boy from below the flower colony."

"Why didn't you stop him?"

"I had no cause, Gerard. I was merely curious. Later his mother and the man called Gel joined them. I stayed outside, barely apparent, but enough so I could hear their arguments."

"So?" ShRil asked. "How is he?"

"The boy is hurt and frightened. His mother is angry. She ordered him never to come here again."

"It's not our concern. She is his mother."

"Of course it is our concern." Fire flashed in ShRil's eyes and she hugged CrRina tighter to her breast. "Hap is linked to CrRina through the flowers. If he feels pain, she feels it. Therefore, his welfare is our concern. Mother or no mother."

Gerard was surprised by her vehemence. Then he realized that it was CrRina far more than Hap that she was worried about. Or was it? "But what can we do about it?"

"Go talk to her."

"And if she won't listen? What then? Shall I grab Hap and run for it?"

"Yes."

"Oh, come on, ShRil. That's stupid. She'd have the station guards up here inside an hour demanding her son back. Then where would we be?"

"All safe." She wiped a small drop of mucus from the end of her nose.

Gerard didn't understand her reaction at all. "ShRil? What is the matter? You're usually the logical one. What you're suggesting isn't—"

"I think she is right," Ronda said.

"Perhaps if we went with youse, Fize..."

"All of you think ShRil's right?" Gerard was more confused than ever.

"Yes." "No." Bertilina and Shttz answered simultaneously.

"Four to two, Shttz," Gerard said with a crooked smile. "Five, if you count CrRina."

"Then you will go?"

"Maybe," Gerard said with a sigh. "I guess it can't do any harm to talk to her. But I can't promise to do any more than that. Maybe I can make her understand that whether she likes it or not, we're all wrapped up in this... this whatever, and for Hap's sake and hers we'd be better off working together."

"That sounds more like a yes than a maybe."

"I suppose it does," he said as he touched her hand. "Well then, who's going with me? And when shall we go?"

Spinnertel's timing had been perfect. He'd done the shortest possible popwarp and braked to within a thousand meters of Askavenhar's ship. After receiving her permission, he docked with an irresistible flair, then disembarked and strode confidently to face his adversaries.

"Greetings, young one," Askavenhar said with the barest of smiles as he walked into the opulent meeting room. "We feared you might not be able to join us."

"I'm here," he said surveying the room. Every member of the Constant was there also. "As I said I would be."

"We have been preparing to observe your Verporchting," Gracietta said with a double smile.

"The supposed Verporchting," Spinnertel said, as he took his seat at the far side of their informal circle.

"As you will. There is much happening on Cosvetz about which we are curious. Gatou-Drin has explained much of it to us, but we hoped you might—"

"I just got here."

"Do not interrupt me, young one."

It was bad enough to have Askavenhar call him "young one," but when the exile did it—

"As I was saying, we hoped you might be able to provide us with details of your idea which would help us evaluate this *supposed* Verporchting."

Spinnertel suddenly realized how tense he was and forced himself to take several deep breaths before answering. "I will provide what I can."

"Good," Gracietta said quietly. "You can begin by giving us the most notable characteristics of its reincarnations, the attributes which formed the continuing threads of its existence."

"As briefly as possible," Askavenhar added.

Spinnertel smiled. "It amuses me," he said softly, "that a body such as this, made up of the most long-lived beings in the universe, should always request brief, concise explanations. We have all the time we could possibly need, yet you always seem to be in a grand hurry to find things out and get them done."

"Some of us no longer have that much time."

Askavenhar's response startled him and he looked hard at her. Could she mean ... "Pardon, Askavenhar, but—"

"Yes, young one. You have finally seen what every other member of this Constant has known for some time. I am dying. So it is I who should request your pardon for asking you to rush like this."

His first reaction was shock. That was followed immediately by the realization that Gracietta would be the oldest living member of the Constant after Askavenhar died. He would be as brief and concise as possible. The last thing he wanted was for Gracietta to lead the final evaluation of the Verporchting.

"I will do my best, Askavenhar." He wanted to tell her that he would miss her presence, but he knew that would be too trite. They would all miss her presence.

"The Verporchting's most enduring characteristics have been insatiable curiosity, a willingness—no, an eagerness—to travel wherever there were new and interesting possibilities, a deep introspection, an immense capability to give and receive love, and a strong tendency to bond with many beings over the course of each incarnation."

"What kind of bonding?" Gatou-Drin asked.

"Spiritual bonding, mostly. But each incarnation seemed to, well, let's just say that the Verporchting never lacked for physical bonding either."

"Anything else?"

"Much, Askavenhar, mostly little things which marked each incarnation and made it instantly recognizable."

"Then those are what you should have told us."

Spinnertel sighed. Gracietta was never content with what he had to say. "I was asked to be brief. I gave you the most important characteristics. The others are more difficult to give concisely because it is the pattern they form, not the individual characteristics themselves which are important to recognition."

"What you have told us thus far is too little and too vague to help us make a final evaluation. Can you describe those patterns for us, please?"

Please? Gracietta had tagged her question with a plea for information? Now that she had brought the Constant this far, was she unsure of her conclusions? Or was she as concerned in her own way about Askavenhar's death?

"Yes, I think I can describe the patterns. But the Constant

must understand that what I tell you in a few minutes or a few hours represents several thousand years of observation."

"We understand."

"The most dominant pattern, that is, the one which always seems to make itself apparent earliest in each incarnation, is an interest in literature which the Verporchting responds to by attempting to write its own contributions to literature— sometimes less successfully than other times, but every incarnation has that pattern of involvement throughout its life."

"And when does that usually become apparent?"

"Sometime before adulthood."

"Essenne knows," Geljoespiy said quietly.

The way the woman stared at her annoyed Chizen, but she was too exhausted from all that had happened in the past two days to complain about something so trivial. "Then she can know that I have made the decision you asked of me."

Geljoespiy would have whooped for joy had he not also been so tired. "I am pleased," he said quietly. "But now we must plan how it will be accomplished."

"I do not care."

"But you must care, Mis Chizen. By representing Jelvo Universal Institute, he also represents the Pleuhockle System. The death of one of its representatives will not go unnoticed."

"Then you tell me what to do." Chizen had made her decision. Now all she wanted to do was sleep. She might even take one of the tranquilizers she had given Hap just to make sure that she could fall asleep without trouble. "But save it for in the morning. I am too tired now to cope with it."

"Yes. Of course. Why don't you get some sleep now? In the morning I will talk to Carson, tell him that you've made up your mind, and get his advice."

"Not here. We cannot take any chances with Hap here. You go talk to him wherever he is. Then later you and I can . . . why are you staring at me like that, Essenne?"

Essenne blushed and bowed her head. "I am sorry, Mis Chizen. I did not mean to stare. I, uh, I . . ."

"You wonder at my willingness to kill this man? Shall I tell you? Shall I?" Chizen saw the eagerness in Essenne's eyes and laughed softly and bitterly. "You would like that, would you not? But you shall not get it. Even your husband does not know the reason. And neither of you ever will. When I kill Gerard Manley, it will be for my reasons, and my reasons only." Reasons I could not totally explain even if I had to, she thought.

"I meant no disrespect, mis."

"None taken. Now, goodnight to both of you."

"Goodnight, Mis Chizen." Geljoespiy waited until she closed the door, then said, "You go to bed, too, Essy. I'll be up for a while. There's work—"

"I'm afraid, Gel."

"Of what? Of her?"

"For you. And of her, too, I guess. She has a cold heart, that one. A cold heart."

"A woman's heart."

"What's that supposed to mean?"

"Exactly what I said, Essy." He smiled slightly and took her hand. "If I had done you a great, great wrong, and on top of that had caused people you loved to die, don't you think you could kill me? Haven't you often said—"

"I know what I've said. But—"

"Hold your voice down."

"I know what I've said," she whispered fiercely, "but saying it and doing it are two different things. If you had treated me like Carson treated Liana, I would have hated you and despised you. I might even have wanted to kill you. But, but, well, I just don't think I could have done it. Now that she's made up her mind, that woman will do it without . . ."

"Without hesitation? I wish I was as sure of that as you are. She seems too humane to be dependable. If she panics, or suddenly has last second doubts, things could get very messy. That's why I have to make sure the plan is right. And that's why you have to go to bed and let me get some work done."

"I still don't like what you said."

"Then I'm sorry."

"No, you're not. You meant it. You think all women are cold down inside."

"Everyone is," he said quietly. "If you push anyone far enough and give them enough reason, they'll find that cold dead center which will let them do anything they need to do. You, me, her. We're all the same."

"Speak for yourself," Essy said, as she rose from her chair.

"But don't lump me in with the likes of her. And if you really believe what you said, then you're not the man I married and whose children I bore."

"Yes, I am, Essy. Yes, I am. Now go to bed."

While Geljoespiy worked in his tiny office, first on the outlines of a plan, and then on a message to send to Letrenn, Chizen worked by the dim light of the glowlamp, stripping and cleaning the small projectile pistol she had brought with her from Sun's March.

She loved that old pistol. It was a fine work of craftsmanship, and over the years she had used it to kill hundreds of rodents which otherwise might have invaded her home. Cleaning it brought her a grim feeling of satisfaction. Learning to use it, and use it well, had given her a small measure of independence and freedom on Sun's March. Now it would have to serve a deadlier purpose for a greater freedom.

<hr>

20

<hr>

Brightseed stirred in the first light of dawn. The time of spreading would soon be upon all the colonies. Then the winds would flourish their pollen. The colonies would bless their ovaries. The Guardians would cherish their seeds in preparation for the long walks to plant their offspring.

When the petals of every heart open, then the seed will be ripe. When we are stripped of seeds and half our Guardians are gone, then we will face again the reality of the One.

The litany did not cheer Brightseed. Through the night its groundsel had tried to monitor Hap's dreams and been met by *kan*, the barriers that would not yield. At the same time kinous Sirreena dreamed of Hap and of dark images which Brightseed could not disperse for her.

141

Too many plants had been sacrificed the night before last. Too much energy had been lost. For the sake of its future offspring Brightseed had forced most of its groundsel and Guardians to rest. Yet it knew that the future could be just as dependent on those two young kinous. Perhaps this was a test. Perhaps Our-Gatou would come in the form of a kinous.

All questions are answers from the Heart-of-One.

(Brightseed? Brightseed?)

Hap, Brightseed answered through the groundsel.

(Brightseed, I was—)

We know. That does not matter. Are you safe now?

(I think so. But I want to get out of here. I promised Mother I'd stay, but . . . but she's changed. I want to leave. Where can I go, Brightseed? Where can I go?)

To the kinous Gerard. He will shelter you.

(But I'm afraid.)

Fear is the wind which drives us to safety. As the mountain wind blows—Wait. He is coming.

(Who? Who's coming?)

Kinous Gerard. He is leaving what you call the ship. Stay where you are for now. We will tell you when he returns.

(I can't go anywhere yet. Mother's still here, and so is Geljoespiy.)

Then be still. The time will come for you to travel to us.

(All right. But if I get the chance I'm going to— I can't talk now. Mother's—)

Gerard knew there were words muffled beneath the buzzing, and for the briefest moment he paused to listen. Then he decided against it. There would be time enough for that later.

With Woltol and Ronda bobbing faintly beside him he skirted through the brush and headed toward the settlement station. Thoughts about Hap dominated his mind, Hap and his connections to CrRina and the flowers.

He thinks of Hap, a Guardian whispered.

That is not clear.

The image is clear. He thinks of Hap. And of us.

Hap. Hap. Kinous Gerard is coming toward you, thinking about you.

(Shhh.)

Be careful, Hap.

142

Spinnertel leaned back with a sigh. "I'm afraid your questions have greatly lengthened my brief explanations."

"Yes, young one, but they have also led us to much understanding. Now that the monitors are in place—"

"Pardon, Askavenhar? Do you mean you—"

"You will know what I mean when you listen before asking. The monitors are in place, three microlenses in stationary orbit, and two ground probes. They were being focused and tuned as we spoke, and, yes . . ." She fingered a small keypad on the table. "Yes, they seem to be functioning properly now."

Seconds later a large screen at the end of the room burst into life. Spinnertel stared at it with a mixture of loathing and envy. Whatever equipment Askavenhar was using was far more sophisticated than his own. But that could only mean trouble if something went wrong down on Cosvetz. He would have a very difficult time hiding anything from—

"You will notice that all four lenses can be focused independently."

The image in one corner of the screen suddenly loomed larger, while the image diagonal to it shrank away.

"And each is equipped with infrared sensors which can track any individual on the planet we choose to tag. For now we will confine three of the lenses to general observation, and use the most refined model to track a particular individual."

Spinnertel held his breath as one image zoomed up and filled the screen. Slowly he let his breath out again when he failed to recognize the male standing like a giant on the screen.

"As you can see, the angle of observation was chosen to give the best possible perspective, but because of the increased distance necessary for that, the resolution of the picture is not all that we had hoped."

"What about sound?" someone asked.

"That is a different problem, one which we can only partially solve with the ground probes. If you will look closely . . ."

The picture shifted, blurred, and cleared. Suddenly a cluster of buildings in the center of open countryside filled the screen.

" . . . you will see we have planted probes here . . . and

here. That will give us a limited ability to listen to what is happening within a reasonable distance of those locations. Like the microlenses, the ground probes can home in on a particular voice once we have that voice's pattern. Unfortunately, they cannot screen out the ambient noise which surrounds that voice, nor can they totally block out..."

As Askavenhar continued her description of the monitoring devices, Spinnertel let himself be distracted by a nasty thought. If the female killed the Verporchting while the Constant was watching, and if they were not totally convinced that she had acted on her own volition, he could be in more trouble than he dared think about.

He immediately rejected that thought. Let the Constant worry about trouble. If the Verporchting died and they accused him, he would deny it. Then what would they do? Question the female? She had no connection to him. His smile revealed sharp teeth through the drooping grey hairs of his mustache.

"You find this amusing, young one."

"But of course, Askavenhar," he said quietly. "I consider it part of the Constant's duty to keep me amused. Don't you?"

"Your humor is out of place," Gatou-Drin said quietly.

"But accurate," Gracietta said with a laugh.

"I'm pleased you two have found something to agree upon," Askavenhar said with the faintest of smiles. "Now perhaps we can all agree on what procedures we are going to follow with the observation."

"We need to locate and tag the Verporchting first—uh, *supposed* Verporchting," Gracietta said with a slight nod to Spinnertel. "Then we can decide on procedures."

"Then that is your task, Gracietta. While she is doing that, perhaps the rest of you would care to join me in a meal?"

Spinnertel reluctantly followed the rest of the Constant out of the room. As he walked through the doorway he looked over his shoulder and saw a tentacled technician helping Gracietta with the controls for the monitors. Spinnertel wished her all the bad luck in the universe.

"Why do you keep looking out the window?" Chizen asked.

"Uh, I don't know." He wasn't sure of anything any more.

"Do not lie to me, Hap."

"I'm not lying. I'm just wondering..."

"Wondering what?"

144

"Just wondering! What's the matter? Is it against your rules now for me to wonder?" What had happened to her since they landed? Why was she being this way? Confusion reigned over his thoughts. No matter how he tried to sort them out, they just got worse. He loved her. But he hated what she was doing. And he hated the distance she had put between them.

She wanted to pull him into her arms, but his antagonism to her at the moment was all too open. "There is no need to talk to me like that."

"Why? Who told me I can't go out? Who made me take that terrible pill? Who said—"

"Enough! I will not be spoken to in that manner. Is that understood, young man?" He stood with his back to her staring out the window and did not answer. "I asked you a question."

His body twitched slightly, but he still refused to answer. Suddenly she could not stand herself any longer. She moved quickly from her chair to stand behind him. After only the slightest hesitation she wrapped her arms around his shoulders and pulled his back to her breast. The bulk of the pistol in her pocket formed a small, hard knot between them.

"I am sorry, Hap. I truly am. But it has to be this way. It will not last for long, but for now it has to be this way."

Hap stared out the window at the hills above the station, seeing nothing, wishing she would let go of him and turn her back so he could run. He didn't know where he would run, but he had to get away, away from everything. Somewhere there had to be a place where he could think.

A flash of movement between two distant buildings caught his eye. He leaned forward and squinted, suddenly acutely aware of his mother pressed against him.

"What is it? What is the matter, Hap?"

"Nothing, Mother," he said as he twisted out of her grasp.

Chizen caught his arm before he could get close to the door and dragged him back to the window. "What is it? Tell me what you're looking for." When he didn't answer they stared rigidly out the window together.

With a sigh of relief Hap let his body relax. CrRina's father had disappeared from view, at least for the moment.

But Brightseed had been right. He was coming this way. And Hap had to get his mother out of the house. He had to protect her, to keep her from . . . She had said she would kill . . . Tears sprang from his eyes. She had said she would kill him.

"Let me go!" he screamed as he tore himself away from her. "Let me go!" He knew if he ran, she would follow him.

"Hap!" Chizen tackled him as he scurried for the door. Fear gave her the strength to hold him as he tried to wrestle out from under her. "Hap," she panted, "stop this. Stop it right now. Stop it."

He grunted and twisted around, his face flushed with anger and confusion. "You're awful," he said through clenched teeth.

"I'm going to be worse if you don't stay still," she said as she pinned his arms to his sides. Suddenly he quit squirming and turned his head. A second later someone knocked at the door. Geljoespiy? No, he would have just come in. Carson?

"Who is it?" Chizen called.

"I've come to see a boy named Hap," a male voice answered.

Chizen released her grip on Hap and pulled herself to her feet. "Who are you?"

Hap scrambled free and opened the door. "Run," he shouted as he ran straight into Gerard. "Run!"

"Easy, easy," he said as he straightened Hap up and peered into the house. With a start he let Hap go and took half a step forward. There in the shadows stood Fairy Peg.

Hap yanked at his arm. "You've got to go! You've got to go! Hurry!"

Gerard shook his arm free and took another step into the house. His mind reeled with images. His legs threatened to collapse. "Is it . . . can it . . ."

"Yes," she said as she raised the pistol in front of her and steadied it with both hands. "Yes."

Woltol flashed past him. Gerard was deafened by an explosion as he crashed to the floor in pain.

"Then you won't do it?" Carson asked in disbelief.

"I can't, Carson. I have to think about—"

"About Liana," Carson finished for him. A sneer curled his lips. "Damn, man, she turned you soft in an awful hurry."

"Leave her out of this."

"Why? She's the one who turned you against me. Are you going to deny that?"

"Yes. She didn't have anything to do with it. You did."

"What do you mean?"

"You, Carson. You." Junathun tried to clear the bitter taste from his mouth and spat on the ground. "I got tired of you. I got tired of putting up with your crazy..." He paused and sought some reaction but his gaze was arrested by the all too familiar light which burned in Carson's eyes.

"The crazy what?" Hate and fear mixed in Carson's voice.

"You know damn well what. All the craziness, the drinking, the drugs, the scheming, the—"

"But that was years ago!"

"It was until the other night," Junathun said quietly. "That's when I knew I couldn't go through it again, couldn't cope with another round of... Look, Carson, I'm sorry I can't help you. I'm sorry I can't be there like I always was. But I can't. I just can't." He looked down at the dirt. There was nothing else to say.

"Liana put you up to this. I know she did. But that's all right," he said, raising his hand as Junathun started to reply. "That's all right. I'll get whoever I can, and I'll do what has to be done. And you and Liana be damned." He turned his back on Junathun and stalked toward the small utility skimmer.

"What about your gear?"

"I'll get it later," Carson said without turning back. Then as he climbed aboard the skimmer he added, "Or you can dump it out in the storage shed if my coming here bothers you."

"There's no call to..." Junathun's words were drowned out by the whine of the skimmer as Carson revved its engine and slewed out of the yard.

Junathun didn't watch him go. He couldn't bear to. But as he went back to his house, a huge wave of relief washed over the ache of grief in his chest. It was over. Done with. Carson's problems were now totally his own. If he had to—

The ringing of the radiophone broke his thoughts. "Hallo," he said quietly as he picked up the receiver.

"What happened?"

"It's over, Liana. I told him I couldn't help him."

"How did he take it?"

"Hard. But no harder than I did."

"What about Gerard and ShRil? Are you going to tell them?"

"Tell them what?"

"You know good and well what."

"Liana, I don't think it's my responsibility to—" The phone

went dead in his hands. His first impulse was to call Liana back. But then he knew they had not been cut off by accident. She had hung up.

"Damn! Damn! Damn!" he said as he forced the phone back into its holder. What did he owe those two? Nothing. But he would talk to them. He would tell them everything he knew about Carson's plans. Liana would make him.

A small, ironic smile crept over his lips. It wasn't over after all.

21

Chizen cowered in a corner, her pistol held shakily in front of her. The ridlow apparition growled menacingly above her, its four arms poised to strike. She pulled the trigger again. Her pistol boomed and kicked in her hands.

"Stop it!" a voice screamed through the ringing in her ears.

Nothing had happened. And now a second apparition stood beside the first. "Put down your weapon," it said, "or I'll let Woltol kill you."

Fear rattled her bones like reeds in the wind. Slowly and reluctantly she laid the pistol on the floor.

"Don't let her move."

Gerard's voice snapped something inside her. Suddenly through the apparitions she saw him climbing to his feet. Then she saw Hap huddled on the floor, crying.

Gerard's back ached from where the boy had hit him, and his right elbow was stiff with pain. "Come on, Hap," Gerard said as he pulled him to his feet. He sat Hap in a chair, then turned to face the figure in the corner. He knew now that it wasn't Fairy Peg. "Who the Krick are you?" he asked as he stepped closer to her.

"I am Chizen Dereaviny," she said in a shaky voice.

"Hap's mother?"

"Yes."

She looked so much like Fairy Peg that—

"You be Inez Nare-Devy," Woltol said quietly, "sister to Princess Peg, Chattel-shi of Kril."

Gerard clutched for the table as another wave of pain-laden images crashed through his mind and threatened to buckle his knees. Inez? Inez? The name rang like a dark bell.

"I am Chizen Dereaviny," she said defiantly. "Inez is dead." Her hand moved slightly toward the pistol and the ridlow growled again. She quickly pulled her hand back into her lap.

"This is Inez," he said, without taking his transparent eyes off her, "the exiled Chattel-shi."

Gerard steadied himself against the pain. "Why?" he asked. "Why did you try to kill me? Did your sister send you?" Each question he asked made him more lightheaded. Inez? Inez? Why couldn't he make the connection?

"We emigrated from Sun's March," Hap offered as he wiped his face on his sleeve. "But I . . ." He shifted his gaze from CrRina's father leaning heavily on the table across from him to his mother huddled in the corner. His tears wouldn't stop. Nothing made sense any more. A trembling filled his heart.

As Gerard forced himself to stand straight, he looked at Hap. His ears rang. His body ached. But he had to have some answers. "Do you know why she tried to kill me?"

"No, sir," he said through his tears. Guilt and love, confusion and loyalty pulled him apart inside.

"Then you'd better do some talking," Gerard said as he turned to face the woman. "Why did you try to kill me?"

"I was asked to."

"Then you're a hired assassin?"

"No, I'm—"

"The Chattel-shi," Woltol repeated.

Memories broke the static shock and crackled in Gerard's mind. Inez! The seduction!

"No! She died in exile on Sun's March, died because—"

"She lies."

Gerard was startled by Ronda's interruption. "Finish your sentence. Why did Inez die?" Even as he asked the question he knew that Woltol and Ronda were both right. It was Inez, the same Inez who had—

"Because there can be no Chattel-shi on Sun's March."

He had to get out of there, had to escape from the syndrome of pain and the crush of memories. Had Fairy Peg actually sent Inez to kill him? "Hap? You're coming with us. Are you ready?"

Hap hesitated. He didn't really want to leave his mother, he only wanted to protect her. But if he stayed, she and her new friends would just lock him up again. Maybe he should—

"Well, Hap? Are you coming with us or not?"

"Yes, sir," he said finally. "Let me get my things."

"No!" Chizen lunged for her pistol. As her hand touched its handle she choked on lungs full of noxious fumes. Spasms racked her body as she tried vainly to breathe.

"Don't! Don't!" Hap screamed, as he tried to pounce on the ghost smothering his mother and fell through it with a thud that knocked the last of the air out of her lungs.

Gerard grabbed the pistol from the floor. "Enough, Woltol," he commanded.

"Mother! Mother!" Hap tried to steady her until her gagging subsided.

"She'll be all right, Hap. Get your things."

Love, fear, and anger ripped through Hap's thoughts. He didn't know what to do, and for a moment held tightly to his mother while staring up at Gerard in total confusion.

"Stay," she gasped.

Come, come, Brightseed whispered imploringly in his mind.

Hap loosened his hold on her a little, then hesitated.

Come, Brightseed repeated. *Come*.

"Hap, you must stay," Chizen whispered hoarsely.

Slowly, ever so slowly he released her and got to his feet. "I can't, Mother," he said, looking down at her through a new wash of tears. "I can't." Then he ran quickly into their room to get his things.

Hurzzz.

"Woltol, you stay with her until we're back aboard Windy. Don't kill her. But don't let her do anything."

"Understood, Fize. Youse understand, Chattel-shi?"

Chizen curled tighter into the corner. Fear and anger

150

foamed on top of grief and doubt in the raging cauldron of her heart. Sobs of anguish racked her body. The muffled wailing of her soul blocked out the sound of Hap and Gerard leaving.

"There," Gracietta said quietly as she adjusted the focus of the microlens. On the screen two male humans and a shadowy figure moved slowly up a hill toward a spacecraft. "There is your Verporchting, Spinnertel."

"Supposed Verporchting," Spinnertel corrected.

"Which one?" Halido asked.

"The adult."

"What is that with them?"

"A spirit," Askavenhar answered, "what some species call a ghost. The soul and mind of a once corporeal creature."

For a moment the entire Constant stared at the screen in silence. Then Gatou-Drin asked, "Where is this danger you called us to see?"

"It all happened too quickly. As I was attempting to locate the Verporchting, the infrared sensors picked up a sudden burst of heat. The two were connected. Some kind of weapon, I think. But the spirits and the boy—"

"Spirits? I only see one."

"There are at least two. One was left behind guarding the female who used the weapon."

"Does it not seem odd," Askavenhar said slowly, "that just as you were about to locate the Verporchting, it was placed in mortal danger?" She directed her gaze at Spinnertel and all eyes in the room followed hers.

Spinnertel laughed and let the tension out of his body. "Forgive me, Askavenhar, but if you are suggesting I had any connection with this danger to that man, I cannot help but be amused. Assuming, just assuming that he were the Verporchting, would it not be extremely foolish of me even to allow something like that to happen? Right before the eyes of the Constant?"

"Foolish, or extremely sly," Gatou-Drin offered.

"Pardon?"

"Sly. Sly. Sly like the Tardepan."

A subliminal shudder ran through the Constant. The Tardepan had set a trap for the Constant a millennium before they sprang it, and their whole method of operation was based on actions which appeared suicidal from the outside. They had almost cost the Constant half its membership.

"That was undeserved," Spinnertel said evenly. This was no time to let his anger get out of hand.

"Perhaps Gatou-Drin only means that such an argument is highly suspect in this body. Besides, I never suggested that you had anything to do with the Verporchting's danger. I only asked whether anyone thought that the timing of it was rather odd."

"And perhaps all of this is unnecessary," Gracietta said with a smile. "There is no way for us to confirm the degree of danger he was in."

"Thank you," Spinnertel said, and immediately regretted it when she continued.

"But I find Spinnertel's protest most interesting."

"So do I," Gatou-Drin said.

"And I," several others responded simultaneously.

"Be that as it may," Askavenhar said quietly, "we appear to be prepared to set up the monitoring procedures."

"Only partially. The sound probe nearest the ship is not working properly."

Everyone turned to the screen just in time to see the two humans and the ghost enter the spacecraft. "Do we have another to replace it?" someone asked.

"Not yet. My technicians are working on one. But for the moment we will have to proceed without it. When are you planning to go to the surface, Gatou-Drin?"

"Whenever the Constant thinks it appropriate."

"Perhaps you should wait until—"

"Why should she go at all?"

"Because, Spinnertel, Cosvetz has developed from her idea. By the rules of the Constant."

"That makes it her right. I know that. But that doesn't answer my question. By the same rules, if that is my Verporchting down there, then I should have the same right."

"Are you admitting it is your Verporchting?"

"No, dammit. But I—"

"Then you do not have the right."

"Of course," Gracietta said softly, "if you wanted to acknowledge your creation now, you would save us much time and tedious observation."

Spinnertel bit down on his anger, aware that all eyes were

152

on him again. "No chance," he said with more vehemence than was necessary. "I want proof before I even begin to consider the vaguest possibility that you could be correct, Exile." His last word hung in the silence of the room.

The lack of willing volunteers angered Carson. After all he had done for many of these people, he could not understand why they were so reluctant to help him burn out the Wheezer's Bane. But there were others who would help. He knew they would. They had to. Especially those with children.

He cut the utility skimmer in a tight arc down the sandy bank and out to the center of the river. The water route was longer, but he knew from past experience that it was faster than maneuvering through the hills. As he advanced the throttle to take full advantage of the skimmer's power, the engine coughed suddenly, stuttered, and died.

"Damn!" Carson turned the skimmer hard for the near bank. It was too far away. The skimmer was already clipping the ripples on the river's surface. "Oh, damn!"

Kinous!

Double panic seized him. The skimmer nosed into the water and flipped over. Carson flew high in the air. A voice screamed in his head.

Kinous! Kinous!

The water stung his face as he plunged beneath it. Air burst from his lungs. Desperately he clawed through the water. He broke the surface with choking gasps. Ten meters away the tip of the skimmer's tailfin sank out of sight.

Carson gulped air as he rolled on his back and started a slow swim toward the closest shore. A faint hum accompanied his thoughts and he remembered a big colony of Wheezer's Bane he had seen on the next bend in the river. At least he was swimming away from it.

The small gratitude he felt for that did nothing to diminish the power of his anger. With every slow stroke in the water he asked himself why? Why had this happened? The skimmer had been running perfectly.

The middle of the river exploded in a geyser of water and bits of the skimmer. For a long second he paused with fascination. Then he started swimming as fast as his poor backstroke could carry him, cursing himself, and the skimmer, and the whole damned universe.

As the pieces started to rain out of the sky he took a deep breath and pushed himself underwater, hoping that would protect him. After holding his breath as long as he could, he pulled himself back to a surface littered with foam and glass fragments, all that remained of his transportation.

His arms and legs ached. His chest burned in the cold water. But anger kept his clumsy stroke steady as he toiled his way to the bank. After he stumbled out of the water he looked back at the river in disgust. Now he would have to try to borrow a new skimmer and then renew his supplies before he could do anything else.

Worst of all, time was running short. He had decided to burn as many of the smaller patches as he could before the pollinating started, using that experience to train his volunteers for the big burns to come. But except for Geljoespiy, and the woman, there were no volunteers.

With teeth clenched in determination he emptied the water from his boots, wrung out his jacket, then buttoned it against the chill breeze and started the long walk to the Nicholsonn place. If he was lucky, he might get there before dark.

22

"I'll get the guards," Geljoespiy said angrily.

"Do not be stupid. What will you tell them? That I tried to kill him? And then he took my son?"

The way she shamed him only made him angrier. "So what do you want to do?"

"I want you to get me a weapon," she said coldly, "and if it's not one I'm familiar with, I want you to teach me how to use it. Then I want you to get him out of that ship any way you can so that I have a clear shot at him. Just one clear shot. That's all I ask for."

"And if I can't get him out?"

"Find a way. Tell him anything. Tell him you had the guards lock me up. You will figure out something."

"Maybe we should wait until Carson—"

"Wait? Wait? Why? What is Carson going to offer us that we cannot do ourselves?" She paused, thinking of Hap, and hating Gerard for taking him from her. "And what is the matter with you, Geljoespiy? You were the one who worked so diligently to convince me. You and your mysterious friend. Now you act as though you are afraid." As she feared losing Hap. "Is that it? Are you afraid?"

"No. But Letrenn hoped—"

"This has nothing to do with Letrenn. It never did. It has to do with *me*! And Gerard Manley." She dropped her voice when she said his name as a heavy discomfort stirred under her heart. Gerard Manley. For her attraction to him she had risked and received exile. And a son, a son he had unknowingly given her and now had taken away—the son she would kill him for.

Her words didn't match the expression on her face. But Gel didn't know what to say. He hadn't expected her to try to kill the man right here, in his own house. And Letrenn's last message had said—

"Well? Do you have a weapon? Can you get me one?"

"I, uh, I have an old three-shot rifle that I used to hunt murples with, but—"

"Does it work?" And can I use it? she wondered.

"Of course it works! Look, Mis Chizen, I'm sorry about your boy, and—"

"By Houn's anger! My son's name is Hap!"

"Look, I'm sorry about Hap, but I'm more concerned, that is, I don't know if we can make it work the way you want it to. Carson was going—"

"Forget about Carson."

"Will you let me finish a sentence?" He slapped the table and rattled the plates.

Despite the situation and the conflicting emotions churning inside her, her years of formal etiquette came to the fore. "I apologize, Geljoespiy," she said sincerely. "I should never have let my emotions run over my manners."

"Accepted, Mis Chizen. I know you're upset. But so am I. What would have happened if you'd killed him here? How would we have . . . oh, never mind," he said with a nervous laugh. "None of that matters now. What does matter is that we do this thing right. Agreed?"

"Agreed," Chizen said quietly. She was no longer sure what was right and what was not. If she had Hap back, and Gerard disappeared, that would be enough.

"Good. Now, I don't think there is much we can do today, and I really would like to wait until Carson comes back. He wants our help burning out the Wheezer's Bane and he'll help us in return. If Gerard Manley dies in one of those fires—"

"Or before."

"Exactly. And his body gets burned up, nobody's going to worry too much about it. Except maybe his family." The thought of family gave Geljoespiy a momentary pang of guilt, but he quickly shook it off.

And his son, Chizen thought. Hap would do far more than worry about it. He'd already proven that. "There are still several hours of daylight left. Isn't there someplace we could practice with your rifle?"

"I suppose there is," he said with a sigh. "Do you want to go now?"

"As soon as possible." Maybe the rifle will . . . what? she wondered. What will it do? Get rid of this feeling that it is all slipping away? Bring Hap back? Make me feel—

"You'd better change into more durable clothes. I'll get the rifle and some ammunition," Geljoespiy said as he got up from the table. "I'd like to get home before Essy gets back." He glanced at the holes in the wall and gave her a quick smile.

"Of course. I shall hurry." Once inside her room Chizen quickly took off everything but her compsage. As she dug in her locker for her heavy jumpsuit, she shivered and suddenly felt naked and vulnerable. Questions and doubts plagued her. She could no more keep them from her mind than the thin material of the compsage could keep out the cool air. Another shiver, then another made her frantic to find her clothes.

ShRil sat down and sighed heavily. "They are both asleep."

"How did you manage that?"

156

"I tricked them. I told CrRina to tell Brightseed that they needed to rest."

"You did what? I don't believe it!"

"Do not look so panic-stricken, my love. We already know they both talk to the flowers. Since I can see no harm in that, I decided to take the easy way out."

"But what if—" Gerard cut himself short. "I guess I'm still pretty keyed up, aren't I?"

"That, my love, is the second biggest understatement of the day. Second only to, 'We had a little trouble.'"

"I know." Gerard took a deep breath and let it out slowly. "What do you think we ought to do now?"

"First tell me how the painkillers are working?"

"Not bad. Woltol was pleased enough with my progress to leave me alone for a while." He managed a half-smile.

"Do you think you can talk about it now?"

"I suppose. But then we need to talk about what we're going to do. All right?" After she nodded, he continued. "You already know the physical details. Hap's mother is Inez Nare-Devy. She is Fairy Peg's sister, and somewhere back in the pit of those years, uh, I think she seduced me."

ShRil looked at him sharply. "You think?"

"Oh, come on, ShRil. You know how it is with these damn memories. They always come in fragments. I remember a few scenes, barely moving pictures with her in them. And the one which keeps repeating itself is one where she is standing naked over my bed, laughing, with Fairy Peg screaming in the background. Not much to know in that, is there?"

He was rubbing one thumbnail with the other thumb and ShRil knew there was more. "What about the others?"

"Just fragments, pieces, nothing I can—"

"Please, Gerard. What about the others?" For a long moment he kept silent. When he finally looked up at her there were small tears in the corners of his eyes.

"I have a son," he whispered. "His name is Orees." The tears broke loose and raced down his cheeks.

ShRil quickly got up and stepped over to his chair. Then she knelt down in front of him and pulled his head to her shoulder. "When did you know?" she asked quietly.

He snuffled. "I'm not sure. Woltol's appearance set the name off in my mind. Then the whole thing with Inez turned on the images. While you were in with the children, I asked

Woltol. He doesn't understand why I can't remember, but he confirmed it. Said that I loved my son . . . that I played with him all the time . . . that we were always doing things—" A heavy sob broke his words.

For a moment ShRil was content to hold him close and rub his back. Then she pulled him to his feet and led him to the bed. His crying eased as she lay down beside him.

"You know the worst part?" he asked as he stared blurry-eyed at the overhead. "The worst part is that I really can't remember him. I asked Woltol to leave. Then I tried to remember. Fara, how I tried. All I could get were images of Fairy Peg, and sometimes Inez, and this small boy who wouldn't stay in focus."

ShRil had to put her head tight against his neck in order to hear him. She gave him a small kiss and whispered, "The memories will come. Others have."

"Maybe. Maybe. But to think that my son, *my son*, is running around somewhere in Ribble Galaxy and I can't even remember him. And I thought I knew how much the mindwipers had stolen from me."

There may be something else, ShRil wanted to say. But she knew this was not the right time. One son and one shock was enough for now.

She pulled away slightly and let her fingers glide lovingly down below his waist then back up to his face. Suddenly he put his hand over hers, twisted sideways, and pressed his lips against hers with a ferocity which had nothing to do with their ordinary passion. Their bodies sought each other's, pressing and crushing for a long, troubled moment until they pulled away only long enough to get their clothes off.

There was no gentle foreplay, no tender attempts to give pleasure. Both of them struggled for physical relief from the pressures on their minds. Yet somewhere in the middle of that struggle they found a mutual rhythm that mounted in fury until it swept them both into the ephemeral blindness of release.

Surprisingly, it was Gerard who fell immediately to sleep afterward and ShRil who lay awake for many hours wondering if, and how, and why, and finding no sure answers which would let her rest. Finally, just before pure fatigue dragged her down to sleep, she realized that Gerard had to be told of her suspicion. It would make a difference in anything they decided to do—especially if she was right.

Again Brightseed sacrificed plants in order to monitor CrRina and Hap. Mixed with its sadness at that loss were two reasons to rejoice. Our-Gatou was coming in time for the spreading of the blessing! With the fourth rising of the sun Brightseed and all of the other colonies would release their pollen in the presence of Our-Gatou.

Kinous Hap stirred in his sleep and Brightseed sent him a soothing, hypnotic message. That Hap was so deeply troubled confused Brightseed. It did not understand why Hap could not and would not accept life as it happened. *As the One changes, so it stays the same.* The murmuring thought ran through Brightseed without bringing consolation.

But in the last light of day Brightseed had realized what was wrong with Hap and all the kinous. They were not truly connected with each other. They could not think and share in the same ways Brightseed shared within itself and with the other colonies. They communicated, but their minds were filled with disconnected thoughts. It was no wonder then that they were so difficult to understand.

There was no word in Brightseed's vocabulary for the difference between itself and the kinous. All it knew was that the kinous were crippled by the lack of a true group. They had no colonies of their own in which they participated, and in which they shared their joys and their sorrows. Thus they were blind to the union of the One, deaf to the voices of truth, and perhaps not fully sentient at all.

As disturbing as that idea was, Brightseed knew it had to be considered. In the Accumulated Words there were no specific references to deformed life, only the directives to respect life itself. There was no denying that the kinous were a part of life, regardless of how limited their minds were.

Were that not enough reason, Brightseed had grown to love three kinous, Amsrita, Sirreena, and Hap, and to respect a fourth, Gerard-called-Dedo. They were not to be pitied for their failings, but cherished for all their valiant attempts to overcome them.

The seventh moon crept over the hill as Brightseed finally quieted its thoughts and left only two Guardians alert. That was a risk it had to take in order to have sufficient energy for the spreading. The kinous of death had been last heard moving away from Low-Riverside-Bend. The night eaters were in their usual retreat before the blessing time. And Our-Gatou was coming. Brightseed had to rest itself and its Guardians for all that was soon to happen.

23

A child's face dissolved. A woman's replaced it. Young voices mixed with old ones. Dull greys washed out bright orange splashes. "Dee it good, Daddy?" the child asked. Fairy Peg laughed. Inez laughed. Gerard laughed. Then he cried.

"No tickle," Orees giggled. "No tickle, Daddy . . . no tickle . . . no tickle . . . no tickle . . ."

Gerard woke up crying in the heat of ShRil's arms. "I dreamed about him," he said as the crying stopped.

"Good dreams?"

"Yes."

"I am glad."

"Me, too." They lay still for a long moment breathing almost in unison. "I love you," he said quietly. "You know that?"

"I know. I am not sure why you say it sometimes."

"Me neither. But I love you anyway."

Soon she rolled slightly away from him and her breathing took on the shallow rhythm of sleep. He absently stroked her thigh as he lay there trying to absorb the thoughts about his son. Why had those memories not come through the mindblocks? How had Self missed something so important? Then as he drifted again toward sleep he knew.

Fairy Peg. Orees looked so much like Fairy Peg that when

the image of Orees had come to him, Fairy Peg's kept replacing it. Yet, yet... that couldn't be the only reason. There was something else, something important he needed to know. "Find it, Self," he whispered. "Find it."

Thoughts tumbled lazily past grand abstractions. Voices echoed hollowly from cold, white walls. "Patients... from security... cases... the hardest... seeeee," a voice whispered. "Seeeee."

The world hung upside down. He was strapped to a table, and far away a dark pool shimmered behind a rising grey mist. As he tried to lean forward, fingers tugged him back. "Seeeee," the voice hissed at him again.

The mist parted. Distant flashes of pain reflected from its calm surface. Then he saw the face, Orees's face, and he knew where he was. But he didn't care. Not this time. Not now.

With slow deliberation he plucked off the hands which clung to him like tiny burrs and cast them aside. For a long moment he stood poised high above the pool. Then he pushed off lightly and soared in a long graceful dive, down, down, down toward the dark peace below. And as he plunged beneath the pool's surface, he knew he was safe. For there, in that sanctuary of his mind, the son was indeed father to the man.

Hap's thoughts twisted and turned and made strange leaps which kept him searching for a comfortable position. He felt abandoned. But he also felt guilty for leaving his mother, guilty in a way that ate at his young soul. There was only one answer for him. Regardless of what she had done, he would have to go back to her, and help her. It wasn't right to leave her with those people who didn't care anything about her.

He cleared his throat quietly and was suddenly aware of CrRina. He couldn't hear her thoughts, not like he had before, but a strange tingling in his mind told him she was awake.

"What's the matter, Hap?" CrRina whispered loudly across the narrow cabin.

"It's too confusing. You wouldn't understand."

"Tell me. Or I'll tell Brightseed."

"Brightseed already knows. Go back to sleep."

"I can't."

The sleepy slur of her words told him otherwise. "You have to. It must be the middle of the night. Go back to sleep."

"Don't you like me?"

"Yes, I like you, CrRina. I like you a lot. But I have to think. I have to—look, I'll tell you what. You go back to sleep now, and when I talk to Brightseed later, you can listen. Okay?"

"I can listen anyway. Tell me now."

She was right. She could listen when he talked to Brightseed, and he didn't know any way to stop her. But there was no way he could tell her what was bothering him. No way at all. "CrRina, I need help. Will you help me?"

"Yes," she murmured. "Yes, Hap."

"Good. You try to go back to sleep now, and then after we get up I'll tell you what's wrong. Please? That will help me an awful lot."

"You promise?"

"I promise."

"Goodnight, Hap."

"Goodnight, CrRina." He lay still until he was sure she was asleep again. Then he slipped out of his bunk and tried to find his clothes in the dark. He couldn't. The textured deck was warm, but the air was cool, and after a few futile minutes of fumbling around in the strange cabin he felt his way back into the bunk and curled up in the covers.

It was foolish to try to leave at night, he reasoned, but the first chance he got he would definitely tell Gerard that he couldn't stay. No. He couldn't tell him that. He would just have to leave without saying anything. Gerard might try to stop him and he couldn't risk that. He had to get back to his mother.

But what could he do for her? And what if she really didn't want him back? Or suppose she was gone?

Hap. Hap.

(I thought you were asleep.)

No. We listened for you. Do not let your troubles keep you from rest. Do not let the thunder stir in your night.

(You're trying to do it again.)

What do you mean?

(You're trying to put me to sleep again. I don't want to go to sleep, Brightseed. I want to go back to my mother.)

162

It is not wise to stand stiff before the wind. Bend with the breeze until the time comes—

(Will you stop that! I did something wrong and I want to fix it. Why is that so hard for you to understand?)

We understand, but do not agree that you committed a wrong.

(I deserted my mother. That's pretty bad.)

Have you deserted her in your heart?

Hap let that question sink in and gain meaning as he absorbed it. (No, but that doesn't change anything.)

You cannot desert what your heart clings to. You cannot abandon a part of your soul. The moons remind us that the sun is always with us. The clouds cannot erase the sky. Be still, Hap. Be still. The time will come to return to your mother.

(How do you know that? What makes you so sure of yourself?)

(Don't yell at Brightseed!)

"CrRina, I told you to go back to sleep."

(. . . back to sleep.)

(I don't) "don't" (have) "have" (to) "to" (do) "do" (what—)

"Hush. Just talk," he whispered fiercely. "But don't try to think-talk and talk out loud at the same time."

(I) "I" (can) "can" (if) "if" (I) "I" (want) "want" (to) "to" (Hap) "Hap."

"Please?" (Brightseed, will you ask her?)

One way is easier, kinous Sirreena.

There was no way to translate the rude image CrRina sent through Brightseed. She was only a baby, and Hap knew that he would have to get away from her if he was going to try—

(Not a baby!)

(All right! You're not a baby.) Now Hap was frightened. He hadn't broadcast that thought, hadn't directed it to Brightseed, yet CrRina had picked it up. A sudden panic hit him. If he couldn't have any thoughts of his own—

We are sorry, Hap. The fault is ours. We are not accustomed yet to multiple conversations.

(I'm sorry, too. Did you hear that, CrRina? I'm sorry.)

(Good. Hap is sorry. Hap is sorry. Good, good, good.)

Hap sighed with resignation. He was too tired to cope with everything else and CrRina, too. (Brightseed? Would you help us both go to sleep, please?)

(Hap is sorry. Go to sleep. Hap is sorry. Go to sleep.)

Thousands of petals dance in the wind, caught in the joy of the spreading of blessings. We are the offspring born of the seeds, swept by the breath from the Heart-of-One, tended by Guardians standing tall—

(*. . . sorry . . . go to sleep . . .*)

Proof of the blessing, proof of her love. From the hand of Our-Gatou the first seeds were spread, casting our lives . . .

The chant echoed fainter and fainter in Hap's mind, insulating him from all thoughts but one: Mother.

"Complete physical exams for both of you?"

"That's right, Davidem," Junathun said quietly. "We're going to sign the bond."

"Marry? But I thought— Oh, bite my tongue!"

"It's all right," Liana said softly. "You're not the only one who had thoughts like that. But it just so happens that you were all wrong."

"Been wrong before," Davidem said with a self-conscious chuckle, "and will be again. But why the physicals?"

"My idea. I want Liana to know what shape I'm in before we take the final step."

"You not feeling well?" Her tone was suddenly professional.

"I feel fine. I just want to be sure."

"This wouldn't have anything to do with Carson's scheme to burn out all the Wheezer's Bane, would it?"

Junathun was startled. "Uh, no. But how—"

"The idiot thought I would help him. Said you would, too."

"You mean he told you—"

"Too much," Davidem said, as she took a handful of forms out of her desk. "Way too much. I think he's lost touch again."

"So do we." Junathun looked at Liana and she gave him a slight nod. "I turned him down, too. But, well, I'd appreciate it if we could talk to you about that, uh, before we start the exam I mean."

"Something I should know? Something medical? If not, then I'm not sure I want to hear about it."

"You decide. I'll tell you what Carson told me, and you decide if it's medical or not. He seems to think the Wheezer's Bane is taking over the minds of the greenie children."

"He told me that."

164

"And? Do you think he's just crazy? I mean, you were the one who tried to treat Amsrita."

"Not really. I just tried to get her to go to Harmony Station. Her case was beyond my training." Davidem leaned back and ran her fingers through her blond-and-silver hair. "I examined one of the immigrant children who had, well, let's just say he was an unusual case. That was before Carson came raging in here with his wildness hanging out."

"His name wasn't Hap, was it?"

Davidem looked at him steadily. "Does it matter?"

"I think so. Hap is one of the children Carson was talking about. Said the Wheezer's Bane was going to enslave them."

"Who are the others?"

Junathun hesitated. "Just one other that he said he knew for sure was talking to the Wheezer's Bane, a little girl, daughter of those researchers, the Manleys."

"Did he say why he was so sure?"

"He's talked to both of them. Said he could tell."

Davidem sighed. "All right. I don't know the Manleys, but I'll talk to the boy's mother—or better yet, I'll talk to the boy and see if he'll tell me anything. That doesn't mean I'm putting any stock in Carson's story, mind you, but it won't do any harm to check up on one of my patients."

"We'll talk to the Manleys," Liana said firmly. "That's what we were planning to do after we leave here."

"I thought you wanted complete physicals? That will take most of the day. You've got to remember that this is pretty much a one-woman operation I run, and what with the other patients I have to see, I can't promise you when you'll get out of here."

"But it's still early."

"I'm sorry, Liana. I'll do my best, but there's no way—"

"Then we'll go tomorrow if we have to," Junathun said. "This comes first. Right, Liana?"

"That was our agreement, but perhaps...no. You are right. We'll talk to them tomorrow."

Junathun gave her a broad smile as he remembered the conversation which followed their lovemaking the night before. Then he turned to Davidem. "Well? What do we do first?"

24

"Why not start with that one?" Chizen asked.

"Right under their noses? We'd never stand a chance. No," Carson said, looking directly at her, "what we have to do is draw them out, far enough away from the ship and help so that we can get them on terrain we select. Then you can get your shot."

"And if they don't come out?" Geljoespiy asked. "What then? I mean, suppose they—"

"They'll come out. They'll have to in order to protect—"

"What about Hap? How will we get him back?" The fire of revenge which had raged so fiercely in her had been almost smothered by her need for Hap. She wanted him safely back by her side more than she cared about burning the flowers or trying to kill Gerard.

"Don't worry. We'll get him back. We'll tell them you've been injured and are asking for him. He'll come."

Chizen was not so sure. She wanted to believe he would, but the anger he had shown made her question. "And if he does not?"

"I said we'd get him back."

"Saying and doing are two different things. What about your mysterious friend, Letrenn?" she asked, turning to Geljoespiy. "Will he be willing to help?"

"Who?" Carson looked hard at Geljoespiy.

Gel cringed inside. He hadn't told Carson about Letrenn and hadn't planned to. But of course she couldn't know that. "I, uh, well, you might as well know, Carson. I have a friend, a very powerful friend, who wants to see Manley dead . . . and I, uh . . . that is—"

"You mean . . ." Carson shook his head. "You mean you have someone who could help us and you didn't tell me? What the Krick's the matter with you?"

"It's not that simple," Gel said after a long pause. "He's not what you'd call an ordinary person. In fact, he's not really a person at all. More like—"

"Dammit, Gel! Spit it out!"

"All right! You don't have to shout at me. But you do have to swear on your life not to tell anyone." They both looked at him questioningly. "Either swear it, or forget it. I can't offer you any other choice. I'm not even supposed to tell you—"

"I'm not swearing anything."

"Neither am I."

"Good," Gel sighed, "then I don't have to break my promise."

"But you can still answer my question," Chizen said evenly.

"Yes, Mis Chizen, I can. As far as I know Letrenn will be more than willing to assist you in any way he can once Manley is dead. Until then, I—"

"I need more than that. I want a commitment."

"And I want to know who the Krick he is!"

"Look, I've already told you—"

"No. You have not told us. You have hinted, Geljoespiy, and suggested shadowy promises, but you have told us nothing." Chizen stared at him. "If you can do no better than that, I refuse to be a party to this any longer."

"Now wait a minute."

"No, Carson. You wait a minute. I have had enough of both of you." Her imperial tones temporarily suppressed their responses. "You want me to trudge around the bush and help you burn out the flowers. Geljoespiy wants me to help you, and in the process sees a way for me to kill Gerard Manley. But neither of you is willing to promise, *promise*, that if I do those things that you will insure that I get my son back. Why should I help either of you when I am now certain I can do better on my own?"

"Mis Chizen, I, uh—"

"Oh, shut up, Gel. Look, lady, I said I'd do everything I could to help you. If that's not enough, then try it on your own. See if I care. He's not my son."

"I'll call Letrenn."

"You do that, Geljoespiy. You do that right now. But if you can't exact a promise from him—"

"And get him to help us—"

"Then I will continue on my own. Is that understood?"

Gel looked down and rubbed his forehead wearily. "I understand both of you. But it's not going to be easy. And he's not going to like it at all."

"How long will it take?" Carson asked suddenly.

"I don't know. I'll send the message in real time, but there's no guarantee when I'll get a response."

"I want to start tomorrow. The Wheezer's Bane can't be more than three or four days from pollinating."

"What difference does that make?"

"It makes all the difference in the world, lady. Once the pollen fills the air, nothing goes on around here. And if you're caught out in it, you're dead."

"Do you not have filtermasks and protection of some kind?"

Carson laughed grimly. "Oh, we do, but the pollen will clog any filter we know about. And without filters you start wheezing, then singing and laughing like crazy, then you die. The only thing that offers real protection is a spacesuit."

"So get us some suits."

He laughed again. "Just like that? Run down to the supply center and pick up three spacesuits? You may have the credits for that, but Gel and I sure don't. It would take five years to earn enough credits around here to buy a spacesuit—if you could find one. No, lady. When the pollen starts, you just retreat, seal the windows and doors, turn on the internal air supply, and wait it out."

"Wait how long?"

"Four, five days. It settles out pretty quickly."

"Then you had better call Letrenn immediately, Geljoespiy." The thought of waiting eight or nine days before she saw Hap again was more than Chizen could bear.

Rolling-Field-with-Thorns announced Our-Gatou's arrival to the other colonies with a message garbled by joy.

Brightseed's welcoming response joined the first chorus of welcome as the news spread slowly across the surface of Cosvetz.

CrRina, Hap, and even Gerard felt the overwhelming sense of happiness which filled the air.

The feedback from their thoughts caused Brightseed a moment of hesitation, then it diverted part of its energy to protect its kinous against the growing hymns of ecstasy. Soon it found the burden unbearable. Too many anthems of praise and glory came too quickly from too many sides. CrRina became frightened. Gerard was in pain. And Hap was on the verge of panic.

As quickly as it could Brightseed soothed all three and lulled them all into hypnotic sleep much to the surprise and consternation of ShRil and the ghosts. But then Brightseed received a curious thought.

(Peace. Your love is understood. I will explain to the others.)

Who are you? Brightseed asked in bewilderment.

(You may call me Bertilina.)

Our thanks, Bertilina. The One reigns.

Whatever responding thoughts the unknown Bertilina might have sent were drowned out by a rising cacophony of voices echoed and relayed by thousands upon thousands of colonies and focused on Rolling-Field-with-Thorns.

Carson screamed in terror. Convulsions wracked his body. Then he screamed again, and again, and again as unseen forces pressed his mind into a black void of silence.

Had he hung onto consciousness a moment longer, he would have heard the stilling thoughts of Our-Gatou.

(Life), she whispered, (life is joy.)

The colonies responded. *Life is joy.*

(Link, and listen.)

Like a great web, strands of thought spread from colony to colony, spanning mountains and lakes, connecting islands with continents, until the farthest colony acknowledged its contact with Rolling-Field. Then when Our-Gatou spoke, her words were transmitted almost instantaneously through the links to every colony on Cosvetz.

(The One, be with you.)

And with you, the colonies responded.

(Soon the blessings of the One will spread once more.)

May our seeds be blessed.

(I will walk among you when the blessings come.)

As the breeze walks the night.

(Listen then to the Accumulated Words.)

ShRil sat with a furrowed brow at the galley table. She had carried CrRina, then Hap, to their bunks, and with the help of the ghosts, had dragged Gerard to bed. Bertilina had assured her they were all right, but she wanted more than that.

So did Shttz. "Tell us precisely what happened."

Bertilina curled into a tighter ball in the middle of the table. "The flowers are participating in a great religious celebration. Their spiritual leader has come to help them celebrate the spreading of pollen."

"Please, Bertilina, be specific."

"I do not understand. What kind of spiritual leader? And where did it come from?" ShRil could not imagine what had happened.

Bertilina purred softly and her luminescence increased. "I am telling what I know—and *feel*," she said softly. "There is no clear image of this one they call Our-Gatou. But she is revered and loved by the flowers."

"But what happened to the children and Gerard?"

"Brightseed protected them. The thoughts of joy when Our-Gatou arrived were so strong that the three of them were overcome. Brightseed feared for their safety and put them to sleep to protect their minds."

"It can do that?"

"The dangerous group mind," Shttz muttered. "I warned Gerard about that."

"But . . . but why was I not affected?" ShRil asked.

"You are not sensitive to their thoughts."

"Then neither are we," Ronda said, indicating herself and Woltol. "But that makes no sense."

"Why do you seek after sense? Why can you not stand in the midst of doubt and uncertainty without questions?" Bertilina's purring stopped and her luminescence dimmed slightly. "Why must there always be this unreasonable search for answers?"

ShRil shook her head. "That is part of life."

"So is the doubt and uncertainty. So are the flowers."

"Dangerous," Shttz muttered again.

"No," Bertilina said quietly, "not dangerous. Only a different form of life."

"But if it hurts my Fize—"

"It protected him from itself, Woltol. Is that dangerous?"

"If it can control their minds, it can destroy them." Shttz's form glowed with such intensity that it gave a blue cast to everything in the galley. "That is the danger. The group mind can control and destroy individual minds."

The galley was silent for a moment. ShRil did not know what to think or who to believe. If Brightseed had protected Gerard and the children, then . . . then what? "How long will this last, Bertilina?"

"I do not know. They are performing some kind of ritual, full of words which have no meaning to me. But their intent has nothing to do with control. They are celebrating life, and love, and the wonder of reproduction."

"A ritual of death if we don't get Gerard and CrRina out of here."

"And the boy?" Ronda asked suddenly. "What would you have us do with the boy?"

Shttz flickered. "Take him with us. Or send him home."

"No," Woltol growled. "His mother deserves no son."

"Woltol. Ronda. All of you," ShRil said quietly. "I think we have forgotten something very important. We *came here* to investigate the flowers, to try to find out whether they are actually sentient beings. We know that answer now, and maybe Shttz is right. Maybe it is time to leave."

"And the boy?" Ronda asked again.

"I do not know what to suggest about Hap. And despite what I just said, I am not sure we should leave. In his directive to us Alvin wrote a very striking passage to the effect that if we met a sentient race that was blind to our gestures and deaf to our words, we should not abandon attempts to communicate with them. For if we failed to make contact, to understand who they were and what their lives were like, we would have failed every sentient race."

"What if this deaf and blind race destroys you? What will be the gain?"

"They are not destroyers," Bertilina said quietly. "You, Shttz, of all of us, should be more open. Was not your race partially destroyed by another which made no attempt to understand you? Is that not how you died?"

"Yes. And that is why I worry. Suppose these, these group minds choose only to control and destroy? What then?"

"I told you—"

"I heard what you said. But you admitted that there was much of what they said that you did not understand."

"That does not keep me from knowing their intent."

"I trust Bertilina's judgment," Ronda said.

ShRil looked at Woltol. "And you?"

"For now I will trust it also. But I will guard my Fize more closely."

With a hiss and a pop Shttz disappeared, leaving behind an acrid smell.

ShRil's sudden brief laugh broke the tension. "I think we ganged up on him. But I hope he does not leave," she added more soberly. "I still value his judgment."

"He will return," Bertilina said. "He loves you too much to stay away and let me overly influence your decisions."

"I hope you are right," ShRil said with a sigh. "And I wish I knew what to do next."

25

A single column of smoke climbed the early morning sky and bent with the wind to form a dark, low-hanging cloud in the south.

Messages of concern, then alarm, spread from colony to colony when the second and third columns joined the first a short time later. Other deaths by fire had been reported in the past, occasionally several in the same day. But never three with such brief intervals between them.

Brightseed received the grim news while still basking in the joy of Our-Gatou's visit the day before. It quickly evaluated the reports as they came in, but could draw no conclusions, could find no quick pattern to explain what was happening.

Low-Riverside-Bend sensed the kinous of death approaching from the direction of the last fire and alerted Brightseed. Then it reported in cold terror that Creekbank-by-Rockspring, its offspring of two seasons before, was encircled by fire.

There was no cry from Creekbank-by-Rockspring. There was no moaning thought echoing under the black smoke. But in the stillness of listening, every colony within range heard the rapidly fading chant of the Accumulated Words. It was the death-chant of the Guardians.

Now as we surrender life, we surrender to the One. One reality alone marks the chosen way. Death can have no meaning when life is passed to greater life. One reality alone . . . the chosen . . . to the One . . .

A great sadness weighed on Chizen as she watched the fourth patch burn slowly down to black ash. It was impossible to convince herself that these flowers were the threat to Hap that Carson insisted they were. It was impossible to understand how so much beauty could enrage him so.

The sound of Carson and Geljoespiy cursing the obstinate engine of the borrowed skimmer behind her gave her no more than grim satisfaction. She had seen enough for one day—enough destruction of beauty, enough madness in Carson's eyes, and enough coldness in Geljoespiy's.

The work on the first patch had been almost interesting to watch as Carson circled the colony in the battered skimmer while Geljoespiy directed the nozzle which filled the air above the patch with a fine mist. She had stood on a slight rise, watching the mist, ready to give them a signal if the wind shifted. But the breeze had stayed light and steady.

Then they had pulled away from the patch until they were well downwind, and with a suddenness which startled her, fired two flares into the heart of the mist.

Chizen had braced herself for an explosion which never came. Instead, the air above the patch slowly turned into a fireball which settled silently on the ground. After a few seconds of staring in awful fascination, she realized that her helmet was blocking out the sound.

Carson had told her not to touch the damper until he

173

signalled it was safe, but she had followed her impulse to switch it off before she even thought about it. Seconds later she switched it back on again, but not before she had felt the pain in her head and heard the hissing and popping of death.

That sound stayed in her head through the burning of the second and third patch, almost as though the helmet had trapped it there. She told Carson she wanted to quit, that she had had enough, but he only laughed at her. And Geljoespiy had reminded her of Letrenn's promise to help if she fulfilled her part of the agreement.

Chizen wished she could laugh at both of them now. She wished she could laugh and walk away. But it was too late. In her heart she knew there was no turning back.

An odd nostalgia mingled with her sadness. Once, fifteen years before, she had known only too well that feeling of being unable to turn back as she had stood naked in the glaring light of Gerard's room, laughing as her sister screamed.

Then she had been impelled to the point of no return by her jealousy of Peg, by her wish that Orees was *her* son, and by her lust for Gerard. She had not reckoned the possible cost then.

Now she was driven by her desire to regain her son, by the necessity of killing Gerard to regain her rightful place in Ribble Galaxy, and by forces too dark and confusing yet to be sorted out. But now she knew what the costs could be.

For want of his first son she had seduced Gerard. For want of his second she had said she would kill him. Yet she knew that cost would be the greatest of all. If she killed Gerard, she would kill part of herself—and part of Hap, too.

Even as Gerard had stood before the muzzle of her pistol, she had known she did not want to kill him. But the rush of the ghost had startled her into pulling the trigger and, after that, after that she had been caught up in a current which would not release her.

Carson and Geljoespiy would fix the engine. They would return to the settlement station, replenish their supplies, and get ready for another round of burning this afternoon. And she would go with them. The trap would be set. Then today, or tomorrow, or the next day Gerard would walk into the sights of Geljoespiy's old rifle at a cost which knew no measure.

*　*　*

Gatou-Drin raged in front of the Constant. "There is no sense to this! It is madness! Pure madness!" She paused and looked across the room at Spinnertel. "Unless... unless, *my dear Spinnertel,* unless some agent among the humans is creating a diversion from our investigation of the Verporchting."

Spinnertel knew better than to respond to her provocation. There was no way she, or anyone else in the Constant, could know about Geljoespiy and the woman. Let Drin rave if she wished. Let her point an accusing finger. Without proof she—

"Perhaps we should address that question," Askavenhar said. "Would you care to make a comment, Spinnertel?"

"There is nothing to be said. According to Gatou-Drin and our own observations, the local humans have always burned out colonies when it suited their needs. I see no reason—"

"But not like this! Never like this. Never a wholesale destruction of multiple colonies at one time! I refuse to believe that—"

"Please," Askavenhar said quietly. "We understand your sense of outrage. However, you yourself have told this Constant about the burnings. What evidence do we have that would indicate these occurrences are any differently motivated?"

"None," Gatou-Drin said after a long pause. "None at all. But that doesn't mean the evidence isn't there. All that means is that we haven't seen it... yet."

"Then perhaps your time would be better spent on the surface gathering evidence than here complaining to the Constant."

"I object," Spinnertel said just loudly enough for everyone to hear him and turn in his direction. "We do have evidence that Gatou-Drin's first visit to the surface caused problems for the individual—"

"The Verporchting, Spinnertel," Gracietta interjected. "You can say it. We will not hold you to it."

"Very well then. We already have evidence that the *supposed* Verporchting was adversely affected by Gatou-Drin's visit. How is the Constant supposed to conduct an unbiased

175

investigation if her mere presence alters this individual's reactions?"

"A point well made. Do you have a response, Gatou-Drin?"

"Yes. I will go in secret."

"Incognito?" Spinnertel laughed. "You don't think your flowers will recognize you?"

"I will avoid the colonies."

"Then how will you get your evidence?"

"As best I can by listening and observing."

"I dare say you won't blend in very well with the humans," Spinnertel said as he slowly appraised her quadripedal form. "I can conceive of no disguise which would—"

"Your point is made again, Spinnertel."

"But, Askavenhar, I never said I would try to mix with the humans. I have resources of my own which will help me gather the evidence you require."

"If there is any."

"Yes, if there is any. But I'm convinced there is."

Askavenhar sighed wearily. The facets of her eyes burned with a dull light. "Then it seems the question before us is whether or not you should be allowed to return to the surface."

"And what she should and should not be allowed to do there," Gracietta added.

"Indeed," Halido said.

Spinnertel was grateful for the temporary allies and relieved that he did not have to suggest the limitations himself. Now if the Constant would only choose the right limitations, he would not have to worry too much about Gatou-Drin.

"That seems fair enough. Are there any other suggestions?" Askavenhar looked around the room and saw none. "Very well. I propose that Gatou-Drin be allowed to return to the surface providing she agrees to do everything within her power to keep from making her presence known."

"Not enough," Gracietta said. Everyone turned to her in surprise. "I am sorry, Gatou-Drin, but I do not believe that is sufficient stricture."

"You want more than my promise?" Gatou-Drin asked in disbelief.

"No. I want an addition to it. I want you to swear that regardless of what you see or hear, regardless of what evidence you gather, that you will in no way interfere with any activities on the surface of Cosvetz."

Gatou-Drin sat back on her haunches. "That means..."

"Yes. That means that if you see the humans burning colonies you must let them do so unhindered in any way."

"Do you want my blood as a guarantee?"

"Unnecessary, Gatou-Drin. What Gracietta suggests is merely a logical extension of my proposal." Askavenhar looked around. "Will the Constant approve those terms?" There was no dissent. "Then so be it. You may leave at the time of your choosing."

The small galley was crowded with four adults, two children, and three ghosts. Junathun looked uncomfortably across at Gerard and ShRil before he started talking. "It's about Carson," he said finally.

"What about him?" ShRil asked.

Gerard was content for the moment to let her do the talking. His head ached from what had happened yesterday and the darkness which had filled his thoughts this morning. CrRina and Hap had also suffered from the experience, and both of them looked pale and drawn.

"Did you see the smoke in the south?"

"We saw it."

"That was Carson. He's set out to burn all the Wheezer's Bane he can before the pollen spreads."

"But why?" ShRil adjusted CrRina in her lap as she leaned forward. "What does he think he is doing?"

"Protecting the children... your children. He has this crazy idea that the Wheezer's Bane is controlling them and..."

Hap shut the man's voice out. He had to think of a way to get off the ship and away from here. He had to find his mother. And now, he had to—

"Hap? Did you hear what Junathun said?"

"Uh, no, sir," he said, barely shifting his eyes up to Gerard's and then down again.

"He said your mother is helping to burn the flower colonies."

"That's a lie," Hap said fiercely. "She wouldn't do something like that! I know it!" He stood up and clenched his fists, ready to strike out if anyone reached for him.

"Easy, Hap. Easy."

"I don't want to listen to this." Hap suddenly saw a way to escape. "Can I go to my cabin?"

Gerard looked uncertainly at ShRil. "Yes," she said, "and why not take CrRina with you?"

"No, Mummum. I want to stay with you."

"All right. You can stay." ShRil wondered what Hap would do sitting in the cabin by himself. "Is there anything I can get for you? There is a microspooler we can hook up in there."

"No, mis. I just want to lie down." Hap made his way self-consciously around the crowded galley and out the door. Suddenly he realized he would have to come past the galley to get from his cabin to the open hatch. "Uh, can I sit up in the pilot's chair instead?"

Gerard looked at him curiously. There was something wrong with Hap's reaction, but he would have to worry about it later. "Sure, Hap," he said with as open a smile as he could muster. "You can go anywhere on Windy you want to—that isn't locked up, I mean."

"Thank you, sir." Hap turned down the companionway and heard Gerard say, "I'm sorry . . ." As quickly as he could he headed for the hatch, determined to get as far away as he could before they missed him. But where would he start looking? If that man had been telling the truth, he should go south, toward the smoke. But if he had been lying, then Hap needed to go to Geljoespiy's house.

When his feet hit the ground, he didn't know which way to turn. As he looked around he saw a new column of smoke rising across the river far to the south. Carson. Hap turned north toward the settlement station.

An hour later Junathun and Liana had told Gerard and ShRil everything they knew, and had been surprised by what they had been told. "I still think you're taking a big chance," Junathun said, as he and Liana stood with them at the base of the hatch ramp. "But they're your children."

"Just one of them," Gerard said with a half-smile. "Listen, I don't know how we can thank you for your concern."

"No need." He shook their hands. "But you call us if you need anything."

"Yes," Liana added. "We'd be glad to do whatever we can."

"Thank you. Thank you both."

Gerard stood with one arm around ShRil's waist and CrRina half asleep in the other arm as they watched Junathun's skimmer skirt the top of the hill and then disappear through the trees. "Nice people," he said finally. "Now, what say we talk to Hap?"

ShRil took CrRina, who immediately nestled her head into ShRil's shoulder and closed her eyes. "There is something I need to talk to you about first—something very important. But before that, let me put CrRina down for a nap. You make sure Hap is doing all right."

Five minutes later they met in the companionway. "Hap asleep?" Gerard asked.

"No. He is not in the cabin. I thought he was up top?"

"I couldn't find him. You don't suppose . . ." Gerard looked back over his shoulder toward the lock which led to the hatch. "That was the way he was headed," he said urgently. He turned but ShRil caught his arm.

"Let him go for now."

"Why?"

"Because he is almost a man, Gerard, and everything that has happened has torn him up inside. You can see it on his face."

As he faced her Gerard saw something else in her eyes. "There's more. What is it?"

"Come back to the cabin. I have the monitor on there in case CrRina wakes up."

"All right, what is it?" he asked as he sat facing her in their cabin.

"I am not sure where to begin, Gerard, but the first time I saw Hap he looked familiar. Then I understood why. He looked like an adolescent version of you. I laughed at the coincidence and let it go. Then—"

"Don't say it." Gerard's head spun with possibilities. He had wondered who Hap's father might have been ever since the boy had said he didn't have one. But what ShRil was suggesting—

"I have to say it, my love. He is the right age. He looks like you. Like CrRina, he has the ability to communicate with the flowers. Add to that his mother's seduction—"

"No! No! I don't want to hear it." It couldn't be. It couldn't be. It absolutely couldn't be. The odds against it were far too great.

"Gerard," ShRil said softly, "all I am saying is that you have to consider it as a possibility. Hap could very well be your son."

"No, dammit. It's not fair. And the probabilities are terrible. One night doesn't make a son!"

"It can. And are you sure it was just one night?"

That element of doubt was the last thing Gerard needed. No, he wasn't sure. He had tried and tried to remember, but like all the other fragments, the one with Inez came with blanks on either side of it—blanks and other erotic images which refused to take a form he could recognize.

Two sons in Ribble Galaxy? And now maybe two sons lost? He had no tears for that thought, only a dry, hollow determination to find Hap and Inez and get to the truth one way or another.

26

"Explain this message, young one," Askavenhar said in a voice which trembled with anger and fatigue.

"There is nothing to explain. It is merely a progress report from one of my agents who—"

"Nothing to explain!" Gracietta stood beside Askavenhar and stared at him. "We receive a message telling you that all is going according to plan, and you say there is *nothing* to explain?"

"As I said, it is a progress report, a routine progress report from one of my agents. What is there—"

"One of your agents on Cosvetz," Askavenhar said shakily.

Spinnertel looked around the room and felt a growing sense of what a lesser being might have called panic. "Not exactly," he said slowly. "The message was only relayed via Cosvetz."

"You expect us to believe that, young one?"

Before Spinnertel could answer, Askavenhar gasped and sat

heavily in her cradlelike chair. All eyes turned to her. Gracietta and Halido stepped to her side. One by one the rest of the members of the Constant stood and approached her.

"Answer me, young one," Askavenhar said with a feeble wave. "Answer me now. Tell me the truth before I—"

A hoarse sound issued from her throat and cut off her words. Her middle sets of arms wrapped tightly around her cephalothorax directly below her mouth. With harsh waves of her forearms she pushed Gracietta and Halido away from her.

"Answer me," she croaked.

Spinnertel leaned toward her. Don't die now, he thought. Don't leave me facing Gracietta, you old spider. "Please, Askavenhar, you are sick."

The dull facets of her eyes glowed with a peculiar light. "Dying . . . dying . . . Tell me." Her arms twitched for a moment then stopped. The light faded from her eyes.

Gracietta bent over her and slipped her hand under Askavenhar's pedicel. "She is dead," Gracietta said softly.

Stillness held the room in a silent grip. Even the sounds of breathing were muffled as each of the remaining twenty-two immortals contemplated the inevitability of death. Then Gracietta stood straight and stared at Spinnertel. "The least you can do in respect for her is to answer her question."

Spinnertel only had eyes for Askavenhar. This was no apparition to frighten him, no superior being who might challenge him. This was the cold face of death staring at him from lifeless eyes. Askavenhar had been there from his beginning. She was immortal, the living proof of the longevity he had to look forward to. Now her corpse was the proof of the end.

"Answer her," Gatou-Drin said.

"Answer her. Answer her," came a chorus of voices.

With a growl of defiance Spinnertel leapt for the door, knocking down several members who blocked his path. "Never!" he screamed. "Never!" As he burst through the door and raced for his ship his heart denounced the immortals, the Constant, and all they stood for. If he had to die one day, his death would be better than that one.

Gracietta looked long and hard at the empty door. Then she let her gaze travel around the room until she had made eye contact with every member of the Constant. "We have lost two of our own," she said quietly. "One we shall mourn. The other, the other we should—"

"Exile!" someone shouted.

"No," Gracietta said quietly, "not until he has had a chance to defend his actions. But we must watch him from this moment on. Is there agreement on that?"

There was.

"Shall I follow him?" Gatou-Drin asked.

"Would you miss Askavenhar's dispersal?"

"If it is necessary."

"Then follow him, Drin. But be careful. He is in a rage beyond understanding. If he flees this system, come back to us. We can always find him again later."

"And if he goes down to Cosvetz?"

"Then you must be doubly careful, and we must watch the Verporchting as well."

"I have to look for him. Don't you understand that?"

"Yes. But I must help you, which means someone must take care of CrRina."

"What about Essenne? No, not if Geljoespiy is with Carson like Junathun said. Bertilina? Would you do it? We could send for Liana, and she could be here in a couple of hours?"

"I will do what I can. But Shttz would do better."

"I know that. She's used to him. But he isn't here and we don't know where he is. ShRil, you explain to CrRina and I'll try to call Liana."

"Ronda could find her faster," Woltol offered.

"True. I have felt her essence."

Before Gerard could respond, Ronda disappeared. "Well, I guess that took care of that. Look, ShRil, why don't I go down to the station and—"

"That I can do," Woltol said. "If the boy is there, I can come and tell youse."

"Should you not go with him and see if you can borrow a skimmer? Or a flyer? We would have a much greater advantage that way."

"Good idea, although I don't remember any flyers down there. But we'll ask. Let's go, Woltol." He gave ShRil a quick kiss and left *Windhover* at a run with Woltol by his side, another long shadow beside his own.

There were only a couple of hours of daylight left, and

Gerard wasn't about to bet any credits that they would find Hap before the sun went down. After dark their chances were no good at all. He almost broke stride when that thought hit him, but instead he ran even faster. He had to know. He had to find out if Hap was his son. And if he was?

Gerard concentrated on the terrain and tried to block the stabbing pain in his side. The answer to his final question would have to wait until he knew the truth.

Brightseed was glad that kinous Gerard was moving away from Hap. Despite the continuing burden of deaths and the agonies they brought, Brightseed had followed Hap, and listened to his thoughts. There was no room in them for kinous Gerard. But there was no room in them for Brightseed, either. Hap was pursuing his mother, driven by needs which Brightseed only vaguely understood, but which it firmly respected.

Hap?

(Don't bother me now.)

Kinous Gerard is looking for you.

(That doesn't surprise me. Let him look.)

He is moving toward what Amsrita called the station.

(Good. Now leave me alone. I've got to find her. And since you can't help me, I've got to find her by myself.)

The kinous of death is across the river.

(I know. I can see the smoke.)

If your Guardian is with her—

(My mother, Brightseed. If she's there, I'll find her.)

We will listen.

(Just don't talk. It's hard enough finding a path around here without you talking in my head.)

All paths lead to the One.

Hap refused to respond again. He had reached the top of a hill from where he could see a bend in the river. He could also see a new column of black smoke several kilometers beyond the river itself. With no idea of how he would cross the river when he got to it, but with a faith in himself which he didn't question, he picked a path among the rocks and scrub trees and headed down the hill.

The brush was thicker than it looked, and as he worked his way through it, he felt sorry that CrRina's father was looking for him. Maybe he should have told them what he was going to do. They had certainly been kind enough to him. Plus he liked Gerard in an odd way. ShRil, too, he thought with a faint blush.

But if he had told them, and they had said he couldn't go, they could have kept him locked up on the ship. No, he had made the right choice. Let him look at the station. Let him look all he wanted to. As long as Hap found his mother first, it didn't matter. Then he would make her see that she was wrong about Gerard. If she really was helping to burn the colonies, he would make her understand how bad that was.

Ever since they'd landed she had acted funny. Now she needed help. She might even be sick. As he pulled himself into a clearing he thought of that medtech, Davidem. She had been nice enough. Maybe she could help his mother.

At the end of the clearing the sandy riverbank dropped into the gently swirling water. It made Hap shiver just looking at it. A warm, calm lake like the ones on Sun's March wouldn't have been a problem. But he had never tried to swim a river before, or anywhere with this many clothes on.

He searched through his pockets, looking for ideas as much as things. He didn't find anything there except the waterproof hood for his jacket. That gave him an idea. As quickly as he could he took off everything but his one-piece undersuit, rolled his clothes into a tight ball, and put them in the hood. By pulling the drawstring as hard as he could, he almost got the hood to form a closed sack.

Then he had a second idea. He took the jacket out and easily pulled the drawstring tight. Winding the drawstring around the mouth of this sack, he hoped it would keep his clothes dry. He hated to leave the jacket, but his boots would have to go with him, and they would weigh him down enough. As he tied them to his bundle by their laces, he realized that his skin was already covered with chill bumps under the thin undersuit.

For a long moment he stood looking at the river, trying to guess how far downstream the current would carry him. Then with gritty determination he pulled his head and one arm through the loop made by his bootlaces and stepped gingerly down into the water.

It didn't feel as cold as he thought it would until it reached his crotch. By then he was committed. He walked slowly forward, letting his body absorb the chill until the water reached the middle of his chest. With a sudden kick he pushed his feet off the bottom and started swimming.

The current caught him sooner than he expected it to, and dragged him in the wrong direction. The bundle of clothes and boots banged and twisted against his body. The laces cut into his skin. The cold numbed his feet. But he kept trying to swim, trying to cut across the current toward the opposite bank. All too quickly he realized that he was going to be swept far downstream. The current was much too strong for him to fight it.

Hap was frightened until he realized that the current was also helping him stay afloat. With renewed hope he tried to cut gradually across the current. Each time he looked up the bank seemed no closer, but when he looked back, the bank he had started from seemed just as far away. And the bundle now hung like a stone beneath him.

He tried to twist it around and get it on his back, but the current kept the laces digging into his skin and he was now drifting feet first downstream. Suddenly he grunted in pain as his foot banged something. As he turned in reaction to the pain, his other foot touched bottom.

Hap shouted in joy. The current was still too strong for him to stand, but he used the bottom to edge himself one push at a time toward shore. Then after what seemed like an eternity, when he shoved with his foot, his knee scraped bottom and he struggled to his feet. By the time he pushed his way slowly through the surging water and climbed up the bank, the sun had sunk to the top of the hills, offering no heat for his shivering body, and taunting him with the disappearance of light.

As quickly as he could he stripped off his wet undersuit, slapped as much water as he could off his body, and opened the bundle. Except for a wet spot on his pants, his clothes were dry. But as he climbed into them, he realized that they were going to offer him little protection from the cold night.

Then as he pulled on his sodden boots, he heard the sound of a skimmer and looked up just in time to see it start out across the water fifty meters upriver from him. In the fading light he could see three people in the skimmer, two in front and one in back. Even as they raced away from him toward the opposite shore he knew the one in back was his mother.

When he tried to shout to them all that came from his throat was a harsh croak of dismay.

Well after dark Gerard guided the skimmer to a slow stop beside Windy. "First light we try again," he said quietly.

"I think we need help."

"Better help than Woltol and Ronda?" he asked as he helped ShRil down. Only then did he see the other skimmer. "Junathun and Liana made it. Maybe one of them would be willing to help."

Liana greeted them at the hatch. "I'm not used to having ghosts pop up in front of me," she said. "But I was surely glad when those two popped up and told us you were coming back."

"Did you have trouble?" ShRil asked with a worried look.

"Sakes, no. CrRina was just fine. But we did feel rather helpless sitting here waiting for you."

"How about something to eat?"

"CrRina showed us where the instafood was," Liana said as she followed them into the galley.

"Can't say as it was very good," Junathun said as he rose to meet them. "No luck, huh?"

Gerard took two blue ration packets out of the freezer and put them in the oven. "No. But I want to go out again at first light and ShRil suggested one of you might want to—"

"Be glad to. Liana can stay here with CrRina." Junathun paused. "If that's all right, Liana?"

"Of course."

"Thank you again," ShRil said. "We appreciate it."

"What are you cooking, Gerard?"

"Oh," he said as he realized his mind had wandered back to the search for Hap, "some special rations we've been saving. Won't be as good as Liana's, I'm afraid, but..."

"As long as it fills us, we'll be happy."

"It will do that. Gerard made these himself, and I suspect you will not be displeased."

Junathun laughed, and Gerard wished he could laugh with him.

27

Gatou-Drin shrieked softly when Spinnertel suddenly appeared beside her.

"You shouldn't have followed me," he said.

She shrieked again as his claws pierced her neck. It was the last sound in her life.

Spinnertel spent his rage tearing out her throat and shredding her flesh with his claws. Then as he stood over her mutilated body he shuddered with a strange mixture of excitement and terror. For the longest moment he didn't understand why he had killed her.

But it was done. There was no sense worrying about the motive now. Yet as he covered Gatou-Drin's corpse with rocks by the pale light of six moons, he knew that by killing her he had killed the living force which bound him to the Constant and the immortals. He had slashed a bloody demarcation line between himself and them which could never be crossed.

Something in Spinnertel had broken loose when Askavenhar died, something primitive and basic, a feral instinct which had been buried under millennia of delusions about immortality. The spectre of death, real death, his death, had stripped away the protective layers and left him totally vulnerable. And that vulnerability was more than his mind could stand.

The paradox was that he felt totally alive, full of an exuberance which had been denied to him before. Whatever dangers the future held for him were now challenges instead of threats. His life was his own, to shape as he wished, with nothing and no one to restrain him.

As the seventh moon crept above the horizon, the silvery

shadows trembled in the wind of a primitive roar which echoed and faded through the hills.

Hap shivered violently as he awoke. An awful sound lingered in the air. Alert with fear he curled himself into a tighter ball under the crude shelter of branches he had made. Nothing stirred around him. Then the harsh sound came again, distant and chilling, like the cry of some huge beast reveling in its kill.

"Have to stay awake," he whispered. "Have to stay awake." But the sound was not repeated. The tiny skittering, snapping night noises resumed their hypnotic pattern. Fatigue crept over his chilled body like a warm blanket of forgetfulness, and in the middle of a gentle shudder Hap fell asleep again.

"Wake up! Wake up!" Shttz squeaked.

Gerard rubbed his eyes and propped himself on one elbow. ShRil turned on the glowlamp over their bed.

"Shttz? What's the matter?"

"Come to the galley. There is someone there you must talk to. Hurry."

Someone aboard Windy? Now? Gerard shook his head.

"Hurry!"

"All right. All right. We're coming." He caught his robe when ShRil tossed it to him and put it on as they followed Shttz down the dim companionway. "Where have you been?"

"Later. Hurry. She may not stay."

"Who may not stay—" His words died in a brief gasp as he stepped into the galley. A huge, spiderlike ghost almost filled one end of the room. Ronda, Woltol, and Bertilina all seemed to be talking to it.

"This is Askavenhar," Shttz said proudly. "She just died and was about to leave when I caught her."

"Unh, hello, Askavenhar," Gerard said as ShRil slipped her arm around his waist. "I am Gerard Manley and this—"

"I know who you are," Askavenhar said. "You are the Verporchting."

Her mutifaceted eyes glowed with internal light, and her body pulsed with energy. Sleep clung to Gerard's brain as he looked at her, and he wondered what in the universe this was all about. "Pardon? I don't know that word."

"Ah, but you do, Verporchting. You do. That was the only reason I accepted Shttz's noisy demand that I pause here."

"I am afraid you have us at a great disadvantage, Askavenhar," ShRil said quietly.

"She's one of the immortals. Or she was." Shttz made a high-pitched sound of amusement.

Gerard's thoughts cleared. An immortal? Like Gracie?

"Hush, little one, and be still for a while. I cannot stay for long." She smiled when Shttz settled down immediately in front of her. "I was indeed one of the immortals until a brief time ago. Now it seems I have changed—but stayed the same."

"Are you, uh, did you know one of, uh . . ."

"Yes, Verporchting. I know your Gracietta. She has been watching you with great care."

"I don't understand." Gerard guided ShRil to a chair and they both sat down. "What's going on?"

"More things than I have time to explain, Verporchting."

"And why do you keep calling us that?"

"Just you, Gerard Manley. You are the Verporchting."

"What the Krick does that mean?" he asked, surprised by the anger in his voice. Somewhere in the back of his mind that name sparked a reaction too fleeting for him to follow.

"It means you are special in a way I have no time to explain. I do not care what happens here, except that you should know the truth of your existence. Then—"

"Tell him, Askavenhar," Shttz said excitedly as his image jiggled up and down.

"If you will all listen, I will. I do not understand this transition yet, but I know I am drawn by a force greater than any I ever felt toward the depths of the universe. It pulls at me even now, so listen closely, for I will not linger to repeat it."

Gerard opened his mouth to say something, but shut it again. ShRil took his hand. Shttz stopped jiggling. "We all listen," Bertilina purred.

"As you should. The Verporchting is an old idea of Spinnertel's which he thought had died after its last incarnation. Then when Gracietta met Gerard, she felt otherwise and commissioned a watch on him which brought her evidence to support her theory. She arranged for a final test by insuring that your offspring and its mother would be here on Cosvetz with you. Unfortunately Spinnertel had other plans, and the Constant has been disrupted by my death. Consequently, there..."

Spinnertel? Constant? Cosvetz? Gerard's head swam with names and terms which made no sense.

". . . they or I can do for you. That is why I paused to give you this truth, and to tell you to beware of Spinnertel. He seethes with anger which has no rational base."

With a slight bowing motion she brought three of her four pairs of legs together in front of her. "Now I must go. Take care, Verporchting."

"But—" Gerard's protest bounced lifelessly off the empty bulkhead. She was gone. Gracie watching him? Beware of Spinnertel? A final test? What in Fara's name was going on?

The ghosts immediately started an unintelligible chatter among themselves. ShRil looked at Gerard with concern. "Do you have any idea what she was talking about?"

"Fara, no." He sighed in frustration and massaged his eyes with his fingers. "How do you cope with something like that?" The names kept spinning in his mind.

"I do not know, my love. I do not know." She squeezed his hand and looked at the ghosts. "Maybe they can tell us."

"In a minute. Something just hit me. Did you understand any of those terms she used? I mean, did any of them sound familiar to you?"

"No. Except maybe—"

"Verporchting?" The word popped unbidden from his mouth.

"Yes. It is as though I had heard it before."

"Me, too. But I don't know where. Damn, I wish she hadn't disappeared like that." Verporchting? The reaction sparked again, but still made no sense to him.

The ghost chatter suddenly stopped. "We have a suggestion," Ronda said.

"You must look in your past."

"For what, Shttz?"

"For the Verporchting. It is there somewhere."

"Windy?" ShRil asked.

Gerard yawned. "Why not?" Fatigue was pushing the confusion in his mind to a quieter lever. "I'll put her on it first thing in the morning."

"Perhaps you should do it now."

"I'm too tired now. And too confused. I wouldn't even know where to begin."

"Then I shall do it."

"You really think all that gibberish is that important?" Even

190

as he asked the question he knew his own answer. Of course it was important.

"I do."

"Then we'll work on it together. But we need to be quiet about it. No sense in waking Junathun and Liana."

"I will make some coffee."

"Lots of it. I have a feeling we're going to be at this for the rest of the night."

"I will monitor CrRina," Bertilina said.

"What about the rest of you?"

"We will watch . . . if that meets with your approval."

"Whatever makes you happy."

Minutes later as Gerard sat at Windy's information console he really didn't know where to start. "Okay, girl," he said quietly, "I guess the first thing to do is figure out some spellings for Verporchting. Then at least you'll have a list of possibilities."

When ShRil brought the vacuum bottle of coffee, he took it from her and offered her the seat in front of the console. "There's my list so far. You play with it for a while and see how many other possibilities you can come up with."

The screen filled with names—Vurpoorching, Vurporcheng, Verporchting, Verpoorching, Verpoorting, Ferpourcheng, Furpurtching, Ferporchting—until they had enough variations for Windy to begin generating them on her own. When she came up with the total, they were both shocked.

"Nine hundred eighty three thousand plus," Gerard said with a shake of his head. "And that's just in the languages our tired old Baird Z-Rangel translator knows. Well, Windy, it looks like all you have to do is scan your data banks and find any references which match up with any of those names. How long do you think it will take?"

When Windy flashed the number, they both laughed. "I can't stay awake that long," Gerard said. "I'm going back to bed. With all due respect, Windy, I think if that thing's in my head anywhere, Self and I have as good a chance of finding it in ten days as you do."

Hap forced himself to climb the hill in the cold morning light. As long as he kept moving he didn't shiver. But moving did nothing for the growling in his gut. He tried chewing on several different kinds of leaves, but each had its own bad flavor and he decided against trying any more.

His only goal at the moment was to get to the top of the hill where he could watch the river. If his mother and her *friends* came back that way, he wanted to be able to see where they went.

Well before he reached the crest of the hill he heard the faint sound of a skimmer. Hap ran as fast as he could and reached the top barely in time to see the skimmer's high tail disappear through the trees. Without hesitation he started following it, jumping over rocks, breaking through brush, trying to keep its high-pitched whine directly in front of him. Then just as he reached an area where the trees and brush thinned, the whine eased and almost faded away.

Hap ran even harder, the sweat cold on his neck and in his armpits, his feet burning from the blisters caused by his wet boots. He was too close to lose them now, too close to finding his mother again.

The whine got louder, a harsh sound which echoed off itself somewhere in front of him. As he ran, Hap was sure he was catching up to them. Then the whine stopped. Hap stopped, too, and strained to listen past the rasping of his breath and the pounding of his heart.

But it was no sound which started him running again. It was a slanted column of black smoke which rose over the trees, and a chant which echoed in his mind.

Now as we surrender life, we surrender to the One. One reality alone marks the chosen way. One reality . . .

The chant faltered and died before he broke through the trees. A colony was burning with dark, red flames under a swirling base of black smoke. "Nooooo!" he screamed hoarsely as he rushed forward with blind, desperate fury to stop the fire. "Nooooo!"

A blur charged at him and spun him around. "Hap! Hap!"

"Nooo," he cried as he beat futilely against his mother's arms. "Please, no."

Chizen drew him tight against her as his struggle broke into sobs and they cried together against a background of death.

28

Brightseed's thoughts twisted in agony. Yet another colony had died before the spreading of blessings. Yet another life swollen with pollen and seeds had burned under the fires of death. And Riverside-Bend reported Hap near the latest death. But when they tried to reach him, they received no response.

Where was he? Had he found his mother? Was he all right?

There were no answers to those questions, and the rapid chemical changes taking place in Brightseed made concentration more and more difficult. When it started releasing pollen with the next day's rising sun Brightseed would be deaf and mute. Its thoughts would fold in upon themselves and all its energies would be directed to spewing every last grain of pollen high into the morning breeze.

It had to set thoughts about Hap aside and deactivate the groundsel which had monitored Sirreena. Those two precious kinous had to be left to the guardianship of the One until Brightseed returned to the outer world with the rising of the fifth sun. Even then it would be weakened as its selected Guardians pulled themselves out of the ground and began the long walk of life.

Brightseed's energy would go to regenerating new Guardians from the tubers left behind, to replacing its torn and damaged roots, and purging itself of the chemical residue left by the spreading of blessings.

Only Brightseed's faith gave it comfort. The One would provide. The One would assure. The One would bless them all.

Liana and Woltol rode with Gerard. ShRil and Ronda rode with Junathun. Their shortrange radios kept them in touch with each other, and for the better part of the day they crisscrossed the hills north and west of the river searching for Hap.

Junathun was sure that Hap could not have crossed the river. The current was too strong for a boy to swim across, and the closest ford was eleven kilometers downstream from the station. At midafternoon the two skimmers rested side by side on a low bluff overlooking the ford. They had found no trace of Hap. But every few hours they had seen a new column of smoke rise across the river in the southeast.

"Suppose we travel upstream and scout the riverbank," Gerard suggested. He and Liana had alternated in guiding the skimmer, but his arms and shoulders still ached from the hours of dodging through terrain where no skimmer had ever been meant to travel.

"That makes as much sense as anything else," Junathun said, with a glance toward the dark clouds hanging over the south bank. "You three follow this side, and we'll follow the other. That way if he did manage to make it across, we might find some sign of it. If we go as slow as the skimmers will let us, it will take the rest of the daylight we have left. But I don't know what else to suggest."

"We're agreed then." Gerard started the engine and followed Junathun down to the ford. As he eased the skimmer out over the water, he turned to Liana. "Can you swim?" he asked loudly.

"Yes. But the water's damned cold this time of year."

"I'll try to keep us out of it, then."

Guiding the skimmer over water while trying to carefully inspect the bank turned out to be no easier than guiding it through the countryside. Only here there was no way to let Liana take a turn at the controls without going ashore, and Gerard didn't want to do that.

All through the day something had been pricking the back of his mind. Now as they crept along scanning the bank with tired eyes for any possible clue, he realized what it was. Askavenhar had said Gracie arranged for *your offspring and its mother* to be here. In his confusion about everything else she had said, and their concern with solving the Verporchting puzzle, that comment had slipped out of sight.

Your offspring and its mother. He knew that didn't mean CrRina and ShRil. Their presence was natural. Thus Askavenhar could only have meant Hap and Inez. And that meant . . . if he could believe her . . . that meant Hap really was his son.

"Watch for that snag," Liana said.

Gerard swerved right and increased the throttle as the edge of the skimmer cut into the water.

"You all right?" she asked.

"Yes." He turned the skimmer back closer to the bank and tried to concentrate on what he was doing. After several minutes he knew he couldn't stand the burning ache in his shoulders any longer and asked Liana, "Can you guide for a while?"

"Certainly. There's a sandy draw up there on the left. Pull ashore and I'll tell Junathun what we're doing." She picked up the radio mike and cupped it in her hands.

Gerard guided the skimmer around another snag, then revved the engine slightly as he pulled up on the bank. Had he not been concentrating so hard, he might have mistaken the grey-blue spot on the bank for a shadow. But as he set the skimmer down, he realized it was something else.

"Tell them I've found something!" he said as he scrambled out of the skimmer. He barely heard them race across the river as he picked up the jacket and inspected it carefully. It was Hap's. He was sure of it.

Askavenhar's death, Spinnertel's defection, and loss of contact with Gatou-Drin had thrown the Constant into turmoil. For all the accumulated wisdom and experience of its membership it had no precedents for this kind of situation.

"And I say we continue," Halido shouted above the noise.

"It is no longer our concern," someone answered.

"Peace! Peace!" Gracietta's voice rang calm and strong through the room. "We will solve nothing this way," she said when their voices quieted slightly. "There are certain decisions we are bound by the rules of the Constant to make. Once we have done that, then we can debate."

"What rules?"

"What decisions?"

"The rules of experiment state that no project may be initiated or abandoned except by a majority vote. They also state that no project may be interfered with by members other than their creators without a unanimous vote of those members present and voting."

The interplay of voices rose again. "What about Gatou-Drin?" Halido asked. "Do we not have an obligation to her?"

"Not by the rules."

"This is her project. Leave it to her."

"With Spinnertel down there?"

"Yes," Gracietta said loudly.

After a long moment Halido again shouted above the noise. "Gracietta is right." He waited for the Constant to quiet and then continued. "If Spinnertel has interfered with Drin's project, it is now between the two of them." His voice was filled with deep sadness. "Those are the rules," he finished quietly, "the rules we agreed to millennia ago."

"But this is different. No member has ever—"

"Those are the rules," Halido repeated. "If we abandon them, we abandon the principles of this Constant."

"I thought we could vote to interfere?"

"Not until Gatou-Drin requests—"

"Where is she?"

"We don't know. The microlenses are searching for her now."

"Then what can we do?"

The corners of both of Gracietta's mouths turned down. "We may observe. We may search for Gatou-Drin and Spinnertel. We may look for cause to interfere without Gatou-Drin's request. Or we may vote to abandon this project."

"Which one? Gatou-Drin's? Or Spinnertel's?"

"Either or both. It is the Constant's choice."

Arguments broke out again. Members shouted at each other or quietly and obstinately defended their points of view. For the first time within the reaches of most of their memories the whole Constant seethed with emotional debate.

Hours later their only consensus was to observe as much as they could of the activities on Cosvetz. Any other decisions would depend upon those observations.

Hap and Chizen sat in the fading light talking quietly. Behind them on the other side of the skimmer Carson and Geljoespiy were arguing about what to do next.

"It's wrong, Mother."

"That is what you have been saying all day."

"But you have to believe me. The colonies—the flowers—are just as alive as you and I are. They think, and love, and everything."

"Carson says they are trying to control your mind."

"Oh, Mother! That's stupid. If they were controlling my mind, how could I have come looking for you?"

Chizen looked at him, saw the sincerity in those familiar eyes, and loved him all the more. Then a dark frown creased her face. "That still does not solve my problem. I have made an agreement which I am bound to keep."

"Break it. You don't owe them anything."

"Ah," she said with a shallow sigh, "but I will."

Before she answered Hap realized what she meant. "Why? Why do you want to kill him? What has he ever done to us?"

His questions tore into her. Chizen knew she no longer had answers for herself, much less for him. As she tried to find words to explain, they were both startled by the sudden appearance of a small flyer coming directly over the trees toward them. "What—"

"Duck!" Carson shouted.

Hap pushed his mother over and lay half on top of her, his eyes wide with fear. It was going to hit them. He knew it. Instead, the flyer settled thirty meters in front of them and a giant, shaggy beast almost as big as the flyer itself climbed out of the bubble over its stubby wings.

"Geljoespiy," the beast's voice boomed in a guttural accent, "why do you hide from me?"

"Letrenn? Letrenn!" Geljoespiy shouted as he ran around the skimmer toward the beast.

Carson whistled. "So that's Letrenn."

Chizen and Hap helped each other up and stared as Letrenn picked up Geljoespiy with a deep laugh and hugged him to his broad chest as though he were a child. "Who is that?" Hap whispered. His insides were shaking.

"A friend of Geljoespiy's," Chizen said quietly. "He has come to help us."

"Burn the flowers?"

"That, too," she said before she could catch the words.

Hap shivered and tightened his grip on her hand. He had never seen a creature like Letrenn, and he couldn't believe that his mother had—

197

"Over there! Look!" Carson shouted, pointing across the river.

Two skimmers hovered at the top of a hill, dark silhouettes against the clear north sky.

"Verporchting," Spinnertel growled, dropping Geljoespiy unceremoniously to the ground. "Verporchting."

Hap didn't know what that meant. But as he watched the skimmers move into the shadows under the hill, he was sure who was in at least one of them.

29

"It's too dark. I think that's the boy and his mother, but I can't be sure about the others," Junathun said as he handed the binoculars to Gerard.

They were high-quality binoculars which gathered every available ray of light, but as Gerard peered through them at the shadows moving between the skimmer and the flyer he couldn't be sure either. "When does the first moon come up?"

"Very soon. But we should be getting back. It looks like the boy's found his mother, Gerard, and there's nothing you can do about that. Besides . . ." Junathun sniffed the air. "Can you smell that?"

The air was tinged with a faint, delicate scent. "Pollen?"

"Not yet. But tomorrow for sure. It always starts at sunrise."

"Do you have any protective gear?"

"Nothing short of a spacesuit can protect you when the pollen starts."

For a long moment Gerard didn't respond. That was his son across the river. And the people Hap was with were bent upon destroying the flowers. Gerard couldn't just run back to

Windy. "All right. You two go back to *Windhover* and get us some suits. Shttz will show you where they are. ShRil and I will stay here and try to keep tabs on—"

"Ver-por-chting!" A deep voice echoed across the river. "Ver-por-chting! You will die your last death!" An insane laugh rolled through the gathering darkness.

"Who the Krick is that?"

"I don't know, Liana. But when you get the suits, you'd better pick up some weapons, too." Gerard took a small case out of his pocket. "Use this to open the weapons locker, Junathun."

"Perhaps Liana should stay with CrRina."

"And maybe ShRil should go back," Junathun said.

"No!" ShRil paused. "I am sorry for snapping at you," she said quietly, "but my place is with Gerard. Liana, will you—"

"Of course. But against my better judgment. We should all go back together."

"Not yet," Gerard said firmly. "Look, there's a good chance that boy is my son."

"You mean—" Liana gasped.

"I don't know for sure, but I have to stay. You don't. And after Junathun brings us the suits and weapons, he doesn't—"

"I'll come back to stay. If Carson's gone crazy, you will need all the help you can get. Let's go, Liana."

As soon as Junathun started the skimmer Gerard turned to Woltol and Ronda. "I want you two to go across the river and find out what's going on over there. Don't let them see you, and don't do anything yet. Just find out what's going on."

"Yes, Fize," Woltol said as they popped out of sight.

After they disappeared ShRil and Gerard settled into their borrowed skimmer and stared across the river. "This could be very dangerous, my love," she said softly.

"I know. But once we get the suits we will—"

The sounds of a skimmer interrupted him. For a split second he thought Junathun and Liana were returning. Then he realized it was coming straight toward them from across the river.

"Kravor in Krick! What do we do now?"

"Get out of here!" ShRil said.

Gerard hit the start button. The engine whined for a second, then coughed and died. He hit it again with no results. As he looked down the hill, he could see the skimmer

199

in the middle of the river. He jabbed the button again and again.

"Time to hide somewhere else," ShRil said. They climbed out of the skimmer and ran across the face of the hill to a small clump of trees.

No sooner had they stopped than the approaching skimmer crashed noisily up the riverbank. It twisted and veered, struck a small tree, and slid directly toward them.

Gerard jerked ShRil back and they ran up the hill. The skimmer bounced once, twice, then ground to a thumping halt against the trees where they had hidden.

Silence followed the descending whine of the skimmer's dying engine. Peering intently through the darkness, neither Gerard nor ShRil could see any movement in the skimmer. Then the insane laugh filled the silence.

"Take them, Verporchting! I have no use for them now!"

The silence returned. Wood snapped. The skimmer settled with a creak. "Youse are all right?" Woltol asked as he appeared suddenly beside them.

"Yes. Come on," Gerard whispered. As quietly as they could they made their way back down the hill, keeping the trees between themselves and the skimmer.

ShRil smelled fuel. "Careful. It is leaking."

"I smell it, too."

The first moon had crept above the horizon and its pale light revealed two bodies slumped over in the wreckage of the skimmer. "It's Hap," Gerard whispered fiercely. He released ShRil's hand and rushed to his son.

ShRil and Woltol were right behind him. Moments later they pulled Hap and Inez out of their seats and dragged them away from the wreck. A crackle of flame issued from underneath it. By the time they pulled the pair behind their own borrowed skimmer, the crackle had grown to a low roar. Orange tongues of flame licked the wreckage, then consumed it.

For what seemed like an eternity they huddled over the two unconscious forms, waiting for an explosion which never came. Woltol stood above them watching and listening. Finally ShRil breathed a cautious sigh of relief and dug the medkit out of their skimmer.

Both Hap and Inez had bleeding gashes in their foreheads, but their breathing was strong and regular. "They are alive, anyway," ShRil said. With Gerard's help she cleaned and bandaged their wounds as best she could by the feeble beam of a small glowlight.

Gerard retrieved Hap's jacket and wrapped him in it. "Woltol, you go back across. We'll be all right." He smiled slightly when Woltol disappeared. Then he and ShRil huddled side by side, backs against the skimmer, to await Junathun's return.

"I think I remember the reference," ShRil said softly.

"What reference?"

"To the Verporchting. It is part of the Tenderfoot legend."

"What do you mean?"

"It is one of the names we found references under. Do not forget, my love, that you and I chose the name for the legend. When we found the first evidence, there were other terms equally available to us. Tenderfoot was merely the one we found most descriptive and convenient, but Verporchting was—"

"Are you trying to say that I'm linked in some way to the Tenderfoot legend?"

"Yes." That idea frightened ShRil and excited her at the same time. To think that—

"But it's just a legend! An old one at that."

"Askavenhar said you were the Verporchting. Whoever is across the river thinks you are, also."

As Gerard remembered all the references to the legend they had found, and all the strangely fascinating Tenderfoot poems, he laughed softly. "That's the craziest thing I ever heard of." Then he looked at Hap and Inez lying in front of him. Who was he to say what was crazy any more?

And once more the insane laughter rolled across the river.

Spinnertel cursed and laughed at Carson and Geljoespiy as they sat across the fire from him. "What do you fear? I have suits which will protect you. My ship is within walking distance. You feeble mortals can walk, can't you?"

"Yes, but we'll need the suits as soon as the sun comes up," Carson protested.

"Then I shall go get them now, and some tools for you to continue your burning of the colonies."

"But we can't—"

"Of course you can! Damn your weak minds! You will burn colonies until I tell you to stop! Is that understood?"

They both nodded silently. Carson was more afraid of this Letrenn, or Spinnertel, or whatever his real name was, than he had ever been of anything in his life. He didn't care what Gel said about how Letrenn would take care of them. Carson was sure he was going to lead them to their deaths—if not from the pollen, then from the offworlder across the river.

"Good. But don't let my Verporchting sneak up on you while I am gone. I want him to face me in the morning, and know that I, Spinnertel, am his creator and his destroyer. Then I'm going to let him die his final death."

Gel looked across the fire, and couldn't see anything. Then a shadow shifted away from them, and moments later he heard the faint keen of the flyer's engines. The rush of air as it flew low over their heads made more noise than the engine. "See," Gel said in a shaky voice, "I told you he was special."

"Special enough to get us killed." Carson spat into the fire and it hissed back at him.

"Don't say things like that. You're the one who wanted his help. Well, now you've got it." Gel felt far less confident than he tried to sound. Nothing had gone the way he thought it would. It had all changed too quickly. Suddenly with Letrenn gone and the skimmer wrecked across the river, Gel would have given almost anything to be home with Essy.

"What'll we do if he doesn't come back?"

"Dammit, Carson, he'll be back."

"Good. You wait for him. I'm going to hike down to the ford, make my way across the river, and run as hard as I can for Beall's place."

"You'll never make it before the pollen starts. I can smell it in the air already."

"I can smell it, too. That's why I'll take my chances." He stood up and brushed off the seat of his pants.

Gel just sat there looking at Carson. Part of him wanted to go, but a stronger part demanded that he stay. "Good luck," he said finally, as he stood and held out his hand.

Carson shook it. "Thanks, Gel. And you, too. I hope your friend comes through for you."

"He will." He glanced up at the four moons already lined up above the horizon. "If you're going to make it, you'd better get going."

Without another word Carson turned and headed into the night. The moons gave him enough light to see by as he picked his way quickly through the trees and brush toward the river. He knew that a well-used game trail ran along the high side of the bank. It was his fastest way to the ford.

A grim smile shaped his lips as he started running down the trail. This route would take him right past the large patch of Wheezer's Bane a kilometer or so above the ford. But by the time the sun came up he had better be pounding on Beall's front door, with every patch far behind him.

30

Low-Riverside-Bend felt the shadow of the void. It stirred from the depths of its preparations for the spreading of blessings and forced an unseeded Guardian to alertness. The kinous of death was approaching.

This was no time to cope with death. There was no energy to spare, no sacrifice it could make to save itself from this sudden shift of the One. Yet even through its cloudy thoughts it knew that if it did nothing, it would die.

As the One gives, so it takes. The One is whole.

That was the answer. Low-Riverside-Bend would release its pollen early, cast it up to the blessed heart of One. Better to die in a moment of holiness yielding itself to eternity than to suffer and burn without tasting the sacred moment.

Energy pulsed. Sepals broke their waxy seals and peeled back. Petals slowly opened then pulled themselves back to form narrow bells. Inside, anthers stiffened and straightened.

Energy pulsed again. With an enormous hiss one hundred thousand anthers spewed millions of grains of pollen high into the air. A rich torrent of life roiled above Low-Riverside-Bend.

Carson screamed in terror. It couldn't be! Not now! Not at night! A second explosive hiss drowned out his thoughts.

He yanked a facecloth from his pocket, covered his nose and mouth, and ran. The scent of the pollen was stifling. He couldn't breathe. But if he could reach the river...

As he gasped for air Carson stumbled and fell. His lungs constricted. Then opened. Then constricted again. He gulped for breath, any breath. A long wheezing sigh emptied his lungs.

It was over. He knew it. But still he struggled to his feet. If only... if only... He stood bent over with his hands on his knees trying to keep his balance, trying to maintain his sanity.

Gradually his lungs cleared. He breathed hard and fast like someone who had run to the point of exhaustion. The air was sweet, nurturing, wonderful. With a sudden giggle he sat down. Then he flopped to his back, looked up at the moons, and giggled again. It was funny. He had almost made it.

Carson laughed like he hadn't laughed since the early days with Amsrita. She would have liked this. She would have appreciated it more than anyone else in the whole universe. He couldn't stop laughing. He wrapped his arms around his chest and tried. Oh, how he tried.

But his body was covered with the same silver pollen which coated his lungs. His eyes were filled with tears of joy. Amsrita. Sweet, wonderful Amsrita. He would see her again.

Thirty minutes later he lay still—happy, contented, serene. All was as it should be. Nothing could be better. Then he died.

"If you're right, Junathun, then you've got to get them out of here!" Gerard shouted as he pulled on his spacesuit.

"But there's no way to protect them!"

"I can," Ronda said. "I can shield their lungs, but you will have to hurry or they will suffocate."

Junathun didn't have time to worry about how it would work. He closed the faceplate on his suit and bent over to pick up Hap. By the time he got him in the back of the skimmer, Gerard and ShRil were right behind him with Inez. "You can come back for us," Gerard's voice said in his ear as they loaded Inez next to Hap. "Now get out of here!"

He had never turned the skimmer off, and almost as soon as he climbed aboard it started moving up the hill with two unconscious passengers covered by a ghost.

Gerard watched them go with a feeling of emptiness. Then picked up his Stearne needle gun from the small pile of weapons Junathun had dumped on the ground. It had been one of ShRil's *dowonâche* gifts and was his favorite weapon.

"You will have to get fairly close to do anything with that," ShRil said as she awkwardly strapped on her Swift blaster over her suit.

"I don't care. It makes me feel better." Their voices echoed hollowly inside his helmet. Suddenly Woltol was standing in front of him waving his arms. For a moment Gerard couldn't figure out what was wrong. Then he remembered to switch on his external communications system. "What's the matter?"

"The immortal has returned."

"Askavenhar?"

"No, Fize. The one across the river, Spinnertel."

"Spinnertel? Do you know him?" ShRil asked.

Woltol laughed. "We visited him on the way here. Afraid of ghosts, he is."

"Then you stick close," Gerard said quietly, "and let's hope that he stays over there until Junathun gets us out of here."

"What about the flowers?"

Gerard sighed and looked at her. His faceplate was clouded, and for a second he thought his sigh had done that. Then he reached up with a gloved hand and brushed at it. Silver glints of pollen smeared across its surface. "Looks like the flowers are already in action." He took out a utility rag and carefully wiped the faceplate clean. "Besides, I don't know what we can do to stop those people if they want to burn more."

"We can try. The flowers are sentient, Gerard. We know that now. We have a responsibility to try to protect them."

Gerard had been too busy worrying about Hap to think about the flowers. "But how? We couldn't even get across the river if we wanted to."

"There is the ford," she offered.

"That's a damned long ways downstream to walk in these suits. And how would Junathun find us when he gets back?"

"We could float across."

That idea didn't appeal to Gerard either. But he knew ShRil was right about their obligation. Since the flowers couldn't protect themselves, it was up to them to do what they could. "All right, as soon as it's light enough—"

"It is light enough now, my love, to walk upstream so that we can try to come ashore above them."

Gerard slung one of the laserifles over his shoulder. ShRil picked up the other one. "Let's do it then."

They were less than a kilometer upstream when Gerard called a halt. "This will never do," he said heavily. "These suits were never made for this. And I wasn't made for carrying this much weight."

"Then what do you suggest?"

"I don't know. How much line do you have?"

ShRil checked her belt. "A full two hundred meters."

"So do I. Woltol? Do you think you can get one end of this line across the river and secured?"

"I will try, Fize. Do youse have a small magnet youse could attach to the end?"

"Let's see." Gerard searched the limited supplies on his suit's belt. "No—wait a minute. How about this? It's magnetic." He held out one of the two extra clips for his needle gun. Woltol reached, and the clip snapped out of Gerard's hand and seemed to hang in the middle of one of Woltol's hooks.

Minutes later Woltol floated out across the river holding the clip in his electromagnetic grip and dragging four hundred meters of light utility line behind him. In what seemed like an impossibly short time he was back. "Done, Fize."

"Good. ShRil, we'll tie our belts together and hope that my reel is strong enough to wind us in. The worst that can happen if the line doesn't break is that we'll have to cut ourselves loose and paddle. Let a little extra air build up in your suit. The higher we float, the less drag we'll put on the reel."

High above, a microlens followed the course of two suited figures as they drifted into the current of the river, then swung ever so slowly toward the opposite bank like the weight on the end of a long pendulum. It relayed that image to the lone observer aboard Askavenhar's ship. Gracietta allowed herself two slight smiles when the figures finally trudged ashore.

They did not need her help, or anyone else's. As he had so many times in the past, Gerard was proving quite capable of taking care of himself.

31

They found Geljoespiy's body at first light of dawn. He was lying with a serene smile beside the ashes of a dead fire.

For the first time since Junathun had left them Gerard felt a prick of fear. No matter how serene the smile on its face, a corpse was a corpse. Gerard shuddered. No matter how sentient and normally benign the flowers might be, their pollen was lethal.

As Gerard and ShRil stared at Geljoespiy's body, Woltol spotted the grey line of smoke which seemed to rise just beyond the trees to the west. "There, Fize."

"Let's check our suits first," Gerard said quietly, glad in a dark way that ShRil couldn't read his thoughts. He didn't want her to know the sense of trepidation he felt.

With quick thoroughness they inspected each other's suits. "No significant damage," ShRil reported. "Your oxygen restoration system shows another forty-three hours of use left."

"Yours shows forty-seven." They each aimed at the ashes and ran their weapons through a test cycle. Gerard's needle gun made a small grey puff. But even on its lowest setting ShRil's Swift blaster scattered the ashes in the morning breeze. For a long second Gerard watched them swirl, then settle lightly on Geljoespiy's cold body.

Grimly satisfied that they were as ready as they could be, he said, "Woltol, from here on we use hand signals. ShRil, turn off your external communications." He turned his off and gave Woltol a nod. "Let's go."

They moved cautiously in the direction of the smoke, rifles at the ready, Woltol leading the way. Gerard was grateful when they picked up a trail which led in the right direction.

As they followed Woltol along the winding path Gerard could hear ShRil's breathing from the speaker in the eerie stillness of his helmet.

He wondered how it had come down to this, and what Alvin would think when he heard their story—if he heard their story. Before he could chide himself for that thought, Woltol signalled a stop, then moved them up beside him.

The path they had been following branched around a colony of flowers which looked twice as large as Brightseed. The smoke was clearly visible rising beyond the trees on the other side of the colony. Gerard hesitated. The path offered them no cover or protection in either direction, but he didn't want to waste time backtracking and circling the open space.

"Gerard!" ShRil screamed.

Claws ripped at his suit and spun him around. The laserifle flew from his hands. As he tumbled to the ground, sweet, fresh air flooded his suit. He twisted around in time to see a shaggy grey giant fling ShRil across the path from him.

ShRil screamed in pain.

Fear and anger charged his muscles. Gerard struggled to free his needle gun from its holster. With a vicious roar the giant slashed at him. He knocked Gerard's hand away from the gun and tore open the front of his suit.

Suddenly Woltol was there, his four arms clinging to the giant's shoulders, his torso pressed against the giant's face.

A blast shattered the air. The giant staggered. Woltol vanished. "I am Spinnertel!" the giant roared as he rushed at ShRil. "I am immortal!" The second discharge from her blaster knocked him backward into a screaming heap.

With great pain Gerard freed the needle gun, but couldn't get to his feet. He couldn't breathe. In anger he yanked open his faceplate. "ShRil?" he wheezed. "ShRil?"

Spinnertel rolled to his side. Pain ripped through his back. Kill, he thought as he forced himself to his knees. Kill.

Gerard saw him rise and fired the needle gun with spasmodic jerks of the trigger as he gasped for air. Still the giant rose like a smoking wall of grey fur and claws.

ShRil fired her blaster again.

For an endless moment Spinnertel hung in the air on the searing edge of life. Bitter anger crammed the last of his energy into a fading roar of defiance. Then his lifeless body collapsed, twitched once, and was still.

"ShRil?" Gerard called in a hoarse, breathless voice.

"Here." She half rose to her feet, then stumbled forward and fell on the path by the smoldering, grey giant. "Here."

Gerard forced his body to crawl. "ShRil," he gasped as he reached her side. His lungs burned. His eyes watered as he stared at the huge rent in the front of her suit which exposed her three breasts. Agony and sorrow gagged his mind.

ShRil fought for breath against the ache and pain in her lungs. A vision of CrRina drifted through her mind. Then a vision of Gerard. The pain retreated, but her lungs closed. A sweet smell lingered in her nostrils. So this is what death is like, she thought.

They clasped each other in a heavy embrace, their bodies deflated by the oppressive pollen. The rising sun warmed their skin through the ragged tears in their suits. Gerard giggled irrationally and raised himself on his elbows. ShRil stared up into his smiling face and returned his giggle with a longer one of her own. With a playful growl Gerard nipped at her nose and they both laughed.

"Take off your suit," ShRil said suddenly. She knew from Carson's description of the pollen's effect that they did not have much time. The last thing she wanted was to have anything between her and Gerard at the end. This really was what death was like.

Junathun had searched for hours in the darkness up and down the riverbank for them, desperately looking for any sign which would tell him where they had gone. He couldn't imagine why they hadn't waited for him unless . . . unless they had been attacked. But other than the burned-out skimmer which he already knew about, there were no signs of a struggle where he left them.

Now as he returned to that spot, he cursed loudly in his helmet. Then he climbed out of his skimmer, scanned the opposite shore, and cursed again.

It was bad enough that his suit wasn't functioning properly and that he didn't know how to regulate it. But he couldn't use the binoculars with the helmet on. And he couldn't get all the pollen smears off the faceplate.

Why hadn't they waited for him? Where had they gone? How was he supposed to find them?

He coughed on the stale air as the questions swirled through his brain. It was no use. There was no sense dying on his own foul breath. He would have to go back and get another suit.

Junathun took one last, long look across the river, coughed again, and reluctantly climbed back aboard his skimmer. No matter what he told himself, he felt like a deserter. But as the engine whined to life he grimly accepted the fact that he had no choice. He kicked over the rudder, jammed the throttle forward, spun around in a cloud of dust and pollen, and raced up the hill.

He would be back. And he would find them. He swore it. He owed them no less than that. If he and Liana hadn't told them about Carson . . . If he hadn't insisted on searching the north shore when they wanted to go across the river . . . If he had gotten back to them sooner . . . Those were all reason enough for Junathun to feel like he owed them something— more than something—everything he could do.

Gerard and ShRil stood naked holding hands by the edge of the colony. Their spacesuits and clothes formed a careless trail back to Spinnertel's corpse. They knew they were dying, knew there was no hope for them, but the pollen had taken hold. A strange joy filled them with the overwhelming beauty of the moment. When Bertilina and Shttz appeared in front of them, Gerard and ShRil looked at each other and giggled.

"We are too late," Shttz said sadly.

Gerard laughed. "Don't be so glum! It's wonderful here."

"No!" Shttz screamed.

"Yes," Bertilina purred quietly. "But you do not have much time." Her pearlescence grew brighter. "Do you still wish to become a ghost, Gerard?"

"What are you—"

"Hush, Shttz."

Gerard looked at ShRil with a thrill of anticipation. "Can we? I mean—"

"Yes," Bertilina said, "I think so. If you join physically as you have in the past, I think you can both remain integrated and become ghosts."

"Become ghosts?" ShRil asked with a disbelieving smile.

"Make love? Here?" Gerard laughed with joy. To make love, here in this glorious setting—what more could they want? He looked into ShRil's eyes and saw the happiness of his life. "Shall we?" he asked.

"Become ghosts in love? Yes," ShRil responded eagerly. It was crazy, but she did not care. With a seductive grin she pulled Gerard to her. "Yes. Here, by the flowers."

Gerard took a deep breath of the cool, sweet air and kissed her passionately. There was no place in the universe he would rather be. What a perfect place! What an absolutely perfect time! "Yes," he said as he relinquished her kiss with a gentle laugh. "Oh, yes, yes, yes."

Slowly they settled down on the grass into each other's arms. Her touch sang to his nerves. Her lips sent fire through his loins. Only happiness hurried them to give pleasure to one another. Only love flooded their thoughts.

ShRil arched against him, pressing his flesh with a lovely, aching desire. "Gerard," she whispered, "love me. Love me now. Love me forever."

"Forever and ever," he answered as the natural gravity of their love drew their bodies together.

Bertilina hovered over them, waiting, feeling, ready.

With gathering momentum Gerard and ShRil rocked in perfect embrace on waves of pleasure they had never known before. Each moment became a sensuous eon, an infinity of mounting sensations. Each movement pulled them closer to one body, one desire, one enthralling passion.

The wild scent of joy filled their lungs and their minds. The universe dissolved except where they touched. Higher and higher they rose in unison until they reached a peak beyond ecstasy, beyond time, and space, and physical life where their love exploded in a glorious shower of eternal fires.

"It is done," Bertilina sighed tiredly as she smothered their still embrace. "It is done."

Somewhere deep in Low-Riverside-Bend's withdrawn thoughts it noted the presence of new life rising past its Guardians.

They were chattering incessantly, still scornful of saying the wonders he and we their presence. They listened about those outside him. But to his world of emotions he felt closer to them and less disrespectful to his problem. For the moment

32

"We are Gerard and ShRil." They said it together, their voices ringing in perfect melodic unison.

"We are the Constant," Gracietta said with a strange double smile for the shimmering ghosts. "You have caused—"

"The death of Gatou-Drin," Halido said harshly, "and—"

Gerard-ShRil groaned with a fierceness which cut him off and brought instant silence to the room. "We carry no death but our own—and no life but our own. Do not burden us with your problems and concerns."

"They are correct, Halido. Would any disagree?"

None did. Gracietta's assumption of leadership had been tacitly-approved by them all. The deaths of three of their peers had left them too weary even to bicker.

"Good. Now, what may we—"

"Gracie, we have come to greet you, to thank you for your help long ago, and to caution you. We do not know what part you and these played, but we suspect it was—"

"Wrong." Gerard's voice broke from ShRil's. "You meddle at a great cost."

Silence was their only response.

"We leave you now," they said in unison again, "and pray that you will leave also. But know this, would-be immortals. Our kind will not always allow you to play your games so freely."

With a bright flash and a quiet pop they disappeared, leaving behind an acrid smell that many members of the Constant would never forget.

Four long days later Gerard-ShRil stood facing their children with the other ghosts in the bright sunlight outside *Windhover*.

Hap held CrRina in his arms, still unable to shake the wonder he felt in their presence. His mother stood close beside him. But in his whirl of emotions he felt closer to them and his sister than he did to his mother. Yet . . . she was his *mother*.

Behind Hap, Junathun, Liana, and Davidem smiled awkwardly as they looked at Gerard and ShRil and the subtle silver glow which surrounded their linked images.

"It has been hard to stay this long and explain so much," Gerard-ShRil said in the melodic tone of their unified voice. "Only our connections to CrRina and Hap have made it possible. Now we must leave."

"Mummum? Dedo? Please, no? Please?" CrRina trembled when the images of her parents reached out and touched her.

"Don't worry, you little spacer. We'll be back. We'll see you again soon. But first we have to . . . have to make our contact. But don't worry. We'll get Alvin to send more help for you and Hap and Brightseed."

They all followed Gerard's brief glance down the hill where four Guardians were walking very slowly away from Brightseed on short, trifurcated roots.

"We trust you to take care of them, Inez."

"I will," she promised through her tears. She owed these two her life—and Hap's. The love/hate she felt for Gerard would have to be sorted out later—if it could ever be sorted out.

"I will guard them from the danger," Shttz said quietly, still watching the retreating Guardians, "until you return."

"Yes, Shttz will help." ShRil's separate voice was like the whisper of the wind. "And we thank you, Junathun and Liana, for all that you did and tried to do. We thank you all."

"Goodbye," Gerard said as he touched CrRina one more time. Then his glowing hand lingered on Hap's shoulder.

Fairy Peg smiled at him through Hap's eyes as Gerard played with Orees in a flood of images. She denied his love, then ordered him to his death. Neutronic bombs exploded high above Evird. Old Marradon's creaking voice warned him of danger. Brunnel's string guarded him. Fianne whispered insane instructions in his ear while Targ slashed at him in the arena.

A second wave of images swept past the first, images of ShRil, and Alvin, of DoOty, and Yuma, and Quadra—all of which swirled with hundreds of other sights and sounds, then settled neatly into the pattern of his life. It all made sense now. It all fit. All the mystery from Ribble Galaxy was gone. The mindwipers' blocks lay with his unneeded body buried next to ShRil's deep in the soil beside Brightseed.

He had become far more than a reincarnation of Spinnertel's Verporchting, far more than a pawn to be used by an immortal, or the Federation, or Ribble Galaxy. He understood with perfect clarity what they had done, and how he had grown. But now he and ShRil were beyond their reach.

The children, ShRil thought. Yes, his response echoed darkly as he looked at his son and daughter.

"Hap, I don't know what the future holds for you, but *Windhover* is yours and CrRina's, to carry you anywhere you need to go. Take care of her. And take care of your sister."

"I will, sir," Hap said softly. Tears edged out of the corners of his eyes as he hugged CrRina closer to him and squared his shoulders. His heart held questions and confusion that no amount of explaining could put to rest. There was too much for his emotions to absorb. He had gained a father and lost him. Guilt rode that thought. Then there was Ribble Galaxy and a brother he had never seen—his brother—CrRina's brother. But he would do his best. "I will," he repeated.

"I know you will. And I want you to know that I am proud to be your father. Goodbye, son."

"Goodbye," Hap whispered.

"Goodbye, Dedo," CrRina sobbed. "Goodbye, Mummum."

Peace, Brightseed whispered weakly.

"And death," Shttz muttered to himself.

As Junathun and Liana, Inez, and Davidem echoed their goodbyes, the ghosts disappeared one by one. Gerard-ShRil lingered one luminescent moment longer, filled with love for CrRina and Hap and concern about their future. But they had to leave. The spiritual pull on them was too great. They had to trust in those left behind. With spirits joined for all eternity, they slowly faded from sight.

Of the ghosts only Shttz remained behind, a wary presence to watch over the offspring of his friend Gerard Manley—The Old Novice, The Verporchting, Tenderfoot.

Peace, Brightseed whispered again. *Peace*.

ABOUT THE AUTHOR

WARREN NORWOOD lives in Fort Worth, Texas. He is the author of four previous books, THE WINDHOVER TAPES: AN IMAGE OF VOICES; THE WINDHOVER TAPES: FLEXING THE WARP; THE WINDHOVER TAPES: FIZE OF THE GABRIEL RATCHETS and THE SEREN CENACLES (written with Ralph Mylius). He is currently at work on a new series entitled *The Double-Spiral War.*

COMING IN FALL 1984 . . .
A TOWERING NEW SERIES BY THE AUTHOR OF
THE WINDHOVER TAPES

THE DOUBLE-SPIRAL WAR
BY WARREN NORWOOD

A saga so large in scope it will take several volumes to tell.
The Double Spiral War is the epic story of an intergalactic
war seen from the point of view of over a dozen key human
and alien characters. On the following pages, you can read
an excerpt from the powerful opening of the first novel
in this magnificent work, MIDWAY BETWEEN.

Frye Charltos read the battle reports with harshly conflicting emotions. So far the surprise attacks had worked almost exactly as he had planned them. He should have been pleased. Yesterday he would have been. Yesterday Doctor Nise had not called him with the final news. Yesterday there was still hope that Vinita might be cured of her disease. Yesterday was gone.

Today the combined task force of the United Central Systems had attacked six of Sondak's most outlying planets and destroyed most of their peripheral fleet. Today war had started between the two spirals of the galaxy, a war which Frye Charltos had been advocating and planning for years. Today was the beginning of freedom for the U.C.S.

Today was the beginning of the end for Vinita.

Frye shut off the microspooler. Leaning back in his chair he closed his eyes and folded his long, pliant hands in his lap. As he thought about Vinita he unconsciously clenched his fingers until they were locked in a rigid hammer of the tan flesh which pounded softly against his thighs.

Vinita had tried to prepare him for this. She had known in some deep, interior way that she was dying. With that knowledge had come a peace that angered him almost as much as her disease did. To Frye it seemed like she was giving up, refusing to fight this tragedy any longer. But Vinita had countered by saying it was better to live with the truth than to hide from it.

Frye smiled slightly and his hands relaxed for a moment.

She had thrown his own words back at him. "Live with the truth," he had told her when she finally understood after twenty years of marriage that he was first and foremost a soldier. "Live with the truth," she had said before she went to Nise-Kim Center for the last-chance tests.

The truth. The truth was that Frye had never loved anyone in his whole life like he loved Vinita. The truth was that he had promised to help her avoid the suffering she faced if these test results confirmed all the previous ones. The truth was that he had promised to kill his wife and Frye Charltos did not want to live with the truth.

The microspooler's tiny bell binged rapidly. Another set of battle reports had been received. Reluctantly Frye opened his eyes. One by one he blocked his emotions off from the immediate present in a way he had done so many times before. This was a great day for the U.C.S., and that was a larger truth than any personal tragedy he would ever face.

The eyes that read his microspooler were calm and professional. The brain that sorted and analyzed the reports concentrated solely on the task at hand. The voice that gave orders into the lapelcom he wore was the stern, controlled voice of Joint Force Commander Frye ed'Laitin Charltos. But deep beneath the conscious levels of his mind a husband cried for his wife in the dry tears of despair.

Frenzy ruled in the Situation Room at Sondak's military headquarters on Nordeen. Scattered reports and pieces of information were coming in from bases on planets in six key systems, each report, each fragment of description seemingly worse than the one which preceded it.

"Who's in charge here?" a harsh voice bellowed above the noise.

The sound level subsided like a landslide slowly coming to a halt. Suddenly a young captain looked up and saw General Mari standing just inside the door. "I am, sir," she said firmly with a salute from half-way across the room.

Other heads looked up, but when they saw Captain Gilbert turn away from the general, they went back to what they had been doing. The information flow did not stop just because a general walked into the room.

General Mari strode quickly through the crowded room trailed by two aides. Despite what appeared to be pandemonium when he had first entered the room, he could see little wasted effort as he made his way to the captain who had answered him. For the moment he would bite his tongue and find out what the hell was going on. Then he would chew that captain's ass up one side and down the other.

"Sorry, sir," Captain Gilbert said when the general was less than two steps away, "but I had to relay some information to BORFLEET Command before we lost our com-window."

"How bad is it?" Mari asked.

"If all this is true, sir, and I can only assume it is, then it's worse than bad. From the reports we have so far I estimate that we have lost close to seventy-five percent of the Border Fleet either heavily damaged or totally destroyed."

"The Ukes?"

"Four confirmed reports say yes. Half-a-set of others still to be confirmed suggest the same."

"Damn. Damn, damn, damn. Who all have you notified?"

"Every major command and commander we could reach. We won't have a com-window for Polar Fleet for another two days, so we sent their message through Mungtinez relay. Should have their acknowledgment in six hours or so."

"What makes you think they haven't been hit also?"

Captain Gilbert barely blinked. "I haven't had time for speculation, sir," she lied. "I can barely deal with the information I've got rolling in on me."

A com-tech demanded the captain's attention, and while she was dealing with the problem, Mari took another look around the room. The total shock of what had happened still had not reached him. He had been one of the leading voices arguing that the U.C.S. would never risk going to war with Sondak. The Ukes were still too dependent on Sondak resources and technology, he had said. They were also too bound by their traditions and culture to enter another war without a long period of loud diplomatic protests and internal rationalizations.

That's what Mari had argued, because that's what he believed. Now all his beliefs were being proved wrong in the worst possible way.

As that thought struck home, the shock of understanding struck with it. Mari was galvanized by anger. "Captain," he said just as Gilbert turned back to him, "I'll be in the Command Center. You will update all information as soon as you receive it and send it there."

"I'm already doing that, sir. Admiral Stonefield has been in the Command Center for the past hour."

Mari was furious. "Why was he notified first?"

"Because he was in the building, sir."

Without a word General Mari turned and left the Situation Room. Captain Mica Gilbert watched him go without regret. All she needed was more top brass giving her orders and slowing down the work her understaffed crew was trying to get done. Moments later she was back in the middle of it, sorting through the new reports, giving new sets of instructions, and waiting for the one report that wasn't due for another six hours. Her father, Admiral Josiah Gilbert, was acting commander of Polar Fleet.

Frye saw the look on her face the moment he walked in the door and knew that she had talked to Doctor Nise. She waited until he was almost to her before she stood up. Vinita always greeted him standing up. It was one of those traditions which started early in their marriage and had stuck for twenty-five years. Now, even though standing was difficult she insisted on maintaining the tradition. It made him love her all the more.

An observer watching them wrap each other in their arms and kiss might have thought them newlyweds except there was no wasted motion, no frantic necessity in their embrace. It was a practiced passion that each of them cherished.

"Today was the day, wasn't it?" Vinita asked as Frye released her.

"Today was a monster," he said wearily.

"Not for me."

He looked at her with surprise as she sat down and the chair adjusted to her frail body.

"Don't look so shocked, darling. I've known about this for a long time. So have you. But I believed it. Now you must too. What else made it a monster?"

"We attacked Sondak today," he said flatly.

Her eyes lit up. "Revenge? Revenge at last? That's wonderful, Frye! But how could you keep it a secret from me?"

"I don't know. It's the only secret I think I've ever been able to keep from you. I wanted it to be a surprise." He sat down beside her and took her hands in his. "When did you talk to Doctor Nise?"

"Before he called you."

"Oh." He heard the disappointment in his voice and wished he had known. "He didn't tell me he had talked to you."

"I told him not to."

"Did you tell him anything else?"

"Yes. I told him I wanted the special prescription. He sent it over and it's—"

"We can talk about that later," Frye said as he released her hands and stood up. A huge chasm had opened inside him and he was afraid that any moment he might fall in.

"I don't want to put it off much longer, Frye," she said quietly. "I don't want to go on like this. Today . . . today I had to write your name down because the first time I called Doctor Nise I couldn't remember it." She looked straight at him with anger burning in her eyes. "Do you understand that, Frye? I couldn't remember your name. I had to *write it down*."

Suddenly she was crying and he was beside her again holding her in his arms. Never had he faced a more difficult decision, nor one so impossible to come to terms with. This most precious of all women was deteriorating before his eyes. She wanted the only escape open to her from the madness that was eating away at her body and her mind, and he had agreed to help her with that escape.

When she finally stopped crying, she looked at him with an expression that he had to turn away from. "You promised me, Frye. You promised to help me before . . . before . . ."

"I know," he said softly as he rocked her gently in his arms. "I'll do what I said. Don't worry. I'll take care of you. I promise."

Dinner was quiet and intimate despite the fact that Vinita kept asking questions about the attack on Sondak. After dinner he told her all he could about the war, and she rejoiced that the U.C.S. was finally going to have revenge—the revenge it deserved for all that Sondak had done to the U.C.S. after the last war.

Frye opened a vacuum bottle of liquor he had been saving for a special occasion. As they sipped the sweet liquor their conversation gradually changed into reminiscence. Then from reminiscence it settled into the quiet, unspoken pleasure they had always enjoyed in each other's presence.

"Lisa Cay will be coming home now," Vinita said. "She'll be coming home to help you, Frye. You can count on her."

"I know," Frye responded with a tiny catch in his voice, "I've been thinking about that." As he refilled Vinita's glass with the last drops from the bottle, Frye added the contents of the small capsule Doctor Nise had sent to her.

"To victory," Vinita said after he handed her the glass.

"To love," Frye answered.

Later he carried her to bed as usual. Then he lay awake all night holding his dead wife in his arms and crying until he had no tears left for anyone in the whole universe.

"That's what our cryptographers believe he said, sir," Rochmon said quietly.

"But you are not sure?"

"Nothing's positive in this business, general. All I can tell you is that we made a major breakthrough in the Ukes code about ten months ago."

"What kind of breakthrough?"

"We discovered they're using a cycling key in their routine subspace transmissions."

"A cycling key?"

Rochman suppressed a sigh. He hated having to explain cryptography to staff officers. "That means they use a cycle of standard keys to encode their messages. Not very sophisticated, but difficult to break because the key changes at random times during the message. Anyway, since then we've been piecing lots of fragments together."

"How accurate is that?"

Rochman bit off his response and took a frustrated breath. "Well, sir, we feel it is pretty yanqui accurate. What you have in your hands has been part of half a dump of messages to high ranking commanders in the past several cycles. The fact that it was repeated in so many interceptions was what led us three days ago to the second major break—one of the cycle keys."

General Mari frowned, then read the message aloud. "In the first year of the war . . . run wild over their systems. Victory will follow victory . . . build a stellar barrier which . . . be indestructible . . . no promise of success . . . not fully prepared for Sondak's counter attack. Then we will fight a battle of wills testing . . . willing to make the sacrifices necessary to defeat us, and whether we are . . . necessary to hold what we have gained."

General Mari laid the message carefully in front of him on the neat desk and loudly cleared his throat several times. "What about all the missing parts?"

"Key changes, sir. But I think what we have gives us a fairly good representation of their intent."

"Yes, I guess it does. How determined are we? And how determined are they? I guess Charltos asked two good questions, didn't he, Commander?"

"I'd say he did, sir. Charltos isn't the type to make threats lightly—not promises either."

"You talk like you know him."

Rochmon smiled slightly. "Not really, sir. I did meet him once, very formally when he visited Drahcir and I was the senior cryptographer there. But, well, general, I guess studying Commander Charltos has become a kind of hobby of mine. Seems like an interesting enemy to me. He's smart, and not just book smart, if you know what I mean."

"So what is your military assessment of him?"

For all that he disliked General Mari, Rochmon admired him as a soldier. There were few men among Sondak's military leadership who had General Mari's skill and understanding. Yet somewhere deep in his heart Rochmon knew that Mari was not equal to the opposition presented by Commander Frye Charltos.

"Well, sir, if you want my honest opinion, I'd say that not only are we up against the best strategist the Ukes have to offer, but we're also up against a man who understands the tactics of interstellar warfare better than anyone before him."

"You're discounting a great number of people when you say that, Commander."

Rochman heard the quiet censorship in Mari's voice, but chose to ignore it. "I know that, sir, but you asked for my assessment. I've been following Charltos's career for the better part of fifteen years, and it seems to me that the only thing we have going for us at the moment is that he has a respect for life that may prove to be his weak point."

General Mari frowned. "Be specific, Rochmon."

"That's hard to do, general. It's just that from all that I've learned about him I'd be willing to bet on the design of his overall strategy."

"Meaning what?"

"Meaning, general, that he will not risk any more lives on the Ukes' side than is absolutely necessary to obtain the victory he's promised them. That's the way he is. He'll fight for that victory—fight as hard and as well as any military commander we know about—but at the lowest possible cost in lives."

"I suppose you have a suggestion of how we can take advantage of that weakness?"

Rochman didn't like the tone of Mari's voice, but that wasn't going to stop him from giving his opinion. "I do, sir, but I doubt if anyone is going to like it."

"Don't second guess my reaction," Mari snapped. "Just tell me what you would do if you were in charge of overall strategy against Charltos."

"I'd back him into a corner every chance I got, sir. I'd raise the cost in lives as high as possible every time we faced the Ukes—in space, or planetside."

"And you think he would back away?"

"Not necessarily, sir. But I think it would make him more cautious. The more cautious he becomes, the better our chances are of defeating the Ukes and whatever allies they pick up from among the neutrals."

"So you are advocating a bloodbath."

"No, sir. Not at all. But I am saying we should make the Ukes pay in lives."

"As I said, a bloodbath. Thank you, commander." General Mari turned, and left the room.

Rochman didn't like having his words twisted like that, but maybe the general was right. Yet when he thought of all the lives Sondak had lost already, he didn't care. Maybe he was advocating a bloodbath. But whatever anyone called it, Rochmon was sure it was the one tactic which gave Sondak a chance. He wasn't willing to bet on anything less.

Frye Charlots stood unmoving throughout Vinita's cremation. Only one of the mourners had been inconsiderate enough to reach out and touch him, and he had glared at her with such ferocity that she shrank back.

Now as he watched the fire burn low on the other side of the thick crystal wall, he almost wished someone would touch him—would grab his arm and scream that it wasn't true, that Vinita was still alive. The military part of his mind scorned his weakness. Nothing could make him like reality. But no amount of self-pity could keep him from accepting it.

A vorian began playing softly in the background, sending a solemn tune like damp mist through the mourners. Frye had heard the tune all too many times before—the Kothhymn of the Dead. The last flame died aay with the last strains of the song. The crystal wall went dark.

There was one more duty he had to perform, and then it would be over. Frye turned, straightened his shoulders, and accepted the mourners one by one as they came to share their grief. Only days later while sitting in his office did he realize that he had not spoken to a single one of them.

"Mellimen," he said quietly into his lapel mike, "I want to see the latest reports."

"Yessir," her voice responded from his desk speaker.

Moments later his microspooler came to life. But before he had time to read half of the first report, Mellimen's voice came over the speaker again. "Admiral Tuuneo here to see you, sir."

"Send him in," Frye said quietly. The last person he wanted to see at the moment was Tuuneo, but there was absolutely no way protocol would allow him to turn away a senior officer. He also realized that having Tuuneo come to see him was an honor directly connected with Vinita's death. He rose when the door opened. "Admiral," he said quietly.

"Sit down, Commander. Sit down," Tuuneo said as he crossed the room. "There is no need for formality with us."

Frye remained standing. "I am honored by your presence."

"Thank you, Commander. Now, please, sit down," he said with a wave of his hand as if the office were his own.

Frye took his seat behind the desk and looked Tuuneo squarely in the face. "What can I do for you, Admiral?"

"The question is whether or not I can do anything for you, Commander."

"I'm not sure what you mean, sir?" Frye thought he detected an odd tone in Tuuneo's voice, but couldn't classify it.

"Well, Commander, I understand how greatly you must feel the loss of your wife, but I certainly hope that has not blinded you to the, uh, shall we say, uh, political realities of the moment?"

Frye had some idea what Tuuneo was referring to, but waited for his senior to continue.

"It seems, Charltos, that several members of the Birdgeforce are concerned about your performance."

Frye was not surprised. "The messages?"

"Not just those, although Decie knows they are not very happy about the messages either. No, this time they seem to be concerned about your judgment—that is, they wonder if you can continue directing our forces in your current mental state."

"Heller's fleet, sir! What is that supposed to mean?" Frye heard more anger in his voice than he felt.

Tuuneo shifted in his chair and looked squarely across the desk. "They are talking about a month's grief leave for you."

"Tell them to take their leave and . . . I'm sorry, sir. I have no right to speak to you like that."

"The wrath of bad news falls on the messenger."

Tuuneo's quotation from the Concordance only mixed Frye's emotions. But he sensed that something more important than Bridgeforce's concern was involved here. A brief flash of insight told him what. "Who else is after me, admiral?"

"Judoff."

Frye laughed coldly. "I should have known. But surely, sir, the Bridgeforce wouldn't put that political rumpsuck in a position as critical as this one?"

"No," Tuuneo said with a faint smile as he smoothed the few silver hairs still left on his head, "not immediately, anyway. But Judoff knows that, too. She and her group have suggested that Commander Kuskuvyet could serve as acting commander until you, uh, recover."

In a steady voice which betrayed none of the hatred he felt whenever that name was mentioned Frye said, "Kuskuvyet is a well-trained officer with a commendable record, but—"

"But everyone on the command staff knows he is no more than a mediocre tactician—and a worst strategist."

"It would be unfair of me to comment on that, sir."

"In Decie's name, Charltos! What's the matter with you? Don't you understand how serious this is?"

"Only too well," Frye said evenly.

"Then why—"

"Why am I not upset? Oh, but I am, Admiral. I am. But showing it isn't going to do any good. Pardon my interruption, but I believe you came here to tell me something you haven't gotten to yet. Until you tell me what that is, I would be well advised to control whatever emotions I feel."

"You seem pretty sure of yourself for a man who could be replaced at any time by an incompetent. If it weren't for the fact that the command staff has been supporting you, you would be gone already."

"So that's it. You almost sound like you regret that support, admiral." Frye had a perspective on the problem which let him see it now with cold detachment. If Bridgeforce wanted to replace him with an idiot, that was their problem. For the moment he was indifferent to their political concerns. His duty was to finish this campaign.

"Charltos, I'm trying to tell you that you're in trouble."

"But you are also telling me that the command staff will not let that trouble get out of hand. Isn't that right, sir?"

Tuuneo shook his head and pressed his lips together. "Yes," he said finally, "we will control Judoff—and Kuskuvyet, too, if necessary. But we need your cooperation."

Frye tensed slightly, then let the air escape slowly from his lungs. "I have the feeling you are about to get to the point of this whole visit, sir. I also have the feeling I'm not going to like it."

"Command doesn't give a finger in space whether you like it or not. We want you to put together a plan to capture and control the Matthews system."

With a grim smile of relief Frye said, "I've already begun working on it."

"You've what?"

"Begun working on it, sir. It seemed one of the next logical steps if our initial plans worked." Frye couldn't tell if Admiral Tuuneo was angry or confused.

"Then why in Decie's name haven't you mentioned it to the command staff?"

"Because it was premature. It still is . . . unless, of course, it is politically expedient to . . ."

Silence hung between them for a long moment before Tuuneo looked carefully at Frye. "It is more than politically expedient, commander. It is necessary if we want to continue leading and winning this war."

Frye finally understood what had brought them to this point. He was not the only one who had doubts about their ability to win the war. Admiral Tuuneo and some of the command staff must share at least some of those doubts. Suddenly he felt much better. A man who knew he could lose would be much better prepared to win. "Now much time do we have?" he asked quietly.

Tuuneo smiled. "To announce the plan to Bridgeforce? A month, at best. After that, who knows?"

"Would you like to make the announcement, sir?" Frye knew he did not have to make that offer, but since they were dealing with politics . . .

"No, Charltos. You make it. As soon as you're ready. That will be more effective against Judoff, I think." Tuuneo stood.

Frye stood with him. "Very well, sir."

The admiral narrowed his eyes, then spoke very quietly. "You keep me posted on this, Charltos. I'll need at least a day's notice before you make the announcement."

"Will do, sir," Frye said as he escorted Tuuneo to the door. "I'll let you know as soon as my staff and I are ready."

Once Tuuneo was gone Frye returned to his desk and sat staring at his folded hands. He was making a mistake. Somewhere deep inside he had been harboring the notion that taking the Matthews system was the wrong thing to do. But he had no logical defense for that feeling.

The Matthews system was a sound military target, and once U.C.S. controlled it, Sondak would have a far more difficult time mounting a counter-offensive. It was midway between the two galactic powers, a strategic base without equal. Yet it was also a high risk target, one which Sondak would even now be preparing to defend.

Frye shrugged wearily and turned on his microspooler. There were many things which had to be done before he could concentrate on the new plan—things which involved life and death for their forces right now. But even as he reviewed new reports which showed fewer than expected losses in the surprise attacks, his uncertainty about the Matthews plan nagged at the back of his mind.

Read MIDWAY BETWEEN, on sale in the early fall wherever Bantam paperbacks are sold.